He gradually sensed she was no longer completely asleep, but nor was she awake. She was lost in a dreaming state between the two.

Her movements had the languor of sleep, but there was no doubt what she wanted when she searched for his mouth with hers. He took her head between his hands, meaning to ease her gently away, but in the end he was too weak-willed to do anything except help her find her target. So she kissed him again. Every part of his body thundered with arousal, but he allowed himself to respond with only the tenderest touch of his mouth against hers. He wanted to taste her. But she thought she was lying with her husband.

'Saskia?' he murmured, his voice tight with strain. Perhaps he could wake her just enough to get her safely back to her half of the cloak.

'Harry?'

He went absolutely still. Her voice had been low and husky, but he was certain she'd called him by his real name. Surely her Dutch husband hadn't also been called Harry?

Claire Thornton grew up in the Sussex countryside. Her love of history began as a child, when she imagined Roman soldiers marching along the route of the old Roman Road which runs straight through her village high street. It is also a family legend that her ancestors were involved in smuggling, which further stimulated her interest in how people lived in the past. She loves immersing herself in the historical background for her books, and taught herself bobbin lacemaking as part of her research. She enjoys handicrafts of all kinds, and regularly has her best ideas when she is working on a piece of cross-stitch. Claire has also written under the name of Alice Thornton. She can be contacted via her website at www.clairethornton.com

RUNAWAY LADY features characters you will have already met in Claire Thornton's *City of Flames* trilogy.

Novels by the same author:

RAVEN'S HONOUR
GIFFORD'S LADY
MY LORD FOOTMAN

and in the *City of Flames* series:

THE DEFIANT MISTRESS
THE ABDUCTED HEIRESS
THE VAGABOND DUCHESS

RUNAWAY LADY

Claire Thornton

First published in Great Britain 2009
Large Print edition 2009
Harlequin Mills & Boon Limited,
Eton House, 18-24 Paradise Road, Richmond, Surrey TW9 1SR

ISBN: 978 0 263 20681 4

Set in Times Roman 15½ on 17¾ pt.
42-1109-80706

Harlequin Mills & Boon policy is to use papers that are natural, renewable and recyclable products and made from wood grown in sustainable forests. The logging and manufacturing process conform to the legal environmental regulations of the country of origin.

Printed and bound in Great Britain
by CPI Antony Rowe, Chippenham, Wiltshire

RUNAWAY LADY

Chapter One

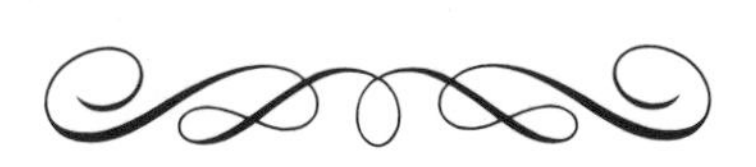

Cornwall—Sunday, 9 June 1667

The sound of footsteps on the gravel path six feet above her head was Saskia van Buren's first warning that she and Anne were not the only ones taking advantage of the warm evening. Both women fell silent as the murmur of conversation grew louder. A few seconds later Saskia recognised the voices of her aunt and the man who'd been introduced to her as her aunt's secretary. They were speaking softly, but the urgency in her aunt's low voice demanded attention.

'Now Saskia's here we don't have to wait. They can both die before the twenty-second of June,' said Lady Abergrave.

'It might be more discreet to continue with our original plan, my lady?' Tancock suggested. 'Wait for Mistress van Buren to return to Amsterdam before we act?'

'No, this way is more certain. There is always the risk that Saskia might challenge any will Benjamin makes in my favour. It's best for her to have a fatal accident now.' Lady Abergrave's voice was chillingly practical. 'She said herself she means to revisit her childhood haunts. No one will be surprised if she falls on the rocks. And no one will be surprised if Benjamin, grief-stricken at the death of his sister, also has an accident. Such tragedies are not uncommon. Grief makes people careless of themselves.'

Shock held Saskia motionless as she listened to her aunt plot her death. Surely she'd misheard. But she saw horror dawning in Anne's eyes, and knew she hadn't misunderstood. She gripped the younger woman's arm in warning and emphatically mouthed the word *quiet.* Anne nodded jerkily.

As long as they made no sound they should remain undetected by Lady Abergrave and Tancock. Trevithick House was built on an area of high ground that sloped steeply down to the river. The house and gardens were surrounded by a retaining wall of Cornish slatestone. Inside, the garden the wall was only four feet high, but it plunged down more than twelve feet on the side facing the river. Saskia and Anne were sitting on a bench cut into the foot of the wall on the river side. They'd only be discovered if Lady Abergrave or Tancock leaned over the wall to look straight down.

'Particularly when the bereaved man already has a broken leg,' Tancock said drily. 'Sir Benjamin's death will take a little more planning than Saskia's, but it won't be difficult. You will receive much sympathy from your friends at the loss of your only remaining blood relatives.'

Beneath her hand Saskia felt Anne begin to shake uncontrollably. She tightened her grip, willing Anne to remain silent. Her own emotions were already locked deep inside her in that place she sent them when disaster threatened.

'Edmund's death was a disaster.' Lady Abergrave's voice hardened with bitterness as she spoke of her dead son. 'But these are necessary. You must do it yourself.'

'Of course. There will be no mistakes.'

'Good.' Lady Abergrave's tone softened into something almost coquettish. 'You will be well rewarded…my friend.'

'My sweet lady. My only ambition is to see you restored to your rightful position.'

Saskia heard the crunch of their footsteps on the gravel as they resumed their promenade around the garden. Until a few minutes ago she would never have dreamed her aunt could be capable of such a heinous plan, yet she didn't doubt her aunt meant everything she'd said.

Isabel Trevithick had been the younger sister of Saskia and Benjamin's late father. She'd been a beauty in her youth. Many men had vied for her hand, but she'd married the second Earl of Abergrave. After his death, she had become the guardian of their son, Edmund. In her position as mother and guardian of the young earl she'd had wealth and influence, but Edmund had been a sickly child. When he'd died the title and inheritance had passed to a distant male relative who'd made only minimal provision for Lady Abergrave. Now the older woman had neither a home nor money of her own. But her late husband had been Benjamin's guardian and Lady Abergrave had assumed the same role. After her son's death she'd brought her remaining retinue, including her stepdaughter, Anne, to live in Benjamin's house.

Saskia had been well aware her aunt resented her reduced circumstances, but until a few minutes ago she'd assumed Lady Abergrave meant to restore her fortunes through a second marriage. Only yesterday her aunt had been flirting with the local magistrate, yet even then Lady Abergrave must have been plotting murder.

Fury surged through Saskia. She started to spring up, intending to seek out and confront her aunt—but almost immediately her anger was overtaken by the terrifying awareness that the first loyalty of every servant in the house was to Lady Abergrave. Saskia's father had died when Benjamin was sixteen, and her brother had been taken from Trevithick House to live with Lord and Lady Abergrave in Gloucestershire. The old family servants at Trevithick had received pensions under her father's will. None of the present household remembered Saskia from when she'd lived at Trevithick before her marriage. They all treated Lady Abergrave as if she was the mistress of the household, rather than her nephew's guest. Saskia didn't dare trust any of them.

Anne opened her mouth to speak. Saskia shook her head, afraid they might be overheard. She glanced both ways and then pulled Anne to her feet and all but dragged her across the path and into the shelter of the band of woodland separating the house from the river.

'What are we going to do?' Anne whispered desperately.

'If we could only get Benjamin out of the house…' But Saskia dismissed the idea before she'd finished the sentence. Her brother's broken leg was in splints and his bedroom was on the first floor. They'd never be able to get him out without attracting attention. And if Tancock and Lady Abergrave discovered them, Saskia knew her fate—and Benjamin's—would be sealed.

'I have to get help.' Saskia gazed intently at Anne, trying to gauge the girl's mood. 'Will you come with me?'

'I…what will be best? I don't want to leave Benjamin.'

'Nor do I. But unless I go now, he'll be in deadly danger. Do you understand?' Saskia had realised what was implicit in Lady Abergrave's conversation with Tancock. 'As long as I'm alive, there is no benefit to my aunt if Benjamin dies before his twenty-first birthday, because in that case our father's will leaves everything to me—and my own will is already written and it does not leave anything to her. It is only if I die first and then Benjamin that Aunt Isabel will gain this estate under our father's will.'

'I hate her.' Anne sounded steadier. 'From the first moment she married my father I have not liked her. Tell me what to do.'

'Wait a while and then go back into the house without drawing attention to yourself. Follow your normal routine, but retire to bed as soon as possible. Don't mention me or draw attention to yourself in any way.' Saskia spoke swiftly as she tried to imagine all eventualities. 'If anyone asks you about me, act as ignorant and confused as the rest of the household will be when my absence is discovered. But if someone does remember we came for a walk together, say we separated because I had a headache and wanted to sit quietly. If you have a chance, tell Benjamin I will be back with help, but only when you are sure no one will overhear.'

Anne nodded jerkily. 'Be careful.'

Saskia pulled the girl into a brief hug. She didn't want to leave Anne behind, but Lady Abergrave had nothing to gain from harming her stepdaughter. Most of the time she barely noticed her. It was Benjamin who was in deadly danger while he was in Lady Abergrave's power.

Saskia moved cautiously through the woodland sloping down to the river, all her senses attuned to her surroundings. Every tiny snap of a twig beneath her feet sounded like an explosion to her oversensitive ears, but she heard nothing except the normal rustles of small animals in the undergrowth. To her relief, the small quay below the house was deserted. Almost as important, water was still rising on the incoming tide. She untied one of the small boats, climbed in and began to row upstream. She knew she needed to make good progress before the tide turned against her.

London—Friday, 14 June 1667

Saskia was lost in London. She rode around a corner and straight into the middle of a riot. A burst of sharp, violent sounds and images exploded into her awareness. A flying brick…a man's contorted face as he bellowed in rage…the bite of axe into a tree. Angry, shouting men were hurling stones at the windows of a grand mansion and chopping down trees in front of it. Her horse shied in alarm, nearly unseating her. Then she regained her wits sufficiently to control the frightened horse and get to safety.

Once she reached the sanctuary of a quiet street she pulled the gelding to a halt. Her heart was thundering, her body trembling with shock. She patted the horse's neck, trying to calm both of them with the gesture. She'd sensed a growing agitation among the people as she'd approached London, but she'd never expected to find herself in the midst of a violent scene. Anxiety knotted her stomach. She didn't have time for this. Benjamin didn't have time. She was acutely conscious of the days relentlessly passing as she sought help. Remembering how the Cornish magistrate had fawned over her aunt, she'd been no more willing to ask him for help than the household servants. When her only other hope of finding help in Cornwall had been thwarted, she'd come to London in search of the one influential man in England she was sure would trust her word—her godfather, Sir Francis Middleton. But first she had to find his house.

As soon as she was calm enough to be confident not to pitch her voice too revealingly high, she asked a porter what was happening.

'Breaking Clarendon's windows? It's his fault we're trapped in this war with the Dutch!' he exclaimed, spitting into the street. Clarendon? After a moment's confusion, Saskia remembered he was the Lord Chancellor.

'How can you not know?' The porter stared at her in disbelief.

'I've been out of the town, visiting friends,' she replied, grateful for the shadows thrown by the tall houses on either side of the street. She was wearing male clothing, and in the poor light she hoped she looked like a dishevelled lad, rather than a frightened woman. 'What have the Dutch done?'

'Broke through the chain at Chatham, burned most of our ships and towed away the flag ship,' the porter said in disgust.

'My God!' Chatham was only thirty miles from the heart of London. The Dutch had pulled off a daring raid on the English. Saskia wondered if Jan had been part of it—then her blood chilled as she realised that revealing her brother-in-law was an officer in the Dutch navy would not be prudent.

'Did they attack the people of Chatham? Have they threatened to attack London?' she demanded.

'Who knows what they've done? Or will do. I've heard they are blockading the Thames. Our ships can't get in or out. This government is a disgrace to us. Oliver would not have let us suffer such a defeat.'

'Thank you for the news.' Saskia extricated herself as smoothly as she could. She had no interest in debating whether Oliver Cromwell's foreign policy had been superior to King Charles II's.

The forced diversion meant it took a painfully long time before she was finally in sight of her godfather's house. From the back of her horse she had a good view over the heads of the people crowding the street and she was sure she'd recognised it correctly. A wash of relief swept over her. Soon she would be with friends—

The front door opened and a man emerged. As he glanced around she had a clear view of his face.

Tancock!

She stared at him in disbelief, shock and weariness making her slow to react. Of course, Aunt Isabel knew Sir Francis was her godfather. She must have guessed Saskia's destination from the first.

Tancock would have been able to reach London quicker than a woman travelling alone.

Saskia suddenly realised it would be as easy for Tancock to see her as it was for her to see him. She started to kick her feet clear of the stirrups, but his gaze—which had passed uninterestedly over her once—returned and locked on to her face. His eyes widened in recognition. The semi-disguise of her men's clothes had not deceived him. It was too late to drop out of the saddle and hide among the pedestrians. She dragged on the reins, intent only on escape. As she did so, from the corner of her eye she saw Tancock lift his arm and point at her.

'Dutch spy!' he shouted. 'Seize her! Dutch spy! Plotting more atrocities on honest, hardworking Londoners!'

As the throng of nearby people murmured first in confusion and then in growing anger, Saskia kicked the gelding as hard as she could, urging him into a gallop. Her most important goal now was to avoid capture by an outraged mob of Londoners.

Covent Garden—London, Saturday, 15 June 1667

The back room of the coffee-house was small and poorly lit. Every time the door opened Saskia felt a shiver of anxiety until she'd seen the face of the man who entered—and even then a residual fear remained that one of those she interviewed might be in Tancock's pay.

But there was no reason for Tancock to suspect she was here. Even Saskia herself had not remembered Johanna for nearly two, panic-stricken hours. Johanna was the cousin of Saskia's late husband, Pieter van Buren. Johanna had married an English tradesman who'd gone into partnership with a silent investor to open one of London's first coffee-houses. After her husband's death, Johanna had continued managing the coffee-house alone. She'd been very willing to help Saskia. Yesterday evening she had sent a message to Sir Francis's house on Saskia's behalf—but the women had been shocked to discover he'd been struck by an apoplexy that same morning. No one knew if Sir Francis would live or die, and Saskia was terribly afraid Tancock might be the cause of her godfather's illness.

Such a hideous mixture of guilt, fear and anger overwhelmed her at the possibility she almost didn't hear the door open. She recovered her composure just in time to snatch up the mask from the table and hold it to her face as the next man came into the room.

She knew at once he wasn't Tancock. He was too tall, too exotic—too obviously *dangerous*.

Her breath caught in her throat. One or two of the

previous men had struck her as uncomfortably disreputable, but she'd called upon her experience of dealing with her late husband's business to dismiss them as quickly and easily as possible. This man was different. A wolf, not a jackal. She could see it in the swift, appraising gaze he cast around the room, the silent, fluid way he moved and the self-assurance of his bearing.

His appearance was a combination of the foreign and familiar. His soft, tan leather boots made no sound on the floorboards. He wore a scarlet sash around his waist from which hung a curved sword. Unlike his boots and his sword, his broad-brimmed hat was English in style, but beneath it Saskia saw his dark hair was cut much shorter than fashion demanded.

He stared straight at her. As she met his dark eyes, even the anonymous mask seemed no barrier to the disturbingly virile, dangerous energy he radiated. Her pulse quickened. She couldn't remember ever being so instantly, compellingly aware of a man's physical—*male*—presence. Nervous tension skittered through her body. She was used to men who obeyed the customs and manners of civilised society. She was already convinced that this man obeyed no rules but his own. She didn't need a wayward, edgy man. She needed one who would follow her commands obediently. Unquestioningly.

She was about to reject him before he'd even said a word. But then she remembered her first impression of Tancock. Until the evening she'd heard him plotting murder she would have said he was punctilious in observing the requirements of civilised behaviour. Perhaps an obviously dangerous, unpredictable man would be better than an apparently placid man. She'd never forget to be on her guard in his presence—and whoever she hired had to be capable of helping her rescue Benjamin.

'Sit down,' she ordered, determined to assert her authority from her first words.

Harry Ward had seen the woman snatch up the mask as he'd opened the door. She'd done it so quickly he'd had no chance to gain more than a fleeting impression of her features. Despite the summer warmth, she was wearing a dark hood and cloak, concealing both her hair and the shape of her body. He hadn't seen her eyes, but he'd glimpsed a well-shaped mouth and a small but decisive chin.

Until a few weeks ago Harry had spent his adult life in lands where the veil was customary for women. One or two European merchants and diplomats took their wives and daughters with them to the Ottoman Empire, but Harry had never seen, let alone spoken to, the womenfolk of even his closest

Turkish friends. Ever since he'd arrived back in England he'd had a nagging sense that he should be chivalrous in female company, without quite knowing what that entailed. From the moment he'd learned that the Dutch agent recruiting men in the back room of the coffee-house in which his brother was a silent investor was likely to be female, he'd been on edge. The confirmation that he was indeed dealing with a woman intensified his unease.

Of course, an Englishwoman who'd turned traitor had forfeited her right to be treated chivalrously. But Harry had been disturbed by the information he'd received. Apparently the woman was motivated by a desire to avenge her dead husband. Harry understood better than most how the burning need for vengeance—for justice—could overwhelm every rational thought. But treason could not be tolerated, nor could her activities be allowed to taint his brother's reputation, even in passing.

Harry steeled himself to deal with the lady as ruthlessly as if she were a man. The mask she held to her face could not disguise the fundamental immodesty of her present situation. The mere fact she was interviewing strange men alone without even a chaperon meant she had forfeited her right to chivalrous treatment. On the other hand, since it wasn't the custom for English women to be veiled, her determination to conduct her illicit business in his brother's coffee-house behind the anonymity of a mask was in itself an insult. All in all, he concluded, she could have no expectation of receiving gentle treatment from him.

'Are you afraid the mere sight of your beauty will make men run wild?' he demanded, a little more scornfully than he'd intended.

'Of course not!' she exclaimed. 'That is…my lord is most complimentary about my looks, but I do not expect to be universally admired.'

'Who is your lord?' Was she talking about her spymaster—or a man with whom she was on more intimate terms?

'That is no concern of yours.'

'And will I be of concern to him?'

'I beg your pardon.' She sounded confused.

'Do you intend to disclose my existence to him?'

'It was his idea I hire you!' she snapped.

Harry was so startled he uttered a short Turkish curse under his breath. What kind of man encouraged his woman to act in such a forward manner? 'Why isn't he interviewing me?'

'Because he's in Portsmouth.'

'Why did he leave you here?' Harry was so distracted by the masked woman's disclosures that for a moment he almost forgot what his former guardian, the Earl of Swiftbourne, had told him that morning.

He belatedly reminded himself that Saskia van Buren was the daughter of a Dutchwoman and an English baronet. According to Swiftbourne's informant, she'd married a Dutchman at the age of twenty and spent the past six years living in Amsterdam. She'd returned to England a few weeks ago after she'd been widowed when her husband was killed in a naval battle with the English. Apparently, it was her husband's death that had driven her to become an agent for the Dutch. If this was Saskia, it was extremely likely her 'lord' was nothing more than a fiction to cover her true plans.

She drew in a deep breath. 'May I remind you, fellow, that you are the one wishing to enter into temporary employment with me,' she said crisply. 'I am the one deciding if I will hire you. *I* ask the questions. Is that clear?'

She didn't sound as if she was overwhelmed with grief. Nor did Harry receive the impression that she was locked into the single-minded, bitter fury of vengeance. She did sound exasperated. Perhaps she wasn't Saskia.

He grinned, amused despite himself at her irritation. He had a temper of his own, though it rarely manifested itself when he was questioning potential employees. There was a plain wooden chair obviously intended for whoever the lady was currently interviewing. He turned it around, straddled it and rested his forearms along the back.

'Ask away,' he said cheerfully.

There was silence for several moments.

'Did you respond to my advertisement so you could entertain yourself by insulting me?' the masked lady demanded.

'I'm here because the Dutch are blockading the Thames,' Harry replied, secretly pleased she'd challenged his deliberately provocative behaviour so directly. When he'd heard he would be confronting a vengeful widow, he'd been afraid he might have to deal with tears and emotional pleas.

Although he couldn't see her face, he saw her gloved fingers tighten on the mask, and sensed an increased tension grip her body. He was satisfied that whatever else might or might not be the truth, the lady was indeed sensitive to mention of England's current enemy.

'And what has that to do with my notice?' she asked sharply.

'I was going to sign up on a merchantman, but until the blockade is lifted…' He shrugged. 'If I don't work, I don't eat.'

'What if the blockade is lifted and the ships sail before you can return to London?' she asked.

'There's always another ship,' he said nonchalantly, which was true, although he hadn't built his fortune by habitually letting the initiative slide. 'I am here, in need of work. What is it you want me to do?'

'With such an arrogant, heedless attitude, I am surprised you ever find anyone willing to hire you,' the lady said tartly.

'They hire me because I am very good at what I do.'

'What *do* you do?'

'Many things.'

'Be more specific. Can you use that sword by your side?'

Harry laughed. 'I'm hardly likely to say no,' he pointed out. 'I have guarded the passage of men and goods along many dangerous routes, from Scanderoon to Aleppo, Smyrna to Istanbul.'

The mask moved slightly as the lady looked Harry carefully up and down.

The fifteen years he'd spent in the Levant meant he was not used to being in the company of women. Whenever he was in the presence of his sister-in-law, Mary, he felt ill at ease, anxious that he do nothing to alarm her or embarrass his brother, Richard. After the Dutch attack on the English ships he'd escorted Richard, Mary and their newborn son to Mary's family home in Bedfordshire. Once there, Harry had been invited by Mary's parents to remain as an honoured guest, but he'd felt so uncomfortable in the presence of his sister-in-law and all her female relatives he'd claimed he had business to attend to in London. He'd given his apologies as courteously as he could, while inwardly castigating himself for his lack of social address. But when he'd heard the news from Swiftbourne that a Dutch agent was recruiting men at Richard's coffee-house he was glad his return to London meant he was available to investigate the matter.

The expressionless scrutiny by the masked lady was an odd, potentially disturbing experience, but it left Harry unmoved. If it had been Richard's wife, or one of her sisters, studying him so closely Harry would have felt very unsettled—concerned he had either offended the lady or revealed his ignorance of the manners of polite English society in some subtle, unintentional way. But he felt no such qualms in the presence of the spy. What the lady saw was what she got. And since she hadn't already dismissed him he was beginning to suspect he could be just what she wanted.

If she really was a Dutch agent, recruiting men to work against England from within its borders, her interest in him might not be so surprising. Not if

Swiftbourne's parting shot was correct. 'You have a lean and hungry look, Harry,' his former guardian had said. 'The kind of man any conscienceless agent would want to employ.'

'You are judging me by yourself, my lord,' Harry had replied drily, and received a characteristically enigmatic smile in response.

'It will be your duty to protect me,' the lady said, her words cutting across his thoughts.

'From whom?'

'My lord's former…former mistress—her servants, that is.'

Harry's eyes widened briefly before he controlled his expression. Would a grieving widow have taken a lover already? Perhaps she hadn't been so distressed by her husband's death? But if she was enjoying her new freedom, it cast doubt over the claim she was determined to avenge her husband.

'She is jealous, you see.' The mask trembled briefly, before the lady's hand steadied once more. Harry noted the tell-tale gesture and immediately suspected this was yet another lie.

'Despite what you said, I assure you my beauty does not drive most men wild,' said the masked lady, and from her tone he was inclined to believe she meant it. 'But my lord is quite fond of me. Very fond of me. Besotted. I mean, devoted,' she corrected herself quickly. 'Unfortunately, his former mistress… Well, she wants to scratch my eyes out.'

'You want to hire me to protect you from a cat fight?' Harry exclaimed.

'Of course not! I would never demean myself…she has servants, of course. They might try to cause me trouble on my journey to Portsmouth.'

'Indeed. And what about your *besotted, devoted* lord?' Harry found her description of her nameless lover very unconvincing.

'What about him?' the masked lady said uneasily.

'Why did so devoted a gentleman ever let you out of his sight? Why is *he* not providing for your comfort and safety? Did he misuse his former mistress or fail to provide adequately for her when they parted? Does he know you are hiring a man-servant in the back room of a coffee-house? For my own future well-being, I must ask—is he a reasonable man, or prone to jealousy—?'

'Very reasonable. Very reasonable,' the lady broke in hastily. 'He is the soul of discretion, of good sense—'

'Yet he left you alone in London at the mercy of his former mistress while he went to Portsmouth?' Harry made no attempt to hide the scepticism in his voice.

'Well, um…it's the Dutch, of course,' the lady said

after a moment's hesitation. 'He cannot leave his post until this business with the Dutch is resolved.'

Harry noticed the almost irritated note in her voice. What kind of spy considered war a *nuisance*?

'Is your lover married?' he asked.

'What? Of course not!' The mask quivered with outrage at the suggestion. 'Do you think I'd have an affair with a married man?'

'If he's not married already, why isn't he going to marry *you*?' Harry asked.

There was another long silence. 'You are right,' she said. 'I hadn't thought of it before, but you are completely correct. He *should* be marrying me and, as soon as the opportunity arises, I will draw it to his attention.'

'Madam, I cannot believe a lady possessed of such firm resolve needs me to protect you from a mere former mistress,' said Harry. 'Let me spare you the expense of my hire—'

'Sit down!' she all but shrieked as he started to stand up. 'I do need you. I definitely *do* need you.'

'Is that so?' Harry relaxed back onto the chair, satisfied his bluff had worked. He had no idea what the lady was up to but, spy or not, he intended to find out. 'And when will I see your face? Or do you intend to hold that mask in front of you all the way to Portsmouth?'

'Masks are very fashionable,' she said, somewhat defensively. 'Respectable ladies wear them to the theatre and even to market or in the street.'

Since Harry hadn't ventured near the theatre since his return to London, he couldn't comment on that. 'But you are not, by your own admission, a respectable woman,' he pointed out. 'At least, not until you coerce your lord into marrying you. I am surprised your ambition needed to be prompted in that regard.'

'I am not hiring you to cast judgement upon my morals, but to protect my person from harm,' said the lady coldly.

'When will I see your face?' Harry repeated. 'I don't work for anyone unless I have looked into their unmasked face.'

'In ten minutes' time,' she said. 'If you accept the post and agree to leave immediately, you will see my face. Do you wish to serve me?'

'Yes,' he replied.

'I will hire you only on condition that you promise to do everything in your power to protect me—and do nothing to harm me.'

'I beg your pardon?' Harry was startled by her demand. It also gave him pause. He didn't believe her story of her absent lover or the jealous former mistress. She hadn't provided any evidence that she was a Dutch spy, but she might yet prove to be a traitor. Harry had never broken a promise, and he wasn't prepared to make a blind commitment now.

'I will protect you as long as you do no harm to anyone else,' he said.

'I just want you to keep me alive.' The words seemed to burst from her of their own volition. A desperate plea she had no control over. Harry's gut tightened as he heard the unmistakable fear in her voice.

'I will not let anyone hurt you,' he said brusquely, even as he damned his own instinctive urge to protect.

'Thank you.' She visibly relaxed, tension ebbing from her body. 'You will be well rewarded.' Without any warning she lowered the mask to the table.

Chapter Two

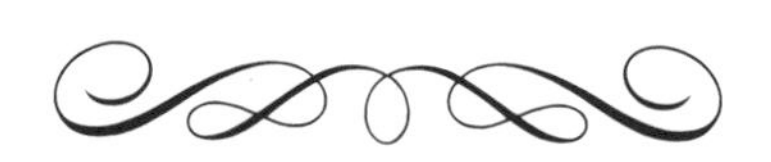

The sudden revelation of her face threw Harry completely off balance. With the mask in place he'd been able to suppress the awareness he was dealing with a woman. He'd even managed to consider her comments about her lover as if they were no more than pieces in an intellectual puzzle.

As soon as he saw her face that illusion was destroyed. She was unmistakably feminine, with a heart-shaped face and smooth, unblemished skin. Her lips were soft and slightly parted, and she was looking at him with vulnerable hopefulness in her large brown eyes. For several heartbeats he lost himself completely in her gaze. He wanted to stroke her cheek and touch her lips to see if they were as soft as they looked. She'd claimed she wasn't beautiful—but now Harry knew that had been another lie. She was captivating. He felt his body stir with more primitive arousal and cursed himself that he had so little experience with women that one glance at a lovely face should have such a potent impact upon him. He preferred always to be in a position of control.

He growled a Turkish curse in his throat. 'Do not look at me like that,' he warned, more harshly than he'd intended. 'You're paying me to keep you alive, nothing else.'

Confusion clouded her eyes for a moment; then she straightened her spine, her lips firmed and temper sparked in her eyes.

'That's all I expect from you,' she said crisply. 'I have already hired a coach. I will give orders for it to be made ready and then we will leave.'

Cornwall—Saturday, 15 June 1667

'I wonder where Saskia is now?' Anne said, her voice low and shaky.

'I hope to God she is safe.' Sir Benjamin Trevithick's hands clenched into useless fists as he tried to control his fear and rage.

'I am sure she is. She was so strong and brave when we overheard…when we…'

'You are strong and brave too.' With an effort of will Benjamin relaxed his hand and cupped the side of Anne's face—the uninjured side. Her other check and her eye were still badly bruised from the back-handed blow which had knocked her to the floor a week ago.

The shocking moment when Lady Abergrave had lashed out at Anne was burned into Benjamin's memory. He'd woken early, restless because he'd had an uncomfortable night. Anne had brought breakfast to his bedchamber, just as she had done every day since he'd broken his leg. He'd known at once that something was troubling her, but before he had a chance to ask what was wrong, his aunt and Tancock had come into the room.

Anne had jumped at the sight of her stepmother, her face paling until Benjamin feared she might faint.

'Where's Saskia?' Lady Abergrave demanded.

'She…she had a headache,' Anne stammered.

'Where is she?'

Anne's eyes grew huge with fear and her voice sank almost to a whisper as she replied, 'In…in bed, I suppose.'

'She's not in bed.' Lady Abergrave advanced on Anne.

'She was going for a walk to clear her head, and then she was going to bed,' Anne said, a little more firmly.

'Liar!' Lady Abergrave struck her stepdaughter so hard Anne staggered and landed in a shaken heap on the floor by Benjamin's bed.

Every time Benjamin remembered that moment he was filled with renewed horror and shame. He'd been trapped beneath the sheets by his broken leg, desperately reaching for his crutches, unable to protect Anne. All he'd managed to do was fall out of bed beside her, powerless to intervene.

He stroked the soft skin of her unhurt cheek with his thumb, trying to comfort her as he remembered how they'd been locked together in his bedchamber while Tancock and his henchmen went in search of Saskia. Anne had told him in whispers about the deadly conversation she and Saskia had overheard. When Lady Abergrave and Tancock returned his aunt had been in an even worse temper, but he'd felt a flood of relief because they hadn't found Saskia. They hadn't given up looking for her. Benjamin knew that Tancock and at least one other man had gone in further pursuit of her. He prayed continuously that his sister should remain safe, but the longer she was gone the more worried he became.

He was also effectively a prisoner in his own house. He wasn't willing to accept that situation without a fight, but he trusted the servants even less than Saskia had. They'd all received their wages from Lady Abergrave for years. They might understand in theory that in a few days' time

Benjamin would be master of Trevithick, but immediate power lay in his aunt's hands, enforced by the core members of her retinue. Men like Tancock, who had already proved they would follow her orders without compunction.

Footsteps sounded in the gallery outside the bedchamber. Benjamin lifted his head, apprehension knotting his stomach. Ned Fenwick, a large, scarred manservant, came cautiously into the room, the knife in his hand very visible. Lady Abergrave followed, carrying Benjamin's crutches. Without them he was completely immobile.

'Come here, girl,' Lady Abergrave ordered.

Anne stood up and took a few reluctant steps forward. As soon as she was well clear of Benjamin, Fenwick reached out and seized her arm. Benjamin's hands clenched.

Lady Abergrave saw the gesture and smiled mockingly. 'Your obedience buys Anne's continued good health,' she said.

'If anything happens to her, you will have no power over me at all,' Benjamin returned, his muscles trembling from the effort to maintain his self-control. Lady Abergrave's willingness to threaten her stepdaughter to force his co-operation limited his options even more effectively than the questionable loyalty of the servants and her regular removal of his crutches.

'Sir William Boscawen has just arrived at the quay,' said Lady Abergrave, laying Benjamin's crutches out of reach as Fenwick took Anne out of the room. Benjamin knew she'd brought them for the sake of appearances in front of the visitor and that they would be removed as soon as Sir William had gone. 'I will bring him up to see you. Remember, if you say anything out of turn, it will be Anne who suffers.'

A few minutes later Benjamin struggled to keep his composure as he accepted Sir William's commiserations on breaking his leg so close to reaching his twenty-first birthday. For nearly an hour he made polite conversation with Sir William and Lady Abergrave while he desperately tried to think of some discreet way of communicating the danger to his visitor. Sir William was a genial neighbour, but he was neither decisive nor particularly intelligent. Far worse, from Benjamin's point of view, he was one of the many men who had courted Lady Abergrave in her youth—and remained equally dazzled by her twenty years later. He would never believe she had murderous intentions towards her nephew. But if Lady Abergrave realised Benjamin had tried to seek the magistrate's help, she would retaliate by hurting Anne.

London—Saturday, 15 June 1667

It took only a few minutes for Saskia to let Johanna know she was leaving the coffee-house and collect the bag containing the few possessions she'd acquired since leaving Cornwall. She set off for the livery stable, very conscious of her new manservant and protector striding beside her. For the first few yards he gained ground on her. After that he moderated his pace to match hers. She had a ridiculous urge to show him she could walk just as fast as he could—which felt very strange, because for so long she had curbed her physical energy in Pieter's presence.

A long-suppressed memory of her first winter in Amsterdam flashed into her mind. It was before Pieter's accident, and they'd both gone skating on the frozen canals of the city. Pieter had been strong and quick, with all the assurance on the ice of one who'd learned to skate almost as soon as he could walk. At first she'd been nervous and hesitant, but she'd quickly gained her balance and her confidence. She'd been exhilarated by her new-found skill, laughingly, perhaps shockingly, challenging Pieter to race with her. They'd had that one winter of carefree joy—then Pieter had been crippled and her expectations for her future had irrevocably changed.

The fugitive awareness flickered in her mind that, even when he was whole and healthy, Pieter had never possessed quite the virile energy of the man walking beside her. Then she pushed aside her memories and her unsettling response to her companion. Now they were in public she was once more holding the mask to her face. It was Tancock she was hiding from, but it was also a relief to conceal her expression from her new manservant's far too intense and disturbing scrutiny. It occurred to her that, even though she had supposedly been the one conducting the interview, he had asked nearly all the questions. She would have to rectify that at the earliest opportunity. She needed to know more about him before she trusted her life and Benjamin's in his hands.

'It would be more efficient if you tied it on,' he said, indicating the mask.

'There's a button I should bite to hold it in place,' she replied, 'but then I would not be able to talk. What's your name?'

'Harry Dixon. What's yours?'

'Sarah Brewster.' Thinking up a suitably English name had been one of the first things she'd done. She owed her Christian name to her Dutch mother, and it was far too unusual to use openly in her current situation. She was still pleased with her new English name. She was less convinced that the story she and Johanna had invented about the jealous former mistress was equally satisfactory, but she'd needed an explanation for why she required protection. Johanna had suggested she hint she was an actress, but the opportunity had never arisen.

'We're leaving for Portsmouth this afternoon, Mistress Brewster?'

'Yes.' Portsmouth was not their destination, but she didn't intend to reveal where they were really going until they were well on their way. Guildford would be soon enough. They wouldn't get that far today, but Saskia was conscious of every minute ticking by, taking them closer to Benjamin's twenty-first birthday on the twenty-second of June.

She had to rescue him before then. She was very afraid that, if she didn't, as soon as Benjamin gained control of his inheritance he would be forced to sign a will in Lady Abergrave's favour and then he would be killed. That had been Lady Abergrave and Tancock's original plan when Saskia had been out of their reach in Amsterdam. Surely Lady Abergrave wouldn't risk killing Benjamin before his birthday while Saskia was still alive? She must know that as long Saskia had breath in her body, she would seek justice for her brother. But Saskia didn't dare predict how her aunt might behave. As fear for Benjamin overrode every other thought, she quickened her pace until she was almost running.

'You are very eager to return to your lover's arms,' said Harry Dixon.

'Oh… Yes.' Jarred out of her preoccupation, Saskia flushed behind the mask. 'That is, I have a great deal to do when I reach Portsmouth,' she added hastily. She was very glad their arrival at the livery stable cut short any further conversation about her supposed lover. But her new servant immediately created another complication by insisting he ride beside the coach rather than sitting next the coachman. A saddle horse was an additional expense Saskia hadn't anticipated.

'You are hiring me to protect you. If you have any sense, you won't interfere with the arrangements I make,' Harry said, when she challenged him.

'I'm paying for your arrangements,' she pointed out.

His eyes narrowed. 'Can't you afford a horse for me?'

'Of course.' The problem for Saskia wasn't lack of resources, but a limited supply of ready coins. She'd arrived in Plymouth from Amsterdam with four bills of exchange concealed in the pocket beneath her skirts. She'd converted one of the bills into English coins in Plymouth on her first day in England, and she'd used that money to pay her way to London. Unfortunately, the Dutch attack meant she was temporarily unable to convert her other bills of exchange into cash. She'd given one to Johanna in return for the clothes and coins the other woman had provided, but she would have to wait before the crisis between the Dutch and the English was resolved before she could present the others to one of London's goldsmith-bankers.

She wasn't yet ready to reveal the existence of the bills of exchange to Harry Dixon, but once they had saved Benjamin she planned to reward him by giving them both to him—and perhaps more besides. Her brother's life meant far more to her than money.

'Choose a horse,' she ordered. 'And then let us be on our way without any further delay.'

Leaving London was a slow business. They drove through the ruins of the burned City and were delayed for over an hour by the heavy traffic of carts and people before finally crossing London Bridge into Lambeth. Saskia wanted to scream with frustration—or at the very least get out and walk.

But she knew that made no sense. Once they were out of London they would make better time.

She relaxed slightly once the coach was rumbling steadily forwards. The first part of her mission had been successfully accomplished. She was on her way back to Benjamin. Now she must plan her next steps. How was she going to rescue her brother when she reached Cornwall? And how was she going to bring Lady Abergrave and Tancock to justice? She had to make sure that neither of them could ever be a threat to her family again.

She still hadn't solved the problems by the time they arrived at the Coach and Horses inn at Kingston-upon-Thames. It was late evening and Harry announced they would stay there for the night.

'We can go a few more miles at least,' Saskia protested.

'Are we staying here or not?' the coachman asked.

'We're staying,' Harry said, and the coachman obeyed immediately without waiting for Saskia's response.

Harry's automatic assumption of command irritated Saskia. She'd managed Pieter's business for years. She wasn't used to having her wishes ignored or overruled. She almost challenged him there and then, but over the years she'd learned to pick her battles. A public argument with Harry was unlikely to enhance her authority in either his eyes or the coachman's—particularly when he was right. Despite her restless need to keep moving, she knew the waning moon would provide little light for the journey. It made sense to stop for the night and continue early in the morning. At least it would give her an opportunity to learn more about her new manservant before she risked trusting him with a portion of the truth.

Harry was well aware of Sarah Brewster's irritation. She was clearly impatient to complete her journey. He thought she was also annoyed with him for giving orders so freely, but that didn't worry him. He was used to taking command and he had two priorities: the first was to establish whether she was indeed Saskia van Buren and a traitor; the second was to keep his promise to protect her. He would do whatever was necessary to achieve those goals. He had no intention of compromising his efforts by pandering to his new employer's whims, even though she was a distractingly attractive woman.

Acting as Mistress Brewster's servant, he took two rooms at the Coach and Horses. He'd expected to guard her from the other side of her closed door, but she disconcerted him by suggesting they eat supper together in her room. Taking a meal with a woman was an unfamiliar situation for Harry in any circumstances. Doing so when they were alone and within a few feet of a bed filled him with more tension than if he were navigating rocks and undertows to cross a dangerous river. He was amazed she didn't seem to be conscious of anything unusual. There were times since he'd arrived back in England when he felt almost as disorientated as he had when he'd first gone to the Levant and had to learn a completely new set of social customs.

They sat opposite each other at a small table. Harry's eyes were drawn constantly to Saskia's face and her uncovered hair. She had long blonde curls touched with hints of warm colour which reminded him of apricots or the first glow of sunrise. He'd been entranced by those shining curls from the moment she'd first put back her hood in his presence. He'd caught his breath and had to restrain himself from reaching out to see if they were as soft as they looked. He still wanted to touch her hair. If he'd been an invisible spirit in the room, he would have been content to simply sit and watch her. A pretty, shimmering angel in the candlelight. But he wasn't invisible, and he was determined not to stare at her like a moonstruck idiot. He'd mastered the art of appearing outwardly self-assured many years ago, so he deliberately adopted a relaxed, untroubled air as he ate his supper.

He'd assumed Saskia meant to take him to task for giving orders to the coachman without her permission, but instead she began asking him questions.

'How old are you?'

'Thirty-four.' For the first time in his life Harry was almost uncomfortable revealing his age. Ever since he'd returned to England, he'd been acutely aware he'd fallen behind his contemporaries in certain crucial aspects of life. On his first day in London he'd been startled and discomfited to see an apprentice more than a decade his junior flirting confidently with the pretty girl behind the counter of a linen draper's. Judging by the girl's twinkling response, she'd enjoyed the apprentice's attentions. But when Harry asked politely for some handkerchiefs her eyes had widened. He was convinced he'd seen alarm in her expression as she hastened to serve him. He knew very well that women had good reason to be afraid of some men. Sometimes, though less frequently than in the past, he still had nightmares about the damage a violent man could do to a woman. He'd had no idea how to assure the draper's girl that, despite his sun-darkened skin and the sword by his side, he wasn't a threat to her safety, so he'd thanked her gruffly and hurried away.

Richard's wife had been nervous in his presence too. Harry knew there were several possible reasons for that, including the natural anxiety any woman might have to make a good impression on her husband's older brother—especially when that brother was also the head of her husband's family. Besides, after so many years apart, Harry and Richard had not yet regained the easy friendship of their youth and it was understandable that Mary would take her cues from her husband. But Mary had led a very sheltered life both before and after her marriage, and Harry had not been able to lose the conviction that she found being in his presence as foreign and unnerving as he found being in hers. Despite his best efforts, they had never managed more than the most stilted conversations. Harry had been acutely aware of Richard's growing bewilderment and unhappiness at their lack of ease with each other. Just before Harry had left Bedfordshire, Richard had even burst out, "I am afraid you don't like my wife."

The accusation had dumbfounded Harry and left him uncertain how to respond. He had no idea how to compliment any man on his choice of wife, much less his brother. He'd assured Richard that he liked his wife very well, but it had been an awkward parting for the brothers.

With his recent experiences with his sister-in-law fresh in his mind, Harry was very relieved that he didn't seem to make his new employer anxious. In fact, she was focusing a distinctly inquisitorial gaze on him.

'Tell me some of the things you've done in the past,' she demanded. 'Why don't you carry an English sword?'

'Because I learned most of what I know from a Janissary.'

She looked surprised. 'Did you spend a long time in the Levant?'

'Since I was nineteen.'

'When did you come back to England?'

'A few weeks ago.'

'Did you not come back at all in the meantime?' she exclaimed.

'No.' The brothers had gone to the Levant together, but the Turkish climate had not suited Richard's constitution. After Harry had nursed his younger brother through three dangerous fevers within a year of their arrival in the Ottoman Empire he'd insisted Richard return to London. Harry himself had stayed to build his fortune, but he'd missed his brother very badly during the first year of their separation. Later, when Harry had accumulated enough wealth and trading contacts to return home, the situation in England—and his future—had irrevocably changed. He'd wanted to see Richard, but he'd had no desire to confront the man whose title and estates he would one day inherit. He'd assuaged his restlessness by moving more frequently within the Ottoman Empire than most European merchants. He'd gone from his original home in Aleppo to Istanbul and ended in Smyrna before finally returning to London.

'Why didn't you come back before?' Saskia's gaze was fixed on his face.

'I was content where I was.'

'Then why did you come back now? Did you stop being content?'

That was too close to the truth for comfort. Harry returned fire with fire. 'What's your urgent business in Portsmouth?'

'None of your—' She broke off and sat back. 'We'll discuss it tomorrow.'

'We will? Let's discuss it now.'

'No. We will discuss it tomorrow *if* you perform your duties successfully in the meantime,' she said firmly. 'I have known several men who returned from the Levant. They were factors. Were you a factor?'

'Do I look like a factor?' She'd guessed correctly and he was curious to hear her response.

'I imagine you might,' she said, surprising him. 'I was told European merchants often adopt Turkish dress in the streets to avoid drawing attention to themselves. Did you wear a turban? Is that why your hair is shorter than fashionable?'

'Franks,' Harry corrected her. 'To the people of the Ottoman Empire, all Europeans are Franks. Tell me the names of your acquaintances. No doubt I know them.' The English, Dutch, Venetians and other Europeans all had their own quarters within each trading city, but Harry had always kept himself well informed about his fellow—and rival—factors.

'I don't recall at this moment.' She evaded his question with barely a flicker of hesitation. 'You didn't tell me whether you wore a turban.'

'Often.' Harry had no idea why she was interested. 'In Smyrna it was usual for Franks to wear European hats, but by the time I moved there I was used to the turban. I'm damned if I'll ever wear a wig.'

Saskia smiled at his forthright statement, but her gaze didn't waver as she continued her interrogation. 'Did you return to England because you'd made your fortune—or because you'd ruined yourself and your principal?'

'Mmm-hmm.' Harry grinned, enjoying their verbal battle. 'Bad bargains, bad luck, misreading the markets—every ship brought another letter from my principal reprimanding me for my poor decisions…'

Saskia gave a soft laugh. 'Yet he still continued to make use of your services. Either he is an indifferent businessman or your decisions were not as poor as you claim.'

It was the first time Harry had ever heard her laugh. When he saw the amusement sparkling in her eyes, he realised just how strained she was usually. For a few heartbeats, lost in her reminiscent amusement, she was completely relaxed, almost carefree—and utterly captivating.

Harry forgot his mission. Forgot why he'd insisted they spend the night at Kingston. Forgot everything except the pleasure of watching Saskia's transitory happiness. Unfortunately, his body wasn't content with just looking. From the moment Saskia had lowered her mask he'd felt the stirring of desire. For a while he'd managed to suppress his awareness of how she affected him, but now his physical reaction to her intensified until it was almost painful. His body was making demands he could neither ignore nor satisfy.

Frustration with himself and the situation eroded his temper. Saskia, blithely oblivious of his edgy, unsettled state, was the cause of his difficulties—and she became the focus of his irritation.

'How will you explain this to your lord?' he demanded.

'Explain what?' Saskia looked up at him, a half-smile still lingering on her lips, confusion in her eyes.

Harry stared at her. Either she was a very good actress or she didn't seem to find anything odd about being alone in the bedchamber with him. 'If you don't know, I must have been away from England longer than I realised,' he said.

'I hoped we won't have to leave England.' Her eyes clouded. 'It would be better to finish it here.'

'Finish what?' Harry's hunting instincts went on full alert at her unwary comment.

He saw her snatch a quick little breath, and the expression in her eyes suddenly became guarded, but she replied calmly, 'Getting safely to my lord, of course.'

Her *besotted, devoted* lord, she'd called him earlier. Harry gritted his teeth and buttered a piece of bread to give himself time to overcome an unwelcome surge of jealousy towards a man whose existence he still doubted. He had no intention of becoming as besotted as her probably mythical lover.

'Will we need to leave England to do that?' he asked.

'No, he's in Plym—*Ports*mouth.'

Plymouth! She'd nearly said Plymouth! Portsmouth was in Hampshire, but Plymouth was in Devon, on the other side of the River Tamar from

Cornwall. Saskia van Buren had come to London from Cornwall. If that was their true destination, it seemed more likely than ever that she was indeed Saskia. Even though Harry was exerting all his self-discipline to control the fiercely conflicting instincts and emotions raging within him, he felt a burst of satisfaction at unravelling her lies a little more.

'If your lord is in Portsmouth, why may we have to leave England?' he said, as if he hadn't noticed her slip of the tongue.

She frowned. 'Please don't ask any more questions. We are going to Portsmouth, and it is your job to protect me.'

'And once we reach Portsmouth, your lord—the one who is opposed to marriage—will take over the task of protecting you?' Despite himself, Harry couldn't hide the scepticism in his voice.

Saskia glared at him. 'You insult *me* when you speak of him so disparagingly,' she said.

Harry felt a stab of guilt at her charge. She'd been lying to him from the first, she might well be plotting against England and she seemed to be completely oblivious that she was directly responsible for his having the most painfully pleasurable, disturbing and frustrating meal of his life. Those learned men who claimed the mere sight of a woman's uncovered hair could rouse a man to undisciplined lust obviously knew what they were talking about. He really shouldn't care whether he offended her—but he did.

'I did *not* insult you,' he said brusquely. 'From what you said earlier, it sounds as if you think you may need to leave England. Is that true?'

She hesitated. For several long moments they stared at each other across the width of the table. Harry was unwillingly fascinated by the swiftly changing emotions in her expression. She was trying to decide if she could trust him. The silence lengthened and the tension between them increased until he could almost hear it snapping in the air.

She looked away abruptly and drew in a quick breath. 'I hope not,' she said. 'But if we need to leave you would not have to come with us—though you will be well rewarded if you do.'

'*We,*' she'd said. A deep instinct told Harry she'd spoken the truth. She really was on her way to join someone else. Had the widow taken a lover within months of her husband's death? A core of ice formed within him at the possibility.

'You would pay me to protect your lover as well as you?' he said, his voice hardening.

'You are a presumptuous, impertinent fellow!' Saskia's temper erupted without warning. 'Eat your supper and mind your manners. We will leave at dawn.'

Her angry reaction—almost as if she'd been trying to hide her avoidance of the question by a burst of irritation—rekindled Harry's doubts about the existence of a lover. And his disgust with himself for caring.

'You are aware that in June it is light by four o'clock?' he said.

'Of course.' The lady rubbed her elbow, almost as if she'd banged it against something, though Harry hadn't noticed her doing any such thing. 'At least I can sleep in a bed tonight,' she muttered.

Harry's eyes widened. If she hadn't been sleeping in a bed, where *had* she been sleeping? And what had she been doing in her unorthodox resting place to hurt her arm?

Saskia wasn't consciously aware she was rubbing her elbow, she was thinking about her journey to London from Cornwall. It had been a long and hazardous journey for an unaccompanied woman, even with the protection of the male clothing she'd worn. The summer weather had made it possible for her to sleep on the ground several nights rather than risk staying alone at an inn, but she hadn't felt either comfortable or safe. The last night had been the worst. She'd been so tired she'd fallen heavily asleep in a small copse of trees, only to be woken by what, in her overtaxed state, had seemed to be the appalling cacophony of the dawn chorus. After her first moment of panic and confusion she'd felt as if every bird in England had taken roost above her head and was now bugling its lungs out within a few feet of her. As she'd flailed about, struggling to sit up, she'd cracked her elbow against a tree.

She was glad that tonight she could sleep safely in a proper bed—but she didn't realise she'd spoken aloud until she saw Harry's startled gaze flicker from her to the bed and back again.

Until that moment she hadn't given a thought to the significance of their surroundings. She almost groaned as she suddenly understood what Harry had meant about the need to make awkward explanations to her lord. How could she have been so stupidly unaware of something so obvious? Especially when she was pretending to be the mistress of a devoted lover. Her cheeks burned with embarrassment at revealing herself to be so unworldly.

She knew why she hadn't considered the implications of being alone with a man in a bedchamber. For more than four years of her marriage she had taught herself to think of her bed as a place only for sleep. Pieter had regained far more strength after the accident than any of them had initially expected. He'd even designed his own wheeled-chair that he could manoeuvre on flat surfaces—but making love was one aspect of their married life they'd never recovered. Saskia had learned not to torment herself with thoughts of what they'd lost. It was shocking—disorientating—to realise that her potential future in this regard had changed. She was a widow, not the wife of an intelligent, but physically incapacitated husband.

She stared at Harry. She'd known from her first glance at him that he was a virile, energetic man, but somehow she had distanced herself from that knowledge, seeing in his strength only a means to protect her and save Benjamin. Now she looked at him again—with the eyes of a woman whose vows of fidelity had died with her husband.

She saw the play of candlelight on the lean sinews of his forearms as he laid his knife down and picked up the tankard of ale. Simple, mundane actions—but suddenly she was very aware that she was looking at a man's strong hands. A man whose whole body was just as strong and deft. His self-assurance, lean, handsome features and piercing gaze commanded attention, but she'd rarely met a man with less vanity about his masculine appeal. An edge of danger always lurked beneath his apparently nonchalant exterior. But though he must know that element of his character was attractive to women, she'd never seen him take advantage of it the way another might. He was intelligent, slightly exotic, physically compelling—and without doubt the most dangerously attractive man Saskia had ever met.

Her thoughts and emotions scrambled. In that moment, as long-suppressed parts of herself flexed back into uncertain life, it was as if Pieter died again—because another man was stirring her feminine interest. As she gazed at Harry, tears filled her eyes.

He froze, his expression suddenly as blank as the mask she'd hidden behind at the coffee-house. He stood abruptly. 'We'll leave at dawn,' he said harshly.

'Wh-what? Where are you going?' Saskia managed to find her voice just as he reached the door. 'You haven't finished your supper.'

'You hired me to protect you—not to sit watching me eat like a lamb supping with a lion.'

Saskia gaped at his retreating back. It took her a few moments to grasp his meaning. 'I am *not* a lamb!' she exclaimed indignantly. But it was too late. The door had already closed behind him.

She'd had tears in her eyes! She must have realised he was lusting after her like a rutting stag and the knowledge had frightened her. Harry slammed his clenched fist into the palm of his other hand. He would have to control his unruly passions better in future. If she was a spy she must be prevented from causing harm to England. But even a spy should not be subjected to fear of abuse at a man's hands. *Never* at his hands. More than two decades ago, filled with disgust and powerless fury, he had made that promise to himself. He would never physically mistreat a woman. But now he was back in England he must take care not to distress them in other ways.

Richard wouldn't have made such a gauche error. He'd always been at ease in the company of others. Though Richard didn't possess Harry's physical toughness, he had a shrewd grasp of business that had helped him advance his career, tempered by a charm of manner that had won him many friends. Harry was confident his younger brother had never made a woman cry, even by mistake.

Harry forced his clenched fists to relax, reminding himself that Saskia had repeatedly lied to him. He must not lose sight of the fact that even if she wasn't a Dutch agent, she was undoubtedly hatching some as yet undisclosed plan.

He didn't like leaving her alone at the inn, but they'd left London so precipitously he had little choice if he wanted to get a message to Lord Swiftbourne. It was Harry's good luck that the regular route from London to Portsmouth went through Kingston. Swiftbourne's grandson and heir had married a lady who owned a house in Kingston. Harry had never met Jakob Balston, but he hoped Balston would be at home and that he'd either be able to take or send a message to Swiftbourne. He stopped to ask for directions. A few minutes later he arrived at the house and was relieved to discover his luck had held.

'Harry Ward!' Balston greeted him. 'Your brother is a friend of mine. I've been looking forward to meeting you.'

'And I you.' Harry shook hands. He'd been aware of Balston's existence for years, but knew Swiftbourne's grandson had only arrived in England from Sweden the previous summer. Balston was a couple of inches taller than Harry's six feet, broad and solidly muscled, with pale blond hair. Harry immediately thought of Saskia's hair. He preferred the warm, reddish glow of Saskia's blonde curls. His fingers still ached to touch them, whereas he felt no urge to touch Balston's hair.

'I apologise for calling so late,' he said.

'I'm glad to meet you at any time,' Balston replied. 'I've just returned from Sussex. My wife is still there, admiring the Kilverdales' new daughter, but I had business to attend to here.'

'The Duke is another of Swiftbourne's grandsons,' Harry remembered. He'd not met any of Swiftbourne's family while he was under the Earl's guardianship, partly because of the divisions caused by the Civil War, but mostly because he and Richard had left for Aleppo within weeks of becoming Swiftbourne's wards.

Jakob smiled. 'Since your father's sister was married to Swiftbourne's oldest son, you can claim cousinship with us,' he said.

'A very distant connection,' said Harry.

'But a connection nevertheless. So sit down and tell me how I may serve you.'

Harry briefly summarised his meeting with Swiftbourne and then the outcome of his interview with Saskia at the coffee-house. 'She insisted on leaving London immediately, so I had no opportunity to take or send a message to Swiftbourne,' he concluded.

'Is she a spy?'

'No.' Harry paused to consider his immediate, instinctive denial. 'I don't believe she has told me the truth,' he said, oddly reluctant to discuss Saskia with Balston. 'But I have no doubt her fear is genuine.'

'You have no idea what the lady is afraid of?'

'No, but I will find out.' Harry stood up, anxious to return to the Coach and Horses and Saskia. 'I will be in your debt if you ensure Swiftbourne knows what has happened so far.'

'I'll go into London tomorrow. To be honest I'm glad of the errand.' Balston smiled a little wryly. 'I find I miss my wife when we are apart. Visiting Swiftbourne will fill the time until my own business is concluded and I can fetch her back from Sussex.'

Sunday morning, 16 June 1667

'You are an arrogant, presumptuous fool! How dare you suggest I would let *anyone* eat me up without a bleat of protest—least of all you.' Saskia kept her voice down, but she made no effort to hide her indignation.

'Bleat of protest?' Harry repeated. They were breakfasting together downstairs at the Coach and Horses. Or rather, Harry was making a good breakfast of cold turkey pie while Saskia nibbled on some bread and butter, most of which she fully intended to save for later. Just because she *could* get up with the birds didn't mean she had to eat her first meal of the day with them.

They were the only customers in the room and Saskia glanced around to make sure none of the inn servants were close enough to overhear her. 'I am not a little lamb,' she stated unequivocally.

Harry had been munching his turkey pie in what

Saskia considered to be a rather grumpy silence. She decided he must dislike getting up early as much as she did. At her announcement he looked up, good humour suddenly—and in Saskia's view inappropriately—softening his expression.

'Ah, I see. Are you claiming that you are a lioness disguised in lamb's clothing?' he enquired. 'Or would you prefer a gentler comparison? A doe, perhaps? Graceful and fleet of foot—'

'I am not any kind of animal,' said Saskia. 'In future, do not use such metaphors for me.' She could foresee that when she finally told him their true destination was three times further than he currently anticipated, his comparisons might be considerably less flattering. 'We are not living in Aesop's fables.'

Harry grinned. 'But how interesting it would be to discuss with a hawk what she sees as she soars in the sky. Or ask a whale what hides in the depth of the ocean.'

Saskia blinked at his unexpectedly poetic response. 'I had not anticipated such whimsy from you, sir.'

'Whimsy? If you are walking over barren, rocky ground, isn't it natural to look up at the hawk and wonder what it would be like to fly so fast to your goal? They use doves to carry messages between Skanderoon and Aleppo. I would rather be a hawk than a dove.'

'I…' Saskia stopped. As a child she'd had such thoughts when she went down to the Cornish coast or walked on Dartmoor in neighbouring Devon, but it was a long time since she'd allowed anything but the most practical ambitions into her mind.

'My husband could not walk,' she said abruptly. 'He designed for himself a chair with wheels. He even made some of the more intricate parts himself—his hands were still quick and strong. But he could only use it on a flat surface. Clambering over rocky ground was just as much an impossible dream to him as the hawk's flight is to you.'

She saw Harry draw in a sharp breath, but he didn't look away as so many had when they'd first heard what had happened to Pieter. She didn't know why she'd told him. Was she obliquely punishing Harry because she was so attracted to the strength and agility he possessed and Pieter had lost?

'He was a man of resolution and determination,' said Harry.

'Yes, he was.' She lifted her chin.

'And ingenuity.'

'Yes.' Her relationship with Pieter had been severely damaged by the impact of his accident, but there had been many times since she'd fled from Cornwall she wished she could call on some of his practical ingenuity. She still had no idea how she was going to rescue Benjamin.

'Why couldn't he walk?'

'He was hurt when a rope broke and a wooden chest fell on him,' she said. 'It was being hauled up to the second floor.' She stopped speaking as vivid, still shocking memories crowded her mind.

Like many houses in Amsterdam, their home had been built with the end wall slanting outward over the street, so that goods could be easily winched up to store below the roof. Pieter had used that method to have a large, finely carved chest lifted, rather than have it carried up several flights of stairs. He'd been overseeing the work when the chest had come crashing down, pinning him beneath it. Saskia had heard the impact from indoors, and the muffled shouts and screams that followed. She'd run outside to find Pieter face down in the street, unconscious, blood on his forehead. In her first moment of horror she'd thought he was dead, and then that his skull must have been cracked. Later she'd discovered he'd suffered only minor grazes to his face. The permanent damage had been to his ability to walk. His legs weren't broken, but after the blow to his lower back he could no longer feel or control them.

'How did he die?' Harry's sharp question dragged her back to the present.

'A fever last autumn,' she said. 'He was more susceptible to illness after his accident—but until that last time he'd always recovered.'

'He was not killed in the war between the Dutch and the English?'

'No.' Saskia frowned with confusion at the unexpected question. 'He was a merchant, but he never left Hol—home,' she corrected herself just in time. She cast her mind anxiously back over all she'd just said. The picture of Pieter lying at the foot of their Amsterdam house had been so vivid she was worried she might have inadvertently said something that gave away the location. She was sure that once she'd explained the whole situation to Harry he would understand her Dutch connections were irrelevant, but she wasn't yet ready to confide in him completely.

Harry's dark eyes were alert and watchful as he studied her. She sensed the contained energy within him and felt a flicker of apprehension. She'd seen a hawk suddenly fold its wings and arrow down out of the sky when it spotted its prey. Was she the unwary prey on which Harry meant to swoop? Was he working for Lady Abergrave after all? Or was her nervousness caused by a far more fundamental reason—the awareness of a woman for a powerful, attractive man?

'Are you going to eat anything?' he asked.

'What?' She blinked and then glanced down at her forgotten breakfast. 'I'll bring it with me.'

'Then let's linger no longer. There's no point in tormenting yourself by rising early if you don't make good use of the extra hours.'

There was a note of amusement in his voice that caused Saskia to look at him suspiciously. 'Do you *like* getting up early?'

'As it happens, I do.'

'I can't stand people who like getting up early,' she muttered as she collected her bread. 'No matter how wayward they are in other respects, they always consider themselves entitled to moralise over the rest of us.'

Harry grinned. 'The early bird catches the worm.'

'Do *not* talk to me about birds,' Saskia said darkly.

Harry rode beside the coach, relaxed in the saddle, though his eyes constantly scanned the surrounding countryside. The lush green fields and woods of southern England in early summer were very different to the dramatic and beautiful Turkish landscape which had become so familiar to him. The sky was a clear blue, and it had turned into a hot June day. The heat was of no consequence to Harry, but he felt the familiar urge to abandon the main thoroughfare and explore the shady woods and tranquil fields and heaths along their way. His tendency to investigate beyond his immediate surroundings had been of great value to him in the past. Experience had shown him that increased knowledge tended to confer increased power and choice. But he knew how to discipline his curiosity. Especially when he had a mystery closer to hand that was far more compelling than any slow-running English stream.

According to the woman in the coach, her husband had been crippled in a mundane accident years ago and died as the result of a fever, not a British cannonball. Had she nearly said *Holland* before she'd corrected it to *home*? The evidence that he was indeed dealing with Saskia was increasingly strong, but he was no closer to knowing her true plans. All he could be certain of was that either Saskia or Swiftbourne's informant was lying. He could see no reason for Saskia to make up such a complicated story about her husband's accident, whereas her lie about the jealous mistress did serve a purpose—it gave her an excuse to claim the need for protection.

He considered what he knew about Swiftbourne's informant. According to Tancock's story, he'd been secretary to the late Earl of Abergrave before continuing to serve the widowed Lady Abergrave. Lady Abergrave was Saskia's aunt. Tancock claimed Saskia had returned to England after the death of her husband fighting the English, and that her bitterness against her former countrymen had soon become evident. Swiftbourne said Tancock had spoken most eloquently of Lady Abergrave's torment as she struggled to choose between love for her niece and loyalty to England.

Even though he'd never met either of them, Harry had taken an immediate, possibly irrational, dislike to both Tancock and Lady Abergrave. He found it hard to warm to a woman who had her servant inform one of the King's Ministers that her grieving niece was a traitor. Had Lady Abergrave made any attempt to comfort or talk sense into Saskia before giving Tancock the order to approach Swiftbourne? Harry knew better than most that grief, anger and the driving need for revenge could propel almost anyone to take terrible actions. But from all he'd seen, Saskia wasn't driven by rage, but by an anxious need for haste.

He wondered when she was going to tell him they were going to Plymouth, not Portsmouth. She couldn't delay much longer. Once they reached Guildford the routes diverged.

It was after one o'clock, and Harry was thinking he'd insist they stop for dinner at the next inn when his instincts suddenly prickled with danger. It was the hottest part of the day and the heath around them dozed in the bright sunshine, the air heavy with the scents of summer. The low-lying heather was studded with birch and hazel trees, patches of yellow gorse and bramble bushes. A butterfly danced past on the warm air. A woodlark singing in a nearby birch was startled into undulating flight by the approaching coach, but there was nothing to alarm him. Yet with every heartbeat Harry's sense of imminent threat intensified.

A casual movement brought his hand close to one of his pistols as he surveyed the landscape with eyes narrowed against the glare of the sun.

There!

The betraying toss of a horse's head as it stood in the shadow of a hazel copse fifty yards away. Two waiting men on horses. One man taking aim with a musket—

Chapter Three

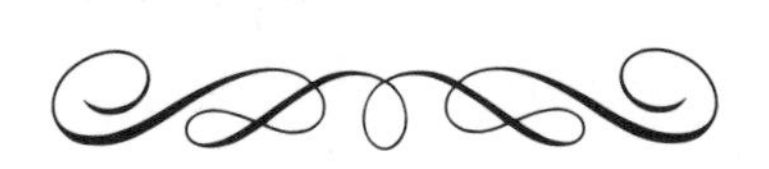

Saskia stared out of the coach window at the heat-hazed heath, considering how much to reveal to Harry. At the very least she had to tell him they were going to Cornwall, not Hampshire. And once she'd admitted she'd been lying about their destination, it might be difficult to retain Harry's trust unless she told him the whole story—

The crack of musket fire shattered the peaceful afternoon.

Saskia jerked upright, so startled she barely identified the sound before shouts filled the air. The coach juddered to a halt, and then lurched forward a few yards before finally stopping. Saskia was flung on to her knees on the coach floor. She scrabbled for purchase on the opposite seat.

Tancock! Her whole body clenched with fear that he'd found her. Then she heard shouts of *'Money!'*

and *'Purse!'* Highwaymen. She let out a gasping breath. Not good, but better than Tancock. He wanted her dead. Highwaymen wanted only her money.

She wore two pockets beneath her skirts. One contained the bills of exchange, the other her coins. She needed the bills to save Benjamin. Her heart hammered against her ribs as she struggled to unfasten her coin pocket. She would hand it over the moment the highwayman appeared at the coach window and hope he didn't find the bills of exchange. She only wished she had some jewels to catch his eyes and satisfy his lust for booty.

The thunder of galloping hooves grew terrifyingly louder. Her skirts were still bunched around her waist, her knees exposed to full sight as she fumbled with her coin pocket. She couldn't be found like this. Her second pocket with the bills of exchange would be discovered. She gave a desperate pull and the coin pocket was safe in her hand. She shoved down her skirts with shaking hands and scrambled forward to look out of the window.

Two horsemen were bearing down on the coach, pistols in hand, their faces hidden by scarves. She threw herself back from the window. Instinct propelled her to the door on the other side of the coach. If she could get far enough from the coach before they reached it, perhaps she could hide on the heath amid the gorse and bramble bushes?

She wrenched open the door. The first thing she saw was Harry's riderless horse galloping away across the heather. The second thing was Harry's body, lying motionless on the ground. Until that moment she'd almost forgotten Harry. She was too used to dealing with crises on her own. A sob of shock and denial caught in her throat. He'd been hit. Dear God, he'd been hit by that first lone shot. Maybe he was dead. He couldn't be dead.

The money *and* her bills would have to be their salvation. She prayed the highwaymen were too sophisticated to place value only on gold. She would give them all she had so they left quickly and she could tend to Harry's wound.

There was a second gunshot, much closer and louder than the original shot, followed almost immediately by a third. She heard shouts of rage and pain through ringing ears. The relentless rhythm of hoofbeats faltered. It was only then she saw Harry's head was up and smoke was rising from the pistols he held in each outstretched hand.

He speared one glance at her as he sprang to his feet. 'Stay out of sight,' he barked, and disappeared from her view as he ran towards their attackers.

He wasn't hurt. She didn't believe any man who'd been shot could move so easily. She sagged with momentary relief—but the danger wasn't over yet.

Harry had told her to stay out of sight, but she had to know what was happening. She crawled to the other side of the coach and opened the door closest to the highwaymen a tiny crack so she could look through it without showing herself at the window.

One of their attackers was on the ground. She was just in time to see the other disappearing into a stand of trees some distance from the road. He was swaying in the saddle, but he didn't fall while she was watching. Sword in hand, Harry approached the prone man, wary and alert as he satisfied himself the highwayman was no longer a threat.

Saskia pushed open the door. Only her hand, clinging to the bottom of the window, prevented her from pitching headfirst onto the stony, dusty road.

Harry looked up at her. In that first searing glance she saw the dangerous predator within him fully exposed. He was still in a state of complete battle readiness, poised to strike at any threat. His eyes burned with feral intensity, his lips were drawn back in a silent snarl of warning. She jolted in shock, but as she stared at him the ferocity faded from his face. He still held his unsheathed sword. His body was taut with readiness, but his expression was now almost disconcertingly emotionless.

'I thought they'd killed you!' she gasped.

'I shot *him*,' Harry said grittily, indicating the man

on the ground. 'I winged the other one.' He looked up at the coachman. 'You did well. When you've calmed your team, catch my horse—and this poltroon's as well, if you can.' He nudged the fallen highwayman with the toe of his boot.

'Yes, sir,' the coachman said in a shaking voice. 'I thought they were going to kill us all.'

Saskia remained where she was, suspended between the floor of the coach and the door, too overwhelmed by the sudden violence to be fully aware of her awkward position or try to extricate herself from it. She watched Harry approach her. He strode across the ground with fluid, powerful grace, sheathing his sword with an ease that spoke of years of practice.

He bent to catch her around the waist and lift her out of the coach. She was trembling so badly her legs couldn't support her. Harry's arms closed around her, holding her up and holding her tight against him. She clutched his coat, pressing her face into his shoulder. She could smell the burnt powder from his pistols. He'd killed to protect them.

She'd been afraid when she'd overheard her aunt and Tancock plotting her murder in Cornwall. She'd been terrified when she'd fled from Tancock in London. But her panic on those occasions had been akin to the fear experienced in nightmares.

Horrifying, but without the gut-wrenching intrusion of immediate, brutal violence. For several moments her teeth chattered so badly she couldn't speak, even if she'd wanted to. She clung to Harry, taking comfort in the steadiness of his hard-muscled body. He was breathing a little faster than normal, but he wasn't shaking. He'd responded to the highwaymen's attack with speed and ruthless efficiency. For the first time in years she allowed herself to lean on someone else's strength. Harry didn't murmur any soothing words, nor did he give her any comforting caresses. But he continued to hold her close while she slowly regained her composure.

As her mind gradually cleared, she realised they weren't standing still. Harry was supporting her weight in his arms as he kept moving slowly around so he could watch in all directions. The feel of his hard body against her was an illicit pleasure. As her shock receded she felt a different kind of excitement flow through her veins. It was so long since she'd been held in a man's arms and been so directly aware of masculine strength. There was nothing lover-like about Harry's behaviour, but his silent embrace was seducing her attention away from everything else that had just happened.

But it was a deceptive seduction. Even as she became aware of the intimacy of their position she felt a change in him. When he'd first lifted her from the coach he'd held her in an undemonstrative but comforting way. Now there was a rigid tension in the arms around her that felt humiliatingly like rejection. He was still holding her, but subtly easing her away from his body as if he'd had enough of her emotional outburst. It wasn't the first time she'd felt that kind of silent rejection. No words spoken, but the unmistakable awareness that the man she was clinging to did not want her so close to him. Hurt and mortification burned through her, but experience had taught her how to hide her feelings and make light of such awkward moments.

She released her grip on Harry, but didn't try to move away because his arms were still a steel band around her and she refused to embarrass herself by struggling. Instead she lifted her head and forced a jaunty note into her voice as she asked, 'Will you drop me if a new danger appears?'

His jaw was locked rigid, his face so stiff she thought he must be fighting the urge to push her away, but to her surprise his expression seemed to soften slightly at her words.

'It would depend on the nature of the threat,' he said. He set her on her feet with precise carefulness and immediately stepped away from her. 'If I see anyone else levelling a musket at us from the shelter of the trees—as I did earlier—I would take you down with me when I drop. But I doubt there will be another attack now.'

'I hope not.' Saskia rubbed her hand up and down her arm. Even though she knew he hadn't welcomed their brief intimacy, she felt exposed and shaky without his steady strength to lean upon. She tried not to feel hurt that he didn't want to be close to her. She'd hired him to get her safely to Cornwall, and so far he'd carried out that task very effectively. He had no obligation to like embracing her. 'What are we going to do now?'

'Take up the body and deliver it to the local constable,' said Harry.

'I don't want him in the coach with me.' Saskia gave an involuntary shudder at the prospect of travelling with the dead man.

'If the coachman manages to catch both loose horses, you won't have to.'

Saskia looked around and saw that so far he'd only caught Harry's horse.

'I'll help him—'

'No, you won't,' Harry said crisply, not looking up from where he was searching the dead highwayman's pockets.

'I'm good with horses,' she said, irritated by his flat veto of her suggestion. She'd managed to take care of her horse all the way from Cornwall to London without any problems.

'If you think I'm going to let you wander the open heath, chirping at a strange horse, you must have taken leave of your senses.' Harry scanned their surroundings once more. 'You hired me to protect you.'

'I didn't know we were going to get waylaid by highwaymen,' said Saskia, torn between annoyance and an absurd feeling she should apologise to him for the inconvenience.

'Hiring me was rather like building a roof to keep out the rain and discovering it does equally well to keep out hail and snow,' said Harry, from his tone obviously not pleased about it.

'I don't see why you're in such a bad mood,' said Saskia, sitting on the floor of the coach with her feet dangling towards the ground. Surely he couldn't still be grumpy because he'd had to hug her for a few moments? 'I'm a novice at being shot at—in fact, this is my first time,' she pointed out, 'but you must be used to it.'

'I'm used to sandflies, but that doesn't mean I like them.'

'We weren't attacked by sandflies. In any case, you've clearly led a very adventurous life. I really don't see how much difference there is between fending off highwaymen or—'

'The henchmen of your lord's jealous former mistress,' Harry interrupted drily.

'Ah...well...' Until Harry's comment Saskia had temporarily forgotten her excuse for needing his protection. She'd told him she wanted him to keep her alive, but he couldn't really have supposed the jealous mistress meant to kill her. More likely he'd assumed the other woman just wanted Saskia to be physically humiliated. No wonder he wasn't best pleased at finding himself attacked by pistol-bearing highwaymen.

She remembered her money pocket and reached back into the coach to retrieve it. 'I was going to give it to them,' she said, when she saw Harry looking at it.

He nodded. 'I didn't make my reputation by letting bandits steal the goods,' he said, 'but it was a wise choice. If a man demands your money or your life, always give him the money.'

Despite the warmth of the summer's day, Saskia wrapped her arms around herself. 'What if he can only get the money after you're dead?' she said.

Harry looked directly at her for the first time since he'd released her from his embrace. His expression was guarded, but his eyes searching. She wondered what he saw and whether she had revealed too much in that involuntary comment.

'I could only catch your horse, sir,' the coachman called.

Harry raised his hand in acknowledgement, but kept his gaze on Saskia. 'You do everything in your power to remain alive until you can remove the threat,' he said.

The highwayman's horse had gone for good, so Harry put the dead man on to his horse and sat beside the coachman on the way to the next village. The coachman was still shaken and he wanted to talk about what had happened. It took all Harry's self-discipline to tolerate the other man's anxieties and questions. He was still experiencing the after-effects of violence himself. That surge of diamond-cold ferocity in response to danger had served him well on many occasions. He knew it always took time to shift from that split-second lethal intensity to his usual equilibrium. But today his fight to bring his body and emotions under his control was much harder. From the moment he'd seen the highwayman levelling the musket he'd been driven by deadly fury at the threat to Saskia. And when the immediate danger was over and he'd seen how shocked she was, he'd been compelled to take her into his arms. To comfort her. To assure himself that she was indeed unharmed…

But he'd never before held a woman while the hot blood of combat still pounded through his veins. While he was still filled with rage at the enemy. Within a few heartbeats his battle-roused body had been invaded by a different kind of lust. A driving compulsion to satisfy his fierce desire for a woman—for Saskia.

He'd wanted to touch her. To stroke her. To press her hips against him—to thrust himself into her—

As she'd trembled with fear in his arms he'd fought a bitter battle with himself, furious and disgusted with himself that he could experience such savage physical need to take her when she was so vulnerable. She'd turned trustingly to him for comfort. If she'd known what he'd been thinking—feeling—she'd have been more terrified of him than of the highwaymen. The image of another woman screaming in powerless fear flashed into his mind. Despite his self-control, he shuddered.

'You did right,' said the coachman. 'Sewer dregs like that don't deserve to live.' With a nod of his head he indicated the highwayman.

'I'll not lose any sleep over him,' Harry said curtly, realising the coachman had misunderstood the cause of his shudder. 'But it's inconvenient. We'll lose some time over this.'

A few minutes later they reached the next village.

It consisted of an inn, a church, a blacksmith's, a baker's and a cluster of houses. The arrival of the coach and the dead highwayman drew a small crowd of interested locals, one of whom was the constable. Several of the men recognised the corpse as Jem Crayford. According to their excited comments, he'd been a notorious local villain who had plagued the neighbourhood for the past eighteen months. But the forms still had to be observed. The constable asked Harry a few questions and then went in search of the magistrate.

After that, Saskia and Harry were urged into the inn, the innkeeper's wife in particular making a fuss of Saskia. Harry's eyes narrowed briefly as he realised Saskia was being taken out of the taproom into the landlady's inner sanctum. He almost protested, but he was used to the separation of the sexes and it made sense to him that, after being exposed to male violence, Saskia needed the comfort of other women around her. Though she was quite calm, she was very pale and he could see signs of strain in her face. She threw one questioning glance at him and then allowed herself to be carried off.

A tankard of ale appeared in front of Harry.

'Good riddance to the villain,' the blacksmith observed. There was a mutter of agreement from the other men.

'He was well known in these parts?' Harry asked.

'Crayford made the Dog and Duck alehouse over yonder his headquarters,' said the blacksmith. 'Boasted about his exploits, so I heard, but there wasn't any solid evidence against him. Those who knew anything were too frightened to speak out—afraid they'd end up at the bottom of a well.'

'Did he often hurt those he robbed?' said Harry.

'He shot coach horses as a warning to his victims.' The blacksmith's expression was grim. 'After that, most people he held up were too terrified to do anything but hand over their valuables.'

'Indeed,' said Harry, thinking of the musket that had been aimed at his heart. He had no doubt that death, not terror, had been the intended outcome of that shot.

Saskia was grateful for the kindness of the local women, but she couldn't afford to relax her guard in their company. Harry had introduced her as Sarah Brewster, and given the impression she was a respectable widow travelling to Portsmouth on unspecified business. Saskia was far more comfortable in that role than portraying herself as the mistress to an unnamed lord, but she still had to watch everything she said. Oddly, it reminded her of times during her married life when she'd found herself surrounded by her female Dutch relatives.

When she'd first arrived in Amsterdam she'd been a new wife. Much had seemed strange to her, but she'd assumed she'd eventually have a secure and comfortable position within Pieter's family. After his accident she'd increasingly felt out of step with the other women. She hadn't been in Amsterdam long enough before the accident to develop any deep friendships, and afterwards she'd rejected the role of 'poor Saskia', instead putting most of her energy into taking care of her merchant husband's business. It was far more common for women to take part in business in Holland than in England, but Saskia had married into a wealthy family and none of the other women needed to take on such responsibilities. The other young wives had babies, and talked endlessly of their children, their husbands and their tasks within the homes they'd created.

Saskia had never confided in anyone her hurt, confusion and even anger at the way Pieter rejected the simplest gesture of affection once he knew he'd never recover any further from his accident. She'd found a way to manage her feelings and gradually their relationship had developed into something resembling a cordial but practical friendship between business partners. She'd greeted each baby into the family with warm smiles, but every time she hugged a new babe in her arms she'd ached with the knowledge she would never experience the pain and joy of motherhood. She hated the pity she saw in the other women's eyes, so she never let her sorrow show—but she always returned the baby to its mother as soon as courtesy allowed.

Now, as she sat in the midst of the English women, grateful for their sympathy over her ordeal with the highwaymen, but longing for the moment when they'd leave and she could finally lower her guard, she wondered for the first time whether she wanted to go back to her old life in Amsterdam. She'd always assumed she would return after visiting her brother. She'd inherited Pieter's business and she was proud of her achievements. But if she remained in Holland would she always be Pieter van Buren's childless widow? She could marry again, but she felt no affinity for any of the Dutch bachelors of her acquaintance.

The innkeeper's wife complimented Saskia archly on travelling with such a fine, handsome gentleman. 'Any woman would feel safe in the hands of such a man.'

'I am fortunate to be travelling with him,' Saskia replied sedately, but her thoughts instantly focused on the exciting feel of being in Harry's arms—at least until he'd had enough of such close contact with her. That memory hurt, and she quickly shut her mind to it.

From the expression on some of the other women's faces, she suspected they were also imagining the pleasure of being in Harry's embrace. She suddenly realised that, for the first time in years, she was the object of curiosity and perhaps even feminine jealousy because of a man. Harry, with his dark good looks, masculine charisma and indefinable air of danger, was the kind of man most women daydreamed about at some time in their lives. And he was with her. No one needed to know it was only because he'd responded to a notice on a coffee-room wall, and that he'd made it silently, but unmistakably, clear he didn't wish to hold her a moment longer than necessary.

'Yes, it is good to be in his hands,' she said serenely, hesitating just long enough before continuing, 'Normally I do not care for travelling, but he has managed every detail of the arrangements.' As the other women glanced at each other, she felt a burst of secret pleasure at her play with words. She had said nothing untoward. A widow unused to travelling might well ask a male friend or relative to assist her—but the picture of herself as the kind of woman who'd attracted Harry's sensual interest was enticing.

She wished it was true. It hurt far more than it should that it wasn't. Then she was angry with herself for caring—and suddenly she was desperate to be alone. She still hadn't told Harry they weren't going to Portsmouth. And somehow she had to persuade him to help her rescue Benjamin. Harry had been in a bad temper ever since the highwaymen's attack. What if he no longer wanted to continue on with her? The possibility he might abandon her was so awful it almost brought tears to her eyes.

She gathered her composure sufficiently to thank the innkeeper's wife and the other women and explain she needed to lie down for a while to recover. When they'd gone she sat at the window, worrying over the enforced delay to their journey and trying to decide how to persuade Harry to help her. As she did so she watched the people who came and went from the inn yard. Always, on some instinctive level, she was searching for Tancock's face. He shouldn't be here—but she hadn't expected to see him on her godfather's doorstep either.

Harry gave his statement to the magistrate and constable in one corner of the taproom. The rest of the village men remained at a respectable, but intensely curious, distance. When they'd first arrived, Harry had identified himself only as Sarah Brewster's escort. Because Saskia wasn't present at the interview with the magistrate, he was able to give his real name to the magistrate and put his true signature to his statement.

'I was given information a month ago I'd find Crayford at the Dog and Duck with his latest booty,' said the magistrate grimly, 'but when I got there he'd gone. You did well to protect Mistress Brewster from his attack.'

'He's not the first bandit I've dealt with,' said Harry. 'I take it you're satisfied with my account?'

'Yes, of course. Your coachman's statement agrees with yours in all essential details. Will you take supper with me this evening? I am eager to hear first-hand the experiences of one who has recently returned from Turkey.' The magistrate's eyes lit with genuine interest. He'd had no difficulty recognising Harry as a gentleman—but then Harry had made no effort to pretend to be anything else during their conversation.

'Thank you. I would be honoured to do so, but I am afraid I must decline,' said Harry, with real regret. He liked the magistrate's down-to-earth approach to his duties. 'I promised I would escort Mistress Brewster safely to Portsmouth. I have not spoken to her since we arrived here and I must consult her wishes for the rest of our journey.'

The other man nodded. 'Perhaps you will have an opportunity to call upon me when you are returning to London,' he said.

Harry took his leave of the magistrate and went out into the courtyard to stretch his legs and breathe some air untainted by the pipe smoke filling the taproom. The hot summer day had become a warm, golden evening. Across the fields he could hear church bells tolling for the evening service. Such a familiar sound from his boyhood, but one he hadn't often heard as an adult. There were synagogues and churches in Smyrna, but though Jews and Christians were free to follow their own religions, church bells were forbidden. Harry was more accustomed to hearing the muezzins calling the faithful to prayer five times a day than the sounds of his childhood.

His memories of the Levant were interrupted when several of the men who'd been sitting in the taproom accosted him with cheerful greetings and eager questions about the highwaymen's attack.

From her window, Saskia saw Harry enter the yard and her pulse quickened. Even at a distance she was immediately aware of his self-assurance and the poised strength in his lean body. He was surrounded by a group of men. She began to feel frustrated because she wanted to speak to him, not watch complete strangers slap him on the back. She was just about to go down into the yard when another man spoke to him. As the man turned more fully towards her, her instincts buzzed a warning. She'd seen him before. At first she couldn't remember where, but she immediately tensed at the sight of a man she recognized, but couldn't identify. It wasn't Tancock, but—

Trevithick House! She'd seen him at Trevithick. He was one of Tancock's underlings.

Sick fear gripped her as she watched Harry speak to him. It seemed to her horrified gaze that, though their conversation was brief, they were making arrangements to meet later. She watched Tancock's henchman slap Harry on the back. For an instant she was overwhelmed by crushing disappointment. She'd trusted Harry—but she knew little about him except he was fast and dangerous with the weapons he carried. Had he been working with Tancock from the beginning?

She dared not challenge him. If he was in league with Tancock, he would never give her the chance to escape once she'd revealed her suspicions. She backed away from the window. For a few seconds despair almost overcame her that once again her plans had gone astray. But she couldn't afford to despair, any more than she could afford to hesitate. She dived across the room to her bag.

Harry extricated himself from his new friends and went in search of Saskia, but the innkeeper's wife was alone when he found her.

'Mistress Brewster said many times how thankful she is you were with her today.' There was a mixture of curiosity and admiration in the landlady's gaze as she looked Harry up and down. 'You have a hardy way with villains, sir, but I'm sure any woman would feel safe in your hands.'

'I did what was needful,' said Harry curtly, ill at ease with both the blatant appreciation in the landlady's eyes and the tone of her compliment. 'I do thank you for your kindness to Mistress Brewster,' he added, trying to make up for his initial brusqueness. 'Where is she now?'

'I put her in a room overlooking the yard. I will show you—'

But to Harry's relief, the landlady's attention was claimed by another customer, so she was obliged to give him directions. He didn't mind being slapped on the back by the village men for dealing with a local villain, but the landlady's admiration was another matter.

Saskia didn't respond to his knock, nor to his voice when he identified himself. The first breath of alarm whispered through him. He opened the door without hesitation. One sweeping glance told him the room was empty. There was a discarded lady's glove lying on the floor. He picked it up, recognising it immediately as one he'd seen Saskia wear. His hunting instincts went on to full alert. He stepped out of the room and quietly closed the door. He hadn't seen any sign of Saskia on his way into the inn, so he continued further along the passage until he came to another set of stairs. At the bottom he found he had a choice of going back into the main yard he'd just left or towards the stables. He went towards the stables. He was in time to catch sight of a stripling in a plain brown coat and brown breeches disappear around the corner of the stables. A stripling with Saskia's hair and carrying her familiar bag.

She was alone. Harry's fear that she'd been snatched by her enemies receded. But was she going to meet someone else? He lengthened his walking stride to a deceptively ground-eating pace until he'd passed two grooms chatting by the stable door. As he turned the corner of the building he saw the apparent lad hurrying away from him, staying in the shadows behind the stable. Now there were no witnesses Harry ran, swift and silent in pursuit of his quarry. He caught Saskia by the shoulder and spun her around.

The instant he touched her, she gave a sobbing gasp of pure terror. He saw the dull glint of a knife blade as she struck wildly at him. He knocked her arm aside, but she kept attacking him in desperate silence.

He could see the panic in her face, feel her wrenching terror in the uncontrolled violence of her attempts to either escape or hurt him. He didn't know if she'd recognised him. If she had, it made no difference to her desperation. In his own defence he caught her wrists, but she didn't stop struggling and trying to kick him. Her hair had fallen over her eyes. Her face was contorted with fear.

His own heart pounded sickeningly against his ribs. Her fear disturbed him on a profound level. Her wrists felt so fragile in his grasp. He could barely tolerate holding her under such circumstances, but he managed to do so just long enough to reverse their positions. Now his back was to the wall and she had open space behind her. A clear escape route. He let her go.

She stumbled back and immediately tensed for flight.

'Don't run.' He was breathing almost as quickly as Saskia, but he managed to keep his voice low and steady. He held both hands out, palms up. 'I'm not going to hurt you. Do you know me? I'm Harry. I'm not going to hurt you.' He kept talking to her the way he would have talked to any frightened animal, trying to ignore the clenching in his gut. He could not stand to see a woman's terror.

She shook her head violently. 'You're working for Tancock.'

'I'm working for you.' He kept his reply simple and direct. It wasn't the moment for complicated explanations.

'No.' She kept shaking her head and backing away. 'I saw you talking to Selby.'

'I don't know Selby.'

'You do!' Her voice rose. 'I saw you. You were making arrangements to meet later.' She dragged in a deep breath and managed to lower her voice again. 'Whatever he's promised you, I can reward you better. Pieter was very rich. I'm one of the richest widows in Amsterdam. You can have it all.' Tears filled her eyes. 'Just don't kill me. I have to stay alive to save Benjamin.'

'Who's Benjamin?' The desperate love in her voice for another man provoked unfamiliar, jagged emotions within Harry.

'My brother,' she whispered.

'My God.' For several tense seconds they stared at each other. Then Harry snapped back to awareness of their surroundings. 'You hired me to keep you alive. Are you telling me you saw one of the men who wants to kill you here at this inn?'

'You talked to him.' Saskia's eyes brimmed with suspicion.

'A lot of men talked to me this evening. I don't know any of them. I am not working for any of them.

Come here. Back into the shadows of the wall.' Harry wanted to make sure she didn't draw the attention of her true enemy while he was trying to regain her trust.

She hesitated and then, very warily, moved closer to him.

'Good.' His nerves were still as taut as a drawn bow, but his tension marginally eased now that she was emerging from her panic.

'If you don't want to kill me, why aren't you angry with me for attacking you and accusing you?' she asked.

'How do you know I'm not?' Harry rasped his thumb along his jaw where she'd managed to land a blow. In truth, he was too relieved she'd calmed down to be angry.

'You don't look angry. And earlier you looked almost as scared of me as I was of you.'

'Scared *for* you,' said Harry stiffly. 'I was concerned you might hurt yourself.'

She nodded. Her eyes still seemed huge in her pale face, and her hand was trembling as she pushed her hair back, but she managed a small smile. 'I'm sorry I hurt you,' she said, looking at his jaw.

'It's nothing.' He lowered his arm. 'Where are you going now?'

'To hide in the woods while I work out what to do next.'

'Good enough.' If Saskia felt safer in the woods, he wasn't going to force her back into the inn. Especially when he had no idea how many of her enemies were inside or what they looked like. He picked up the knife she'd dropped and her bag. He returned the knife to her hilt first, but kept the bag. He glanced around to decide on the route that would give them the best cover.

'This way.'

Chapter Four

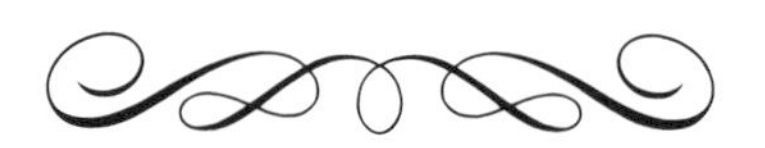

Saskia's nerves were still jumping as she walked through the twilight with Harry. Was she being wise or foolish to trust him? Now she'd had more time to consider, she could see no reason why he'd have made such ruthless efforts to protect her when they were attacked by the highwaymen if he was working for Tancock. But at the very instant she decided she was right to trust Harry a sliver of doubt intruded that perhaps he'd only been protecting *himself* from the highwaymen.

Then she remembered his expression when he'd caught her behind the stable. She hadn't been lying when she'd claimed he looked scared. He hadn't been afraid when two armed men were shooting at him, so she tried to puzzle out why he'd been so unhappy confronting *her*. She was hardly a physical threat to a man of his abilities. And any honest man whose employer first tried to run away and then attempted to stab him had some justification for being angry. Why had he been bad-tempered with her after the highwaymen's attack, yet not when she'd assaulted him and then insisted they hide in the woods?

She glanced sideways at him. Harry's strong profile was towards her. He'd had no opportunity to shave since the previous day and short dark stubble covered his jaw. The backs of her fingers still tingled with whisker burn from when she'd hit him. At least she hadn't found her target with the knife. She'd never before struck another person. She'd been angry many times in her life, but she was shaken to realise she could be driven to such mindless, panic-stricken violence.

As she looked at Harry he glanced at her, his expression unreadable, and then returned his attention to their surroundings. At intervals he checked behind them and a couple of times he made her stop while he listened intently. Though he appeared relaxed, she realised there was nothing casual about his actions. She drew in a breath to speak and then thought better of it. If Harry considered it worth listening to hear if Selby was following him, she would remain silent until Harry deemed it safe to speak.

They walked on into the gathering darkness until Saskia was sure they'd gone at least two, if not three, miles. She hoped Harry had a good sense of direction because she was thoroughly disorientated. At last he stopped by the shelter of a group of trees next to a small stream. There was no moon in the sky, only the pinprick lights of the stars far above them.

'Where are we?' she asked, feeling an almost superstitious need to keep her voice low, just in case there was someone else nearby.

'The inn's back there. Guildford's that way,' he replied, gesturing confidently. 'What have you got in your bag?'

'My dress. Cloak—'

'Anything to eat?' he interrupted.

'Bread.' She was momentarily disconcerted by his question.

'Hmm.' Harry gave a dissatisfied grunt. 'Get your cloak out.'

'Are you hungry?' Saskia asked.

'I've been hungry since before the highwaymen attacked us,' he replied. 'The magistrate invited me to sup with him this evening; no doubt I turned down a veritable feast.' He took the cloak from her and spread it on the ground. 'Sit.'

Saskia dropped down and scrabbled through her bag for the remains of the bread she'd saved from breakfast, remembering Harry's hearty appetite at that meal. He was probably starving by now. He might well consider being forced to miss his dinner and his supper a worse offence than being shot at by highwaymen. And she really did want him in a good mood while she told him all about Tancock and Lady Abergrave and the need to rescue Benjamin. Fortunately the innkeeper's wife had given her some cake, which she'd shoved into her bag along with her speedily removed dress before she'd left the inn.

'Cake or bread?' she said, producing the food with some relief. 'The bread's a bit dry and the cake's somewhat crumbly, I'm afraid, but there's quite a lot of it.'

'Aren't you hungry?' Harry didn't take any.

'I hadn't thought of it until you said.'

'And now you have thought of it, you are,' he correctly interpreted. 'Eat first. You must keep your strength up.'

'It's more important *you* keep *your* strength up,' Saskia pointed out. 'For both our sakes. I don't suppose you could catch a fish from the stream or a rabbit or something, could you?' she asked hopefully.

'Yes, but I'm not going to.' He sounded mildly amused as he sat cross-legged beside her. He reminded her of a picture she'd seen in a book about the Ottoman Empire, and she recalled being told that the Turks sat on cushions on the floor and did not usually have tables or chairs in their homes. Harry had obviously adjusted to their customs.

'Short commons for one day won't harm us,' he said. 'We'll be able to buy more food tomorrow.'

'We'll share,' she said, as she realised that now her anxiety had receded she was also hungry.

He nodded, and didn't wait for a second invitation to start eating his portion of dry bread.

Saskia hesitated. She knew she wouldn't feel completely at ease until she'd told him the truth and seen his reaction. 'I'm not going to Portsmouth, I'm going to Cornwall,' she announced baldly.

'I know,' Harry said, slightly indistinctly.

'How?' She was stunned.

Harry swallowed his mouthful. 'You nearly said Plymouth once and then changed it to Portsmouth,' he replied, and continued before she had time to respond, 'What's your involvement in the war with the Dutch?'

'What?' Saskia gaped at him. 'The war? What's that got to do with anything?'

'That's the question. Are you planning to use me to carry out some act of vengeance against the English? Blow up any of the King's ships we find at Plymouth, for example?' Despite his deceptively light tone, she sensed he was fully alert to her answer.

She opened and closed her mouth several times

before she finally managed to form a coherent sentence. 'No! The sooner the stupid war ends the better! It's made everything ten times more difficult. A *hundred* times more difficult!'

'You're definitely not any kind of Dutch agent or spy, then? Don't shout!' he added quickly.

Saskia took a deep breath. 'Is that what you thought? Is that why you answered the notice in the coffee-house?'

'Information was received,' he said obliquely. 'And you were hiding behind a mask. Not to mention the not entirely convincing story of the jealous former mistress.'

Saskia glared at him for a moment, and then sighed. 'Johanna and I were so pleased with that story when we first thought it up, but I knew it was a mistake once you started asking all those questions. What do you mean—information was received? It was Tancock, wasn't it? He didn't just stand in the street shouting I was a spy. He told someone important!' She was torn between furious indignation and horror. It had never occurred to her that Tancock would go to such lengths to blacken her reputation. It wasn't just the local magistrate in Cornwall she couldn't trust; Tancock had even tried to blacken her reputation with powerful men in London.

'He did,' said Harry. 'And that important man told

me because you'd put up your notice in my brother's coffee-house.'

'It's Johanna's coffee-house,' Saskia protested.

'My brother is the silent investor.' Harry took another large bite of bread.

'I am not a spy,' she said emphatically. 'You *must* believe that. *Do* you believe that?'

'Yes.'

Saskia stared at Harry in the darkness. Now her most immediate fear had been allayed, she had time to unravel what he'd revealed about his involvement in her affairs.

'You and your brother are both merchants,' she said. 'I am sure that, far from losing your money, you were a very successful factor. It wouldn't be suitable for your brother to participate directly in trade so he hired Johanna's husband to manage the coffee-house. And you didn't care whether the ships sailed before you got back to London because you aren't a sailor. But I don't understand why you chose to investigate me yourself. Surely you have trustworthy servants you could have assigned to the task?'

'I was curious,' said Harry. 'I've never played spy-catcher before.'

'Spycatcher!' Saskia didn't know whether to laugh or cry. 'I'm sorry to disappoint you, but I'm not a spy.' Now his mission had been accomplished, would he abandon her?

'I'm not disappointed,' said Harry. 'Now you know I'm not going to drag you back to London to be hung, drawn and quartered for treason, you may relax and eat up.'

'Not yet.' She knelt up beside him and caught his wrist as he lifted the bread to his mouth. 'I heard my aunt plotting to kill Benjamin and me so she can inherit Trevithick,' she said in a desperate rush. 'Will you help me save him? Will you?' She tried to shake Harry's arm.

'Yes.'

'What?' She wasn't sure she'd correctly heard or understood his one-syllable reply.

'Yes, I will help you,' he repeated patiently.

Saskia stared at him for a few agonisingly hopeful seconds. Then she covered her face with her hands and burst into tears. She hadn't meant to cry. She tried to stop, but now her self-control had been breached she couldn't.

After a few moments she felt Harry's hand on her shoulder. He hesitated briefly and then pulled her against his side. At first she leant into the silent comfort he offered, but then she remembered his equally silent rejection earlier in the day and tried to pull away. His grip tightened slightly. She couldn't sense any reluctance in him, so she stopped resisting. Almost at the same time his arm loosened, but he didn't remove it. Instead he gently patted her shoulder a few times with his free hand. She couldn't understand why he'd disliked holding her when she was reasonably calm, but didn't mind when she was almost hysterical, but she'd never understood how men thought. If she'd understood more, she might have managed things better between Pieter and herself.

Harry hesitated a few seconds before he tried to comfort Saskia, but it wasn't in him to ignore her tears. He tightened his hold instinctively when she momentarily tried to pull away, then realised what he was doing and was ready to release her just as she sank against him once more. It was the second time she'd accepted his comfort, and this time he was determined not to let his own reaction interfere.

She was weeping in uncontrollable, but almost silent sobs. He hated the idea she'd considered her situation so desperate that his mere promise to help prompted such an emotional catharsis. But she wasn't hurt and he knew she wasn't frightened of him because she was clinging to him for comfort almost like a child. She wasn't a child. He was well aware it was a woman he held in his arms. But he'd comforted more than one distraught child in the past, feeling his heart twist with sympathy at their acute distress, even knowing that within half an hour or less they'd be smiling again. Although the intensity of her emotions distressed him, he wasn't as disturbed as he would have been if she'd shown fear of him.

He patted her shoulder, and then allowed himself the illicit pleasure of stroking her hair. But since she didn't seem aware of what he was doing, and therefore couldn't protest, he decided it wasn't an honourable thing to do. Particularly since it led him to think of other illicitly pleasurable things he would like to do with her, which was having an inevitable effect upon his body. He feathered one last caress over her curls, patted her shoulder, then picked up a piece of cake in his free hand and chomped down on it, resolutely ignoring his other physical appetite.

Saskia's tears gradually subsided, but for a while she seemed content to lean against him while he ate cake. Harry would have appreciated a cup of coffee to finish his meal, but all in all he had no complaints about his situation.

'You have no soul,' Saskia said at last, without moving. Her voice was still thick from her tears, but she sounded mildly amused. 'I'm crying my eyes out and you're *eating.*'

'I have got a soul,' he said. 'It was hungry, so I fed it.'

'I suppose I've got crumbs in my hair now.'

'I don't think so.' But her curls fascinated him, and she'd given him the perfect excuse to touch them again, so he checked. He thought he felt her give a little quiver as he stroked her hair, but she pushed away from him before he had time to decide what her reaction meant.

'Thank you,' she said. 'I'm sorry. I didn't mean to cry all over you. It was just such a relief when you said you'd help. I just haven't known what to do—' She gave a little hiccoughing sob, and he knew her emotions were still very near the surface.

'Eat,' he said firmly.

For a little while they sat in silence, Harry pondering all he'd now discovered, while Saskia regained her composure.

'Tancock is my aunt Isabel's secretary,' she said eventually. 'My aunt is Lady Abergrave. She was married to my father's brother. I ran away from Cornwall when I heard her plotting to have me and my brother die in accidents so she can inherit what should rightfully be Benjamin's. I can't believe Aunt Isabel can do such a thing!' she burst out, her voice anguished. 'How can she turn against her own family so cruelly? How can she plan to harm us? Over and over I keep hoping that somehow I misunderstood. Or that it is really Tancock alone—but then I remember what my aunt said, she was by no means in thrall to Tancock. She was giving him orders.'

'Shared blood does not guarantee affection or loyalty,' said Harry, his voice harsher than he'd intended. 'How exactly did you overhear them and how did you escape?'

He listened carefully as Saskia explained the layout of the grounds of Trevithick House and how she'd rowed upriver when she'd realised there was no one she could trust in the household to help her.

'I hoped they'd think I'd gone down to Plymouth,' she said. 'So I went upstream. I know the Marsh family from my childhood. I'd hoped Tom Marsh would be there and he'd be able to help me get Benjamin out of Trevithick. But Tom had gone on the fishing boats. His mother guided me across Dartmoor to Chudleigh. She had a friend there who took me on to Exeter where I hired a horse—and then I rode to London.'

'All alone?' It was nearly two hundred miles from Exeter to London.

'Yes. I got lost several times. I was always afraid Tancock might catch me. I dressed as a man—well, you can see—' Harry sensed rather than saw her gesture towards her clothes. 'But I still didn't feel safe staying at inns. I don't think I'm a very convincing man. I slept on the ground most nights. I was *so* glad to reach London. But then Tancock was on my godfather's doorstep…' Her voice wavered.

Harry resisted the urge to take her back into his arms. She was sitting several feet from him and hadn't given any indication she wanted further comfort.

'Your brother's leg is broken?' he said.

'Yes. He slipped on some wet rocks just before I arrived in Cornwall. He's taller than me. Heavier. Even if we'd had Pieter's wheelchair I couldn't have got Benjamin safely out of the house and away without Aunt Isabel's servants catching us. I just keep thinking—I have to stay alive. As long as I'm alive they need to keep Benjamin alive too. But I left him behind in d-danger.' She scrubbed a jerky hand across her cheek and turned her head away.

'That was the only choice open to you,' said Harry. 'If you'd stayed, the chances are high you would both be dead by now. You did what you had to do to save your brother. Such decisions are not easy and there is often a price.'

He thought back to the decision he'd made to send his own brother back to England. The thin, fever-weakened lad he'd put on a ship at Skanderoon had turned into a healthy, prosperous London merchant. But Harry had paid a high price in loneliness after his brother had gone, and for months he'd been haunted by the debilitating fear Richard would not survive the journey. He'd wept with relief when, nearly a year later, he'd received the letter telling him Richard was safely home in London and in good health. The echoes of that decision still lingered. Now he was back in England he was saddened to realise he was more at ease in the company of the magistrate he'd met at the inn than he was with his own brother.

'You said you know an important man,' said Saskia. 'The one Tancock told I was a spy. Now you know I am not, can't we ask him for help?'

'At the first opportunity I'll send him a message,' said Harry, 'but I'll lose time if we go back to London. We need to go on.'

'Oh my God, no, we can't lose any more time!' Saskia exclaimed. 'It was such a mischance we were attacked by the highwaymen. Though if we hadn't been delayed at that inn so long I might not have spotted Selby. At least we know Tancock is prowling close and we can be extra careful.' She glanced around at the darkness with a hint of her earlier nervousness.

Harry didn't blame her for being edgy. He was sure they hadn't been followed from the inn, and it was unlikely Selby would stumble upon them by chance in the darkness. But Harry was glad it was a summer night and there was no need for a fire for warmth. He hesitated. His natural instinct was to protect Saskia from further distress, but she had proven her ability to deal with bad news.

'I don't believe it was a mischance we were attacked by highwaymen,' he said quietly. 'You could not have seen this, but he took careful, deliberate aim at me before they charged down on the coach. He wasn't trying to fire above our heads to frighten us.'

'Oh.' Saskia sounded shaken, and Harry saw the movement as she pushed her hair back from her face. 'No wonder you were in a bad mood after the attack.' She gasped suddenly. 'I'm so sorry! He was trying to kill you and it's my fault for involving you.'

'As you pointed out this afternoon, I've been shot at before,' said Harry calmly. 'In any case, it is Tancock himself who inadvertently involved me. If he hadn't informed on you as a spy, I would not have responded to your notice.'

'But the highwayman was a local villain. How did Tancock manage to hire him? And how did he know when and where to attack us?'

'According to the locals, Crayford was well known at the Dog and Duck alehouse. The magistrate didn't manage to catch him there red-handed with stolen property, but I'm sure it wouldn't have been difficult for Tancock or Selby to make contact with him. As to how he knew where to attack us—' Harry shrugged. 'I might have been followed on the way to the coffee-house, although I didn't notice anyone. I imagine one of the reasons Tancock informed against you was simply in the hope the greater resources of a King's Minister would find you for him. But if I was Tancock, I would have set a watch on your godfather's house, to see if you returned yourself or sent a message. Then I would have followed the message bearer. You said Johanna sent a message to your godfather on your behalf…'

Saskia groaned in horror and put her face in her hands. 'I tried so hard not to make any silly mistakes.'

'As far as I can see, that's the only possible mistake you've made since leaving Cornwall,' said Harry. 'In any case, we don't know for sure that's how Tancock tracked you. Insisting we left London as soon as you decided to hire me was very sensible. I didn't expect you to act so quickly, and I don't suppose Tancock did.'

'What are we going to do next?'

'You're going to sleep,' said Harry. 'You said you rode all the way to London from Cornwall?'

'Yes.'

'When did you arrive?'

'Friday.'

And it was only Sunday night now. For someone who'd just completed one arduous journey, immediately embarked on a second and survived several frightening situations, she was holding up very well. He'd been watching her surreptitiously as they walked away from the inn. There were dark circles under her eyes, but though he could see she was tired, he hadn't seen any signs of serious flagging. He knew that to some extent she was being sustained by anxious determination to save her brother. But he also recognised a physical resilience in her similar to his own. He hadn't expected to discover such a quality in a woman, and he was both intrigued and impressed. He didn't want to push her too far, but her stamina was an advantage now.

'So you'd be willing to continue on horseback rather than in a coach?' he said.

'Oh, yes,' she said immediately. 'We'd have to make that change eventually, anyway. The coach wouldn't be able to travel on the roads further west.'

'We'll rest now and obtain horses as soon as possible in the morning,' Harry said.

Tancock stood in the shadow of the trees close to the inn, waiting for Selby to return. He'd been profoundly irritated when he'd discovered his plans for

Saskia to die at the hands of the local highwayman had been thwarted by the foreign-looking manservant she'd hired in London. He'd been forced to come up with a new plan—but it hadn't taken long, and now he was even more pleased.

Just as with his plan for dealing with Saskia's godfather, his scheme took advantage of the training he'd received as an apothecary's apprentice, before he'd managed to claw his way up to better things by convincing Lady Abergrave he had more skill than any of the physicians to keep her ailing son alive. Most likely that had been the truth. He hadn't enjoyed the lowly status of apprentice, but he'd learned his craft well, and valued the power over others his knowledge gave him.

He'd kept the young, weak Lord Abergrave alive as long as he could, because doing so was his guarantee that he would continue to receive lavish rewards from Lady Abergrave. But he'd always known the boy was not likely to survive into adulthood. When the child died, Tancock's own life of luxury would end—unless he made plans. So all the time he'd been extending the boy's life he'd ingratiated himself further and further into Lady Abergrave's favour. By the time her son died and the power and wealth Lady Abergrave had wielded on his behalf were snatched from her hands, Tancock had established himself as her close and loyal companion. When she'd had to leave her marital home to live at Trevithick House, he'd gone with her as her secretary. But his sights were set much higher. Lady Abergrave thought she was controlling him with her combined appeals to his lust and his greed but, as far as Tancock was concerned, it was the other way around. By the time he was through Lady Abergrave would be his wife, and her murderously gained inheritance would pass into his control. But that was for the future. He had urgent matters to deal with tonight.

Had Saskia already made accusations against her aunt to her new manservant? Would she guess Tancock had been behind the highwaymen's attack and share her suspicions with her foreign manservant?

Tancock had seen the fellow from a distance. That brief glimpse, coupled with the memory of the highwayman's body, had been enough for Tancock to decide it would be foolhardy to have Selby try to overpower Saskia's new protector. It would be better to ensure that nobody, including the foreign manservant, believed any wild claims Saskia might make that Lady Abergrave wanted her dead. Tancock didn't want his future wife's reputation spoiled by such potentially deadly rumours.

He'd already tried to discredit anything Saskia

might say by his counter-accusations that she was a Dutch agent. His new scheme would completely destroy any chance of others trusting her word—and then anything she'd said would no longer matter. Within days she would be dead, her memory tainted by the madness which had driven her to make deluded, unfounded accusations.

Selby knew which room Saskia had been given. Now Tancock imagined him creeping through the inn towards her. Saskia was far too much the prudish Dutch matron to allow a strange man into her room, no matter what the circumstances, so Tancock was certain Selby would find her alone. Selby had orders to subdue her first without leaving any obvious marks, and then apply to her bare skin the ointment Tancock had given him.

'Wear your gloves,' Tancock had ordered. 'Do not allow any on your skin. Take particular care to smear it under her arms and between her legs.'

The ointment contained a mixture of ingredients, including henbane. Tancock had first encountered the use of such ingredients in stories about women claiming to be witches, and he'd been sufficiently interested to experiment further. There was always an element of uncertainty in such applications but, if all went according to plan, Saskia would soon begin to experience vivid hallucinations of a most bizarre kind. Tancock hoped she would rave about her visions, though there was also a possibility she would fall into a deep, unwakeable sleep.

There would be many witnesses to Saskia's descent into confusion and madness and Tancock was sure none of them would guess her behaviour had been induced by his ointment. One or two of the villagers had seen him when he'd watched the coach arrive, but none of them knew his name or would be able to connect him to Saskia's madness. Any accusations Saskia had made against him or Lady Abergrave in London or to her foreign manservant would be discredited. Everyone knew lunatics were unpredictable and prone to accidents. Within a day at the most Saskia's death could be arranged in a way that would arouse no suspicions, and then Tancock would race back to Cornwall to bring Lady Abergrave and Sir Benjamin the sad news. Grief and shame at the taint of lunacy in his family would make the unfortunate Sir Benjamin fatally careless…

Tancock's musings about the many entertaining ways to bring about Sir Benjamin's demise were interrupted by Selby's return.

'She's not there,' said Selby.

'*What?* Are you sure you went to the right room?' Tancock demanded.

'I did. I went to his room too. They're gone.'

'Where?'

Selby lifted his big shoulders in a shrug. 'I didn't see them go. Here's your salve.'

Tancock's hand clenched around the pot of ointment. Now he had to make another new plan. But first he had to find Saskia again.

Harry slept lightly, waking fully at frequent intervals to listen for possible threats, though he believed the real risk of discovery would come tomorrow, because the route to the West Country through Winchester was predictable. He'd considered bypassing the city, but he had friends there and, if they made good time, Saskia would be able to sleep in a safe bed tomorrow night.

She was lying a few feet away from him on her cloak. He was amazed and humbled that she'd had the courage and resolution to travel from Cornwall to London, without help or protection. The first time he'd spent a night alone beneath a hedge he'd been driven by desperate emotion just as Saskia was, but he'd still jumped nervously at every strange sound. He'd been eleven at the time, and Saskia was a grown woman, but even at that young age he'd known an unguarded female was vulnerable to terrible insult and injury. Harry had seen Saskia's knife, but he'd also seen how ineffectively she'd tried to use it against him. He doubted she'd have succeeded in fighting off any man determined to rape or steal from her. The mere thought of her being violated caused his stomach to clench with fury. One thing was certain: he would never leave her unguarded again.

She murmured in her sleep and he shifted instantly to full wakefulness. She stirred restlessly and a small whimper escaped her lips. He raised himself on his elbow, looking in concern across the small distance that separated them. He suspected she was having a bad dream. It was hardly surprising after all she'd been through. He was hoping she'd settle into peaceful sleep once more when she muttered again, her words indistinguishable, but her tone distressed. He hesitated. If she'd been an infant he would have rocked her crib, spoken softly to her, or even cradled her in his arms until she settled again. Was that what he should do now? He couldn't rock her, but he could soothe her and hold her. She hadn't objected when he'd comforted her earlier.

He closed the distance between them, quietly speaking meaningless words meant only to reassure. He eased down on to his side next to her and put his arm over her waist. She stirred and he held his breath, afraid she might wake from her nightmare and be made even more frightened by his unexpected proximity. But she was still asleep. And somehow she was closer than she'd been before, snuggling against him. He exhaled very carefully and rested his head beside hers on the rolled-up skirts she'd used for a pillow. He could keep an alert ear on their surroundings just as well here as he could several feet away. He listened to her breathe and was conscious of the gentle rise and fall of her breasts. He resisted the urge to touch her hair. He could not take advantage of her sleeping trust, but lying with her in the velvet darkness his ever-present awareness of her surged into full, insistent arousal. Even though his body demanded he push forward, he eased his hips back so that she would not inadvertently press against his erection.

But in her sleep Saskia had no such reticence. She sighed contently and moved closer until their faces were almost touching and her hand rested on his chest. He could feel her warm breath on his skin. His heart beat fast with excitement and desire. Her lips were only a whisper away. There wasn't enough self-discipline in the world to stop him brushing his own mouth gently against hers. Once—he only meant to do it once. But once wasn't enough. The second time he let their mouths touch, her lips parted and she seemed to return the kiss. His whole body jerked slightly in response. Every coherent thought in his mind fused into a white-hot pool of desire. Every instinct demanded he roll her on to her back and settle himself between her thighs. But the image of her trapped cruelly between the ground and his hard, pounding body jolted him back to a semblance of sanity.

She was still asleep. She didn't know she was in his arms. His own overheated passions made him imagine things. His blood rushed in his ears. He almost didn't hear her sigh of apparent pleasure as she pressed herself against him—against his erection. He hadn't imagined that! She was definitely responding to him in her sleep. He sucked in a ragged breath. She must be dreaming she was back in her husband's arms. She would be shamed and mortified if she woke now and realised what she was doing. Harry summoned all his resolution and tried to move away from her, but as he half-turned on to his back, she went with him, until she was sprawled across his body the inside of her breeches-clad thigh resting on his groin. His hips flexed upwards once before he managed to still them. He bit back a groan. She was inflicting sweet torture on him, but when she woke she would be horrified.

He gradually sensed she was no longer completely asleep, but nor was she awake. She was lost in a dreaming state between the two. Her movements had the languor of sleep, but there was no doubt what she wanted when she searched for his mouth with hers. He took her head between his hands, meaning to ease her gently away, but in the end he was too weak-willed to do anything except help her find her target. So she kissed him again. Every part of his body thundered with arousal, but he allowed himself to respond with only the tenderest touch of his mouth against hers. He wanted to taste her. To press his tongue between those soft, seductive lips. But she thought she was lying with her husband.

It hurt worse than he could have suspected to know that she was kissing him believing he was another man. The twisting wound of sadness, tinged with jealousy because she was still devoted to the memory of her husband, was far more distressing than the physical discomfort of unrelieved passion.

Somehow he had to separate them and allow her to sleep on with no further disturbance. In the morning she would wake and perhaps she would believe her dream of her husband had been unusually vivid—and perhaps that would cause old grief to resurface. But at least she would not have to bear the embarrassment of knowing she'd kissed a stranger. He made another attempt to ease her off of him. She made a small, wordless sound of annoyance. She couldn't have made it any clearer she liked it where she was. Harry thought he might explode from the effort he was expending to remain still.

'Saskia?' he murmured, his voice tight with strain. Perhaps he could wake her just enough to get her safely back to her half of the cloak.

'Harry?'

He went absolutely still. Her voice was low and husky, but he was certain she'd called him by his real name. Surely her Dutch husband hadn't also been called Harry?

'Yes.' His fingers were buried in her hair. He could feel the shape of her body resting on his. Her leg still touched his erection, though there were layers of cloth between them.

'Mmm.' Her lips brushed his again.

With unimaginable effort he kept his body unmoving, but he couldn't resist her kiss. His only tenuous grip on sanity was that he let her lead, holding his own passion in check, as he responded to each seductive caress of lips and tongue.

Saskia had fallen asleep almost immediately. The ground beneath her was no softer than the ground on which she slept during her journey to London, but she was a hundred times more comfortable because she felt safe with Harry. He would protect her—and he had promised to help her save Benjamin. After days of carrying the full weight of her mission herself, it was an almost unimaginable luxury to be able to place her trust in someone else. It meant far more to her than a soft bed or a fine meal.

But then Tancock and her aunt, dressed as highwaymen, began to pursue her through her dreams. She half-wakened in distress, but when she heard the comforting murmur of a familiar voice she drifted back into a deeper sleep. Harry was with her, a far more desirable companion to welcome into her dreams.

They were walking in a garden and the scent of roses filled the warm afternoon air. Harry was bareheaded and she could see the sunlight glinting on his dark hair. He picked a rose and she watched, her heart beating in anticipation, as he stripped it of thorns. He offered it to her, and when she reached for it, he took the opportunity to pull her into his arms and brush his lips across her mouth. She sighed and put her hands on his shoulders as he drew her down to lie on the sweet grass. One tantalising kiss wasn't enough, and she lifted her head for more. The body pressed close to hers was lean and excitingly hard-muscled, but his lips were warm and gentle, his mouth almost hesitant against hers. She'd expected him to claim her with the same decisive confidence he'd done everything else, but his tender hesitancy was very stimulating. Her body began to heat with slowly building arousal. Warmth pooled between her legs.

For long, uncounted seconds she slipped between dreaming and sleepy wakefulness. She was lying in Harry's arms in both states. When he spoke her name she answered, but was only half-aware they'd both spoken aloud. As she wakened further the vivid dream gradually became reality. Even without opening her eyes she knew they were lying on her cloak beneath the tree by the stream. And she wasn't just in Harry's arms; she was sprawled across him as he lay on his back.

For a few heartbeats she was still too hazed with sleep and desire to think beyond the pleasure of her position. She liked the feel of his mouth on hers, so she teased his lips with the tip of her tongue, tempting him to claim her more boldly. He did return her kiss, but his restraint frustrated her, and it was her frustration that brought her to full wakefulness—and then to full awareness of her situation. She was lying on top of Harry, silently demanding kisses like…like a passion-starved widow!

She'd been in this mortifying position before, trying to elicit physical affection from Pieter after he'd recovered from his accident. She'd been too modest to make her gestures brazenly bold, but she'd lain beside him, gently touching or kissing him as she had done in the first five months of their marriage. She'd needed that comfort and thought he must need it too, but he'd been rigid and unresponsive, even with actions she knew were well within his scope. He'd regained enough strength in his arms to lift himself from the bed to the wheeled-chair he'd designed for himself, so why wouldn't he put his arms round her any more? There were many times since his death she wished she'd had the courage to confront him with that question. Now it was too late.

She was frozen in a moment of unreality. As soon as she moved she would have to explain to Harry why she was clinging to him like a lust-starved limpet. If only some miracle would intervene so they were safely separated by a few feet of turf and they could pretend nothing untoward had happened. But pretending nothing had happened was how she'd ended up a business partner, not a wife, to her husband. Besides, despite the potential embarrassment of the situation, deep down she *wanted* to be in Harry's arms.

In those first few seconds as she absorbed where she was, she also began to notice more. Harry's body was rigid with tension, but it was the rigidity of fiercely imposed self-control, not rejection. His breath rasped in his throat and she could feel his erection pressing against her thigh…

She could feel his erection.

He wanted her. He couldn't hide it. But he was doing his honourable best not to succumb to her dream-induced attempt to seduce him. The most excitingly attractive man she'd ever met was aroused by her fumbling kisses! An image of how shocked he must have been when she'd crawled all over him in her sleep flashed into her mind. A slightly hysterical giggle escaped her.

'Saskia?' She heard surprise and concern in his hoarse voice.

'I'm s-sorry. I know it's not really f-funny.' She allowed herself the luxury of briefly dropping her forehead to his shoulder.

'Funny?' he said disbelievingly.

'I was thinking how shocked you must have been when I—' She stopped, because she couldn't bring herself to put into words what she'd done.

'I thought you—' He broke off in turn.

She wondered what he thought, but wasn't bold enough to ask. She could sense his uncertainty in the way he was touching her. His hand was resting lightly on her upper arm, and it seemed to her he wasn't sure whether he should lift her away from him or put his arms around her properly.

'You are a good man.' Tears suddenly choked her throat. She touched his face, grateful for the protective darkness, yet wishing she could see his expression.

'I am…a man.' There was a warning in his voice, but he turned his head so that her fingers brushed his lips.

'Mmm.' She braced her hand on his shoulder so that she could very carefully lift her leg from him and roll away.

She stared up at the branches above her and wondered what on earth she could say now. She heard Harry exhale and thought it must be a sigh of relief. Though of course he hadn't achieved relief. Neither had she. She was acutely aware of the hot, swollen place between her legs, of the pulsing need within her that had not been satisfied. Harry was only a few feet away, and she was sure his need was just as acute. For a wild moment she almost suggested they went back to where they were—or wished she hadn't fully woken up until their embrace had reached a natural climax.

But from what she'd seen of Harry, he'd never have let that happen, even if he'd had to drop her in the stream to shock her awake. The picture of Harry, his body hard with desire, his jaw rigid with honourable determination, as he dunked her in the water to slacken her lust startled another unwary, nervous giggle from her.

'Are you…upset?' he asked.

She looked towards him and saw from his silhouette he was propped up on his elbow, looking at her. He must have mistaken her giggle for tears.

'I was just imagining you dropping me in the stream to wake me up,' she explained.

'Oh.' He sounded thoroughly bemused.

She smiled, rolled on to her side away from him, tucked her hand beneath her cheek and settled down to sleep once more. She didn't want to find herself inadvertently plastered all over him in the morning, but she wouldn't object to another pleasant dream about kissing him.

Harry listened to every small sound in the grass and trees around them to take his mind off his physical state. Did Saskia have a history of sleep-walking? He'd known a factor who'd left his bed, dressed and gone out into the night, only to have no recollections of his actions the following morning. Perhaps Saskia would have forgotten all about their kisses tomorrow. But that still didn't explain why she'd been amused rather than embarrassed by what had happened. If all women were so unfathomable in their behaviour, how would he ever learn how to deal appropriately with them?

But right now he didn't need to fathom out any other woman, only Saskia. And even though he was somewhat shocked that *she* hadn't apparently been shocked at waking up on top of him, he was grateful she hadn't burst into horrified tears.

He gritted his teeth against the uncomfortable ache in his groin. It wasn't the first time he'd suffered such inconveniently unquenched lust. He'd expected the problem to become more frequent on his return to England, but only Saskia had aroused his passion to such an acute degree. He could not deny that his casual interest had been stirred by many of the pretty women he'd seen at a distance in London or elsewhere. But invariably whenever he'd been within conversational distance of females, he'd been so ill at ease he'd not felt the slightest twinge of physical desire.

The mere idea of choosing a bride made him feel awkward and reluctant. He knew he would be considered a good match by any matchmaking father seeking a wealthy, high-ranking husband for his daughter. But Harry didn't want to buy a wife. Didn't want to fear the only reason his wife submitted to his wishes was because he'd paid for the privilege of having her in his bed. His thoughts flew back to Saskia. He couldn't doubt that, in her dreams at least, she had no objection to lying in his arms and experiencing his kisses.

Chapter Five

Monday, 17 June 1667

Saskia dreamed she was surrounded by a flock of birds wearing turbans and carrying an assortment of wind instruments. As she turned round and round in horror trying to find an escape route the birds got bigger and bigger until they were the same size as her. A starling put its trumpet to its beak, leant closer and blew straight in her ear.

She jolted straight out of her dream and into the equally noisy real world. After staring in confusion at a squashed daisy for several seconds, she groaned and pulled her cloak over her head in an attempt to muffle the dawn chorus.

She heard a masculine chuckle and memories of the previous night flooded back. She'd tried to kiss Harry while they were both asleep. She almost groaned again, this time with mortification. She couldn't believe she'd lost all sense of decorum during the night. Had she really laughed and joked about Harry dropping her in the stream? Waking up stiff and uncomfortable on the hard, dew-damp ground with a dreadful cacophony all around, her sense of humour seemed to have deserted her. Her eyes felt puffy, probably because after her tears the previous night she hadn't bathed them. Her hair undoubtedly resembled a haystack, and there was nothing she could do about her appearance before she stopped hiding under her cloak and revealed herself to Harry.

A pulse started to beat in her throat. She hadn't felt this nervous and shy the morning after her wedding night. Of course, on her wedding night it had been Pieter who had taken the lead and everything that had happened had been meant to happen. Last night…

Her thoughts scrambled with a mixture of embarrassment and guilty pleasure as she remembered how Harry's body had felt against hers. He'd been aroused by her sleepy overtures, even though he hadn't taken advantage of her. She didn't dare imagine what he must think of her now.

She took a deep breath, pushed back the cloak and sat up, keeping her back towards Harry as she blinked around her surroundings. It had been dark when they'd stopped for the night. Now the trees and fields were lit by the glow of sunrise.

'Good morning,' said Harry from behind her, sounding irritatingly wide-awake and composed.

She pushed back her hair and twisted around to look at him, a blush warming her cheeks. She briefly met his eyes, but that was too awkward and her gaze automatically lowered to his lips. She'd kissed him in the dark. In the light of day she could hardly believe her mouth had touched his. Unthinkingly she sucked her lower lip between her teeth and lifted her hand to her mouth. She heard his quick intake of breath and looked up. Her gaze locked with his. Hot, restless energy gleamed in his dark eyes. His voice might be calm, but the expression in his eyes gave him away. It burned into her soul, rendering her temporarily deaf and blind to everything but Harry. She didn't even hear the exuberant birdsong all around them.

For a heartbeat or two she almost expected him to close the distance between them and carry on from where they'd left off the previous night. Desire kindled inside her. Images of Harry flooded her mind. His hands on her skin. The power of his body surging into hers. Her pulse and her breathing both quickened.

A low growl escaped from Harry's throat—but then he looked away. Saskia felt simultaneously bereft and relieved she was no longer in thrall to his intense gaze.

'As soon as you are ready we'll set off,' said Harry, his voice no longer as smooth as it had been a few minutes ago.

'Yes, of course. Let me wash my face.' Saskia stumbled to her feet.

At least her male breeches were more practical than her petticoats—for most things anyway. But she'd had several days of travelling alone to get used to them, which made it easier for her to attend discreetly to her needs now. When she returned to their makeshift camp, she saw that Harry had already replaced the few things she'd taken out of her bag. There was nothing to show where they'd spent the night apart from some flattened grass.

'Do you think Tancock and Selby are close?' she asked.

'I doubt if they are far away,' Harry replied, 'but with luck they won't yet realise we've left the inn. Unless they are aware of your penchant for dawn starts, they may not expect us to continue our journey for another three or four hours.'

'I hope not.' For a little while Saskia had been distracted from her fear and anxiety, but the thought of Tancock lurking somewhere out of sight made her shudder. 'Let's get as far away from here as possible.'

'Wait.' Harry stopped her with a brief touch on her shoulder.

She looked up into his face, feeling a flutter of expectation and uncertainty beneath her breast. His hand brushed against her hair and she felt a disproportionately powerful ripple of sensation through her body. He coiled a tendril around his finger. She glanced sideways and couldn't stop herself from moistening her lower lip. Did he want to kiss her as much as she wanted him to kiss her? That couldn't be possible or she'd be locked in his arms right now. Perhaps even lying entwined with him beneath the tree.

'Have you got a hat?' he asked hoarsely.

'What?' His question disorientated her.

'Your hair is unforgettable.' He filled his hand with the soft, apricot-blonde curls.

'Oh.' No one had ever looked at her hair or touched it the way Harry was looking at it. The heat of arousal in his eyes was unmistakable.

She put her hand on his chest. The moment stretched out between them like a tight, sweetly singing harp string.

Harry bent his head a fraction.

She stood on tiptoe.

Harry bent his head a little more and she put her hand on his shoulder. He brushed his mouth across hers. Her lips parted and her hand slipped behind his head, unconsciously holding him in position. His lips curved against hers, almost as if he was smiling. Then he kissed her. She was wide-awake now, and so was he, but she did not hesitate to respond to him. She could sense the energy thrumming through his body, but his mouth was gentle on hers. He explored her lips with exquisite tenderness and only when her tongue crept out to touch his lips did he become more demanding. Her lips parted at the first gentle pressure of his tongue, unconsciously inviting him deeper. Between one heartbeat and the next the kiss intensified until she was breathless and dizzy with overwhelming sensation.

His right hand was still buried in her hair, but he slid his left arm around her waist, clamping her to his hard-muscled body. Even through their clothes she could feel his erection pressing against her stomach. Between her legs she was swollen and throbbing with the need to take him inside her. Her muscles were weak with desire. She gave a soft whimper of pleasure and longing. He lifted his head, but for a few seconds she hardly noticed because she was so lost in a haze of glorious sensations. The arm holding her tight against his body relaxed its grip so suddenly she nearly folded in a heap of boneless desire at his feet.

She gave a gasp of protest and clutched at his

shoulder. At once his arm closed around her again. But she was no longer completely lost in the sensuous experience. She opened her eyes to look at him. He was staring down at her, his eyes dark with passion and other emotions she couldn't decipher.

'Did I distress you?' he asked, his voice hoarse.

'No,' she said, in confusion. Then she blushed, because she should have been distressed—or at least shocked—at being kissed by a man she barely knew.

'It does not frighten you when I hold you so tightly?' he persisted.

'No. If another man did it—' She broke off, blushing even more intensely and looked away. She was suddenly aware that she was still in his arms. She could still feel his erection and they were having what must be one of the most disconcerting conversations of her life.

'You would not like it if another man held you like this, but you do not mind if I do?' said Harry.

'Ah...that's right.' Saskia couldn't look at him. She began to twist the button on his coat instead. 'Do you always stop in the middle to ask if the lady is frightened of kissing you?"

'Didn't your husband?' said Harry, after a moment's silence.

'Pieter never talked of such things at all,' Saskia replied, unable to keep a note of bitterness out of her voice. It occurred to her that, embarrassing though it was, Harry's apparent willingness to discuss intimate situations might have some merit after all.

'So you have not kissed anyone except your husband and me?' said Harry.

'N—' Saskia broke off. On the one hand, she instinctively wanted to defend her virtue—and therefore her honour. On the other, she was annoyed by the interrogation and disinclined to feed Harry's masculine pride.

'If you tell me how many ladies you have kissed, I *may*...' she emphasised the word '...tell you how many men have kissed me.' As she spoke she extricated herself from his embrace.

'That would not be gentlemanly,' he replied after a brief pause. His expression was inscrutable when she glanced at him in mild surprise.

'Then I hope you are equally discreet about me,' she said after a moment.

'Of course.' He drew in a breath and she sensed he was not as much in control of himself as he wished to appear. 'A hat,' he said suddenly. 'Do you have a hat?'

'I lost it.'

'Take mine. Your hair is too noticeable—and too memorable,' he said, putting it on her head. 'Push your hair up inside it. I know it is not the fashion, but it will attract less attention.'

'You are hardly forgettable yourself,' Saskia said, doing as he suggested. She couldn't help but be flattered by his comment, even though he hadn't really phrased it as a compliment.

'I'm just another man.' Harry shrugged. 'Though I grant my sword is unusual.'

'And the scarlet sash it hangs from, and your boots,' Saskia pointed out. 'You look like a well-bred pirate.'

'Their coach and the coachman are still at the inn—but they've definitely gone,' Selby announced. 'No one at the inn knows when or saw them go.'

Tancock gritted his teeth. He'd had some small hope that Selby had been mistaken about the rooms. Or that Saskia and her foreign servant would return for the coach in the morning. 'Were any of the horses stolen from the stables?' he asked.

Selby frowned. 'No one has said anything about that. I wonder why they left.'

'She must have seen and remembered you,' Tancock said impatiently. 'I didn't think she would.'

'What are we going to do now?'

'Be quiet.' Tancock looked around, as he considered the alternatives available to him. It was important to remember that Saskia's actions, just like his own, were driven by the rapid approach of

Benjamin's twenty-first birthday. She'd been on her way to Portsmouth when the highwaymen had attacked her coach. She might be trying to get back to Holland to find help there—though surely she knew that would take too long. But there was another reason why she might be heading to Portsmouth. Hiring a boat to take her along the south coast from Portsmouth to Plymouth would be faster than negotiating the roads between Guildford and Plymouth.

Tancock weighed his choices. He and Selby could cast around here until they picked up Saskia's trail. They could head overland towards Cornwall as fast as possible, hoping to come upon Saskia during the journey. Or they could continue south to Portsmouth, gambling she'd gone in that direction. Tancock fully intended to emerge from this current adventure with a fortune to his name. It was important to take the course of action that best guaranteed his future wealth.

'You ride well.' Harry glanced sideways at Saskia before resuming his scrutiny of the countryside.

'Thank you. Until the last week I hadn't ridden much for years.' Saskia hesitated. Even though it was mid-morning, she still felt self-conscious in his company. 'Thank you for paying for these horses and for breakfast,' she added. 'And my hat. Of course, I will reimburse you—'

'That's not necessary,' he interrupted.

'I think it is.' But then she paused. She could no longer consider herself his employer and, despite the kisses they'd shared, he was neither her betrothed nor her lover, with an obligation to protect her. She could think of no name or precedent for their relationship.

'You don't think I'm a Dutch agent any more, do you?' she said.

'No.'

His brief answer was reassuring, but didn't encourage further conversation. A sudden thought chilled her.

'Are you married?' She was so agitated at the possibility that the question burst from her as soon as it popped into her mind.

'No!' He threw her a startled, almost disapproving glance.

'I beg your pardon,' she apologised hastily. She hadn't meant to offend him. 'You are somewhat old to be a bachelor,' she tried to explain. 'Unless you are a widower, like me.'

'I am not a widower,' he replied stiffly. 'Nor am I the only factor to return to England unmarried. It is easier to make a fortune in the Levant than it is to find a suitable bride there.'

Saskia looked at his rigid jaw and couldn't resist teasing him. 'Did you meet any pretty Turkish ladies?' she asked.

'No.' He stared straight ahead.

'They weren't pretty?' From her conversations with Dutch merchants who'd returned from the Levant, Saskia suspected that wasn't what Harry meant, but a devilish little impulse prompted her to continue teasing him. She didn't like it when he was so controlled and monosyllabic.

'I was not introduced to any Turkish ladies at all,' Harry said. 'When I visited Muslim friends I did not meet or even see their womenfolk. If I spent the night as a guest in a friend's house, it would always be in the *selamlik*, the separate quarters set aside for male visitors. Besides, subjects of the Sultan are not allowed to leave his empire—and I always knew I would eventually return to England.' There was an unexpectedly grim note to his voice as he concluded.

'Didn't you want to come back?' she asked.

He glanced at her and away again. 'Of course,' he said lightly. 'My brother is here, and my new young nephew.'

'My brother is here too,' she said, familiar anxiety rising within her. The danger to Benjamin was never far from her mind.

'Are you close?' Harry asked.

'We were as children. It was hard to leave him when I married. I meant to visit England more often, but after Pieter's accident I became so busy. Pieter trusted me to take on a large part of the management of his affairs,' she added by way of explanation. There had never been any problems in that aspect of her relationship with her husband. They'd been good business partners.

'Wasn't that difficult?' said Harry. From his tone she couldn't tell if he was disapproving or simply surprised. 'To obtain the proper respect from those you did business with?'

'I did not find it unduly difficult,' she said, tensing a little because there had always been some who'd doubted the ability of a woman who hadn't grown up in Amsterdam's merchant elite. She wondered if Harry shared their views, though probably for different reasons. 'I had much to learn. But there is perhaps more independence permitted to women in the Dutch Republic than here. And many women in Holland are forced to be active in business because their husbands are absent or dead. Many men work for the Dutch East India Company. They're away for years and may never return. Their wives would suffer if they could not do business on their own account and the law allows for that. It is true that I now have more complete legal independence as a widow than I had when I was a wife, but the only reason I am unusual in Amsterdam is because Pieter's commercial interests are so extensive. No one thought I should have an escort every time I stepped out of the door, though I have noticed…'

'What?'

Saskia hesitated, not sure if she should say what she was thinking. 'Since I have been back in England, I have seen respectable ladies wearing scandalously low dresses,' she admitted, remembering in particular the gown her aunt had worn when she flirted with Sir William Boscawen. 'We dressed more modestly in Amsterdam.'

She glanced at Harry. 'Are you shocked at the idea of me conducting business?' she asked. 'Does my description of the Dutch Republic seem as foreign to you as the things I've heard about the Ottoman Empire seem to me?'

He did not immediately reply and she wondered if he did disapprove and was trying to find a courteous way to say so. 'I am not shocked,' he said at last. 'I am…curious. I know there are women in Turkey who own property and even engage in business—but usually through the intermediary of a male relative. I had not imagined a lady would enjoy such activities—but I think you do?' He raised an enquiring eyebrow.

'Oh, yes,' she said immediately. 'It has been very satisfying to achieve so much.'

'It is,' he agreed and smiled. 'I have learnt much since meeting you. Until yesterday I did not know ladies could enjoy business. Nor had I thought a lady could travel unaccompanied from one side of England to the other. Now you have proved both are possible. Your journey should never have been necessary—but that is a different matter.'

Saskia twisted around in the saddle to stare at him. His hat brim shaded his face from the overhead sun. He still hadn't shaved. The dark whiskers on his jaw, the dangerous curved sword hanging by his side and his constantly roaming gaze as he watched their surroundings made him resemble a bandit far more than an English gentleman. Yet he had just made one of the most astonishing statements Saskia had ever heard. She did not believe her father or Pieter would have been sufficiently flexible in their thinking to adjust their prejudices in such a pragmatic manner.

'So if I…if I—' As she searched for an example her gaze fell on his sword. 'If I demonstrated I was a master swordsman, you would accept I possessed that skill and allow me to fight my own battles?'

'No,' said Harry. 'I have seen you try to defend yourself with a knife,' he continued, as she gasped indignantly. 'You are not a master swordsman.'

'I didn't say I was. It was just an example.'

'Pick a better one.'

'I was trying to find out if you are willing to accept me as I am, for my true capabilities—or whether you expect me to behave according to your notion of how ladies are supposed to behave,' she said.

Harry glanced at her, a gleam in his eyes that looked very like amusement. 'I have been away so long I have very little notion of how English ladies are supposed to behave,' he said. 'No doubt the longer I remain in your company, the more I will learn.'

It was well past noon when their route brought them in sight of a small group of buildings clustered around a water mill. Saskia was tired, and though she doubted Harry was equally weary, she was sure he was hungry. She'd grown used to Pieter's lack of interest in food, but Harry had demonstrated he had a healthy appetite.

'We can check whether we are still headed in the right direction,' she suggested.

'If you wish,' he replied. 'I'll see if the miller can sell us some food,' he added, and she suppressed a smile because she'd guessed right. But when they dismounted from their horses, it was a woman who emerged in response to Harry's call.

'Good day, good woman,' said Harry.

Saskia had been surreptitiously stretching her stiff muscles, but when Harry spoke she glanced at him in surprise. She'd never before heard him use such a stilted but deliberately gentle tone. It was almost as if he expected the mill woman to be afraid of him. Then she saw the wary expression in the other woman's eyes and realised that could well be the case. Any lone woman was likely to be alarmed by the unexpected appearance of two strangers, especially when they looked as disreputable as she and Harry. It was only an hour ago that she herself had thought Harry, with his unshaven face and unusual sword, looked more like a bandit than an English gentleman. Saskia decided she couldn't blame the mill woman for being wary.

'Hello.' She smiled and stepped forward to draw the woman's attention. 'We're going to Winchester and we wanted to make sure we're still headed in the right direction.' Despite her clothes she didn't try to pretend to be a man. It wasn't unheard of for women to travel in men's clothes in times of necessity, and since she'd been in England Saskia had learned that Queen Catherine had even made it something of a fashion for Court ladies to wear male costume.

The woman from the mill looked at Saskia for a few seconds. What she saw seemed to reassure her, and she gave directions willingly enough. Perhaps she was just anxious to hasten them on their way.

'My husband said we didn't need to stop for directions,' Saskia said, 'but I wanted to be sure.' She threw a teasing glance at Harry, mainly to show the other woman they were no threat, but partly to see how Harry reacted to her claim.

For a few seconds his expression became so inscrutable it was almost forbidding, but then he smiled. 'To tell the truth, I am more eager to obtain food than directions,' he said, still speaking with slightly exaggerated gentleness. 'I would gladly buy some bread and cheese or any other food you might have to spare.'

'There is some rabbit stew on the hearth, if that would please you.' The mill woman glanced between Saskia and Harry, before her gaze rested briefly on Harry's sword. It was apparent she was still not at ease with them, but equally obvious she didn't want to do anything to provoke Harry.

'Only if you can spare it,' said Saskia. 'Thank you.'

'There is plenty,' said the mill woman. 'Please come in.'

'I will tend to the horses first and join you,' said Harry.

Saskia saw him glance at the woman's retreating back before he met her gaze. There was a troubled expression in his eyes, as if he was disturbed by the mill woman's nervousness in his presence. Saskia had a sudden suspicion he might not come in at all, but simply ask her to bring some bread out to him when she was finished.

'Don't take too long with the horses,' she said in a low voice. 'I shall not eat until you are sitting beside me.' He'd insisted she should take her share first the previous night, so she hoped what she'd just said would be sufficient inducement to make him follow her inside.

The lit hearth meant the kitchen was hotter than comfortable, although the scent of the fragrant stew was some compensation. After the bright sunlight outside, the interior seemed dark, and it took a few moments for Saskia's eyes to adjust. She sank down on to a bench beside a solid wooden table.

'Thank you,' she said. Since Harry was still outside she felt safe to admit the truth. 'I am so tired it is a relief to sit on something with four legs that isn't moving.'

'Have you travelled far?' The mill woman spooned stew into two bowls.

Saskia hesitated, reluctant to reveal they'd come from London in case Tancock or Selby passed this way and asked questions, but too lacking in local knowledge to offer a plausible alternative.

'From Canterbury,' said Harry, ducking his head as he came into the kitchen. 'My wife received news that her sister is dangerously ill. Speed has been our priority on this journey—though I wish it could be more comfortable for my lady.'

The mill woman glanced at him, then set one of the bowls in front of him as he sat down. 'My family all live in the village,' she said. 'I cannot imagine being so far away from them that I must travel for days to reach them.'

'Sometimes it is very hard,' said Saskia, remembering the wrench of leaving England and all that had been familiar to her when she'd married Pieter. It had hurt when she'd kissed her father and her brother goodbye before setting off for her new life in Amsterdam. She had not seen her father again. He'd died before she'd been able to visit England.

Saskia was too weary to make further conversation while she ate and Harry made no attempt to engage the mill woman, so for a while the silence was broken only by the sound of the turning watermill and the foraging chickens near the open kitchen door. Then Saskia heard a shout from outside. The mill woman glanced at Harry, who was still placidly eating his stew, and then hurried out to answer the call.

Before Saskia had time to say anything, she was distracted by small, whimpering cry. She looked around, half-expecting to see a dog lying in the shadows, and for the first time noticed a crib beneath the shuttered window. She'd only just realised there was a sleeping baby in the kitchen when it whimpered again, then started to cry in earnest. Saskia froze. She glanced uneasily towards the kitchen door and then back to the crib. Surely the mill woman would come back soon? If she didn't…

Saskia managed to swallow a suddenly unappetising mouthful of stew as she wondered whether she ought to try to comfort the babe. While she was still agonising over what to do, Harry stood up. For an instant she thought he might be exasperated by the noise and her anxiety spiked even higher in case he stomped out and left her completely alone with the crying infant. But then, to her astonishment, he went over to the crib. Saskia stared at him, not quite believing what she saw as he picked up the red-faced babe and spoke soothingly to it. He sat down again with it cradled securely in the crook of one arm. To her amazement, the baby stopped crying. She could see that it was not fully awake. Its eyes were open, but it rested its head against Harry's broad shoulder and blinked vacantly as he continued to eat, using his free hand.

Harry saw her looking at him and frowned in concern. 'Are you not well?'

'I am quite well,' she replied hastily. 'I…shall I fetch its—I mean, his mother?'

'She will come back when her business is done, I am sure,' Harry said, sounding unconcerned.

'But—' Saskia didn't know what to say. It wasn't that she disliked babies. But once she'd realised she'd never have any of her own she'd found it too painful to spend much time with other women's children. She would have been unsure of herself trying to comfort one of her nieces or nephews, let alone a stranger's child. How had Harry acquired confidence in such an unlikely skill?

The baby was more alert now, holding his head up to look at Harry and then lean forward to look into the bowl of stew. When the babe made a grab for Harry's spoon, Harry laughed softly and held it out of the way.

'Well, you are a sturdy lad. Are you eating stew already?' Harry looked at the baby and the baby looked solemnly back at Harry. It was one of the most incongruous yet touching things Saskia had ever seen. Harry was all hard, lean angles, and the two days' growth of stubble only added to his dangerous appearance. The baby was soft and round and unblinkingly curious.

Harry put some gravy on the spoon and offered it to the baby. The baby opened his mouth obediently and from there on Harry alternated between feeding himself substantial mouthfuls of the remaining stew and the baby smaller amounts of gravy.

'I do not know what his mother gives him,' Harry said apologetically, when he noticed Saskia was still staring at him. 'But gravy will not hurt him and it is not fair to make him watch us eat when he is hungry.'

'Of course not,' she said, still feeling bemused. She doubted if her male relatives would consider it their job to spoonfeed their own children, let along a stranger's.

'You have not finished.' Harry glanced down at her bowl. 'You need to keep up your strength. We still have a long ride ahead.'

Saskia nodded. Now she'd eaten something she was already starting to regain her energy. She finished her stew and sopped up the last of the gravy with a piece of bread, most of her attention still focused on Harry and the baby. When had he learned to be so good with infants? She felt a pang at the thought he must have children of his own. He'd never been married, but he could easily have a mistress. He would keep his mistress and children secure from the dangers and alarms of the outside world. She imagined them all together in a sheltered courtyard garden, a happy harmonious family in all but name. Tears pricked her eyes and she didn't know if her grief was for what she'd lost when Pieter had been crippled—or because Harry's heart already belonged to an unseen and perhaps distant family.

A shadow darkened the kitchen door as the mill woman returned. When she saw her baby in Harry's arms she gave a gasp of mingled surprise and alarm. The baby saw her and reached out both arms towards her. Harry laughed and surrendered him immediately. 'I am a poor substitute,' he said. 'But he was sad when he woke up without you.'

'Thank you. He is a good baby normally,' said the mill woman breathlessly.

'He was a good baby today,' said Harry. 'What is he? Ten—eleven months old?'

'Ten.' The mill woman was gazing at Harry in astonishment.

'He is a strong, sturdy fellow.'

'Yes, he is.' The mill woman smiled suddenly, the remnants of her anxiety in the presence of strangers vanishing in her pride in her son.

To Saskia's disbelief she listened to Harry and the mill woman talk about babies for several minutes. Whereas he'd seemed ill at ease when he'd first arrived, he was obviously perfectly at home discussing infants, and the mill woman was equally happy to talk about her son. Now it was Saskia who felt awkward and out of place. She was a woman, yet she knew hardly anything of matters such as teething or the age at which a babe first walked or talked. To hide her discomfort she busied herself pulling coins from her purse to pay for their meal.

'Do you and your wife have many children?' asked the mill woman.

'We have not been married long enough for children,' said Harry, as Saskia struggled to produce a coherent reply.

'But you know so much about them!' the mill woman exclaimed.

'I come from a large family and I have spent much time with my siblings' children,' Harry replied easily.

Chapter Six

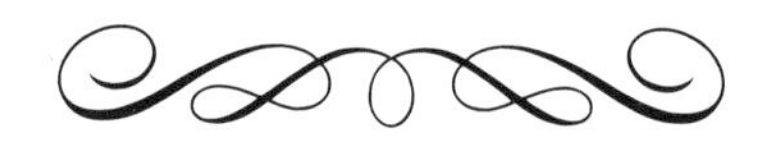

'I thought you only have one brother you hadn't seen for years until recently,' said Saskia, when they were well away from the mill.

'That's true.'

'Then you surely must have children of your own to be so good with them.' She tried to keep her voice light so he wouldn't realise how much she cared about his answer.

Harry grinned. 'I am not always good—I was lucky he was such a placid babe. Selim would have howled the place down if a stranger had picked him up—but I thought it was worth a try so that we could finish our meal in peace.'

Selim? Saskia seized on the name of the unknown child. She had already guessed Harry must have had a great deal of experience with children to be so confident with the mill baby. She tried to conceal a pang of distress she had no business feeling at the affection in his voice when he spoke of Selim.

'Is Selim your son?' she asked, hoping her voice did not betray how much she cared about his answer.

'No. I have no children of my own,' Harry replied. He was gazing forward between his horse's ears, and Saskia was glad he wasn't looking at her, for she was afraid her expression might have revealed how disproportionately relieved she was at his reply.

'Then who is Selim?'

'The youngest brother of my former servant Yusuf.'

'You tended a servant child!' Saskia exclaimed before she could stop herself.

'All children need proper care, no matter what their birth or rank in life,' he replied.

'Yes. Yes, of course,' Saskia said hastily. 'I did not mean to imply… It is just that I was surprised that a man would care for *any* child in such basic matters as feeding and—' She broke off, flushing.

Harry smiled faintly. 'I also changed Selim's linen and bathed him at need,' he said, apparently amused by her reaction to the possibility that he might have cleaned a baby's dirty bottom. She could sense no awkwardness in him at the admission. She found his lack of self-consciousness both attractive and intriguing, particularly in comparison to his initial lack of ease with the mill woman.

'How did you come to care for Selim?' she asked. 'What happened to his mother?'

'She died,' said Harry. 'I never met her. Yusuf was twelve and his father and other siblings were already dead. He was working for me to provide for his mother and Selim, when she too died. Yusuf could not bear to be separated from his only remaining brother, so I took Selim into my household.' Harry said it as if it had been the natural thing to do, but Saskia wondered how many other men would have made the same choice.

'That was generous of you,' she said, feeling a surge of warmth and admiration at his compassion for the children.

Harry shook his head slightly, as if he didn't agree, but most of his attention was clearly focused on the past. 'It was not right that the brothers should be separated when I could help. Yusuf knew more about babies than I did, of course, but I learned quickly. Selim was seven months when he came to me. Too young, perhaps, to be to be denied his mother's milk.' Harry smiled ruefully. 'But Yusuf and I knew nothing of wet nurses, and we were careful with what we fed him. He grew into a strong, quick lad. He is nearly fourteen now.' There was no mistaking the pride and affection in Harry's voice.

'Where is he?' Saskia asked.

'I became good friends with a Turkish architect in Smyrna. Selim is training with him.'

'And Yusuf?' Saskia didn't imagine Harry had taken such pains for only one of the brothers.

'By the time I left Turkey, Yusuf had already become quite a successful merchant.' Harry sounded equally proud of the older brother. 'Of course he is not as yet a member of the Levant Company, or part of the English Factory, but his contacts there are useful to him.'

'It must have been hard, leaving them behind,' said Saskia, and saw Harry's lips press together and his gloved hand tighten on the reins.

'I miss them, of course,' he said quietly after a moment, and Saskia was sure that simple statement covered a greater depth of feeling than he was willing to express openly. 'But I knew from the first it would be necessary. As I said earlier, the Sultan's subjects cannot be taken out of the empire. I began the process of ensuring Selim and Yusuf's future years before I left the Levant. But Selim was not the only infant I cared for. There were other children who stayed a few weeks, a few months, or sometimes longer. It became known I would not turn a child away. The other factors were inclined to laugh at me.' His sudden grin lightened his sombre mood—and also revealed the opinion of the other factors had been a matter of indifference to him. 'I came close to causing a diplomatic incident on a couple of occasions, but we managed to sort it out with the *Kadi*.'

'*Kadi?*'

'An official, something like our magistrates,' said Harry. 'We came to a good understanding in the end.'

Harry's revelations amazed Saskia. Until she'd seen him with the mill woman's baby she had never guessed he would even spare a second glance at a child, let alone respond with such practical compassion. None of the children he had provided for were related to him. He'd had no expectation of watching them grow up to inherit his business or continue his family name, yet she suspected he had done everything he could to ensure the future security of all of them.

'Why did you do it?' she asked.

For the first time he seemed reluctant to answer. 'Children have no power,' he said eventually. 'No choices. At the very least they should be well fed and safe. Haven't you known many children?'

Saskia's gaze shot to his face. 'What makes you think that?' she said, disconcerted by the way he'd suddenly turned the tables on her.

'Something in your expression when the baby started crying,' he said.

'What kind of something?' she asked, embarrassed and worried that he might think badly of her for lacking the nurturing qualities expected of a woman.

'Panic.'

'It was not—' she began indignantly.

He grinned.

She sighed. 'How did you know?' she asked, feeling foolish and inadequate.

'I've seen that look before on my friends' faces when they thought they might be left holding a crying infant,' said Harry. 'Even my brother is not yet fully confident holding his new son.'

'I *like* children,' Saskia assured him. It was suddenly very important to her that Harry didn't think she had an aversion to them. 'I just haven't spent much time with them. I didn't know what to do.'

'Don't you have any female relatives in Holland?' Harry asked, clearly puzzled.

'Oh, yes, lots of them.'

'So they are all of an older generation, without young children?'

'No. My husband had several brothers and sisters and they are all married. I have many sisters-in-law and cousins and they all have children,' said Saskia.

'Didn't all you womenfolk spend time together, with the younger children of those who had them?' Harry said. 'While you did your…needlework…'

he hesitated '…and whatever else women do when there are no men present.'

'Yes, they did,' said Saskia.

'Do you mean they did not include you?' To her surprise, Harry sounded indignant. 'Because you are not Dutch?'

'I am Dutch,' she corrected him. 'Or half-Dutch. My mother was Dutch and I can speak it as well as I speak English. I was a stranger when I arrived, but everyone welcomed me.' She bit her lip as she considered how to continue. 'After Pieter's accident I had less time for my needlework,' she said. 'I had to manage his business. I suppose it was natural that after my life became so different from the other women's we had less to talk about. I did not mean to hold myself aloof from them. It hurt to hold a baby and know I would never have one of my own.' She gasped and turned her face away as she realised how much she'd revealed.

'Your husband's accident meant there could be no children?' Harry said gently.

She nodded jerkily, still not looking at him, furious with herself because she was on the verge of tears.

'When we have rescued your brother, are you going back to Amsterdam?' Harry asked, after a little while.

'I don't know.' It was difficult to look beyond her

immediate goal of rescuing Benjamin, but her visit to England had thrown up questions about her future. 'At first I took it for granted I'd go back. I have many responsibilities in Amsterdam. Now I am not sure. But at least I have a position and a role there. If I come back to England I will just be Sir Benjamin Trevithick's widowed sister. There would be nothing for me to do except manage his house until he takes a wife. He will be twenty-one on Saturday. I am sure he is smitten with Anne. Perhaps he will ask her to marry him soon.'

They rode in silence for a few minutes as Harry considered what he'd just heard. Before he'd met Saskia he had never had such a conversation with a woman. He was deeply interested in even the simplest of details of her everyday life, and he was intrigued and pleased to discover that Saskia's revelations did not seem entirely alien to him.

'Your situation is not so different to mine,' he said. 'When I was nineteen I went to Aleppo and had to learn to live among strangers, just as you went to live in Amsterdam. Now I have returned to England and I must learn to be part of an unfamiliar world all over again. It is a fascinating challenge.'

'A fascinating challenge?' Saskia echoed. 'But it is different for a man. You have more choice in what you become. I can carry on doing what I do in Amsterdam because everyone knows I am Pieter van Buren's widow, continuing to run his business. I do not think it would be easy for me to do the same thing in England as Sir Benjamin Trevithick's sister.'

'Are you determined to continue in business?' Harry asked.

'I enjoy it,' she said. 'It gives me more freedom. I believe I have spent more time in the past few years talking to men than to women—about business matters, of course,' she added hastily.

'No one tried to take advantage of you?' Whenever Saskia was near Harry was constantly aware of her in every particle of his body. He couldn't believe the other men hadn't been equally captivated.

'Sometimes. Merchants can be very hard-headed. But I can strike a hard bargain too.' Saskia smiled proudly.

That wasn't what Harry had meant, but he supposed that if anyone had offended her feminine modesty she would have grasped his meaning at once, so he didn't pursue the matter. He was more curious how her husband had felt about his enforced dependency.

'Your husband must have been very proud of you?' he said, approaching the matter obliquely.

Saskia flushed slightly. 'We worked well together,' she replied after a few moments.

Harry couldn't tell if she was uncomfortable with the implicit compliment or whether there was something else behind her hesitancy. 'If I were married, I would find it difficult to let my wife spend a great deal of time with other men,' he said.

'That is because you have spent so many years in places you did not see *any* women,' Saskia responded energetically. 'Pieter understood very well that our business often required me to meet other men when he wasn't present.'

'In such circumstances, were I unable to walk, I would be a very jealous husband,' Harry said quietly.

Saskia's colour deepened. 'Only once,' she said in a low voice. 'The first winter of our marriage we skated on the frozen canals. I loved it. So fast and exhilarating. The next year Pieter could no longer skate. One of his brothers persuaded me to go on to the ice with him. It was wonderful. I had not felt so free for months. But when we came back, and I saw Pieter's expression… I never went skating again. Can we gallop?' Without waiting for a response she urged her horse to go faster, veering off to one side to gallop along the brow of the hill running parallel to the road.

As he spurred after her, Harry wondered exactly

what she'd seen in her husband's face that day. Disapproval? Jealousy? Resentment? Whatever it had been, she'd sacrificed her own pleasure for Pieter's peace of mind. She was galloping full tilt. He wondered if she was running from her memories or simply indulging in the taste for speed she'd revealed when she described her pleasure in ice-skating. Harry swore as he saw her new hat blow away, but he didn't stop to chase it. As he watched her, fearlessly urging her horse faster, he felt a thrum of hope and excitement. She was smaller than he was, her body soft and womanly, but she was also physically robust and courageous. And she liked kissing him. He was beginning to feel more optimistic about his own future than he had done for months. In the meantime, he had to be practical. He gave Saskia another few moments before he shouted for her to slow down.

'I'll try to obtain fresh horses soon, but we do not know how long these beasts must carry us,' he said, as she threw him a mutinous glance. 'Your hat's gone,' he added, as their horses slowed to a walk. He couldn't resist reaching out to touch the tangled curls gleaming apricot-gold in the afternoon sun.

'Oh, no!' She looked back in consternation and then at Harry. 'I'm sorry. I never thought.'

He grinned and plopped his own hat on her head. 'Don't lose mine before we get you another one.'

'I am not usually so careless,' she assured him, dropping the reins so she could stuff her hair into the crown of the hat. Then she looked at him hesitantly. 'What is it?'

'Nothing.' He shook his head, unwilling to reveal the powerful effect her feminine beauty had upon him. He hated it when she hid her hair, even though he still considered it a sensible precaution. At the same time he experienced a flash of relief that other men would have less provocation to lust after her. He was beginning to understand on a very visceral level why a man might want to keep his woman hidden from the eyes of other men, even though on a more intellectual level he believed concealment in itself heightened the fascination.

The sun was throwing long shadows when they stopped a mile outside the walls of Winchester. Saskia followed Harry off the main thoroughfare so that they could rest in the shelter of a hedge. Grazing rabbits darted away at their approach, and then settled down to continue nibbling the grass at a watchful distance. Every muscle in Saskia's body ached as she slid out of the saddle. If not for Harry's hands on her waist, she was afraid her knees would have crumpled. She was so tired she didn't consider the intimacy of their position until she looked up, straight into his face. For a moment she was snared by the intensity of his dark eyes. She was suddenly, dizzyingly aware that the last time they'd stood this close he'd kissed her. At the memory, tiny sparks of energy began to fizz through her weariness.

Harry squeezed her waist and then stepped away from her. 'Not long now before you can rest,' he said encouragingly.

'It has been a long day,' she admitted.

'You've had several long days in succession,' he said. 'We need to discuss our plans before we enter Winchester.'

'I thought you were hoping we can stay with your friend,' said Saskia. She walked around in a small circle, suppressing a wince of discomfort as she attempted to relieve the stiffness in her legs.

'I am,' Harry replied, 'but he won't be expecting me, and he certainly won't be expecting me to be escorting an unchaperoned lady.'

'Oh.' Saskia had been so focused on pushing forward to Cornwall she hadn't considered how their situation would appear to an outsider. She thought about it for a few seconds. 'If you trust him, why don't we just to tell him the truth?' she suggested. 'Or do you think he won't believe us?' Her lower back was aching and she decided stretching to the side might help, so she leant over, feeling the gentle pull in her muscles.

'I intend to tell him some of the truth,' said Harry, his gaze fixed on her unconventional movements. 'But the whole truth is a little...unusual.'

'The whole thing is utterly bizarre and unbelievable.' Saskia shrugged out of her man's coat. She'd have to put it back on before they rode into Winchester, but now it was a relief to feel the breeze through her coarse linen shirt. 'I still cannot fully comprehend Aunt Isabel's callous greed.' She put her hands on her hips, arching and hollowing her back a few times in an attempt to ease her overworked muscles.

There was silence for several seconds, before Harry cleared his throat. 'That's not the aspect of our story Nicholson will have difficulty with,' he said hoarsely. 'It is the fact that you hired my services in a London coffee-house that will excite his comments.'

It took a moment for Saskia to catch Harry's meaning—and then indignation made her forget all about her aching body. 'It was the only practical thing to do in the circumstances!' she exclaimed.

'That's debatable,' Harry retorted. 'And though I am aware women have more licence in England than they do in Turkey, I am sure many people would not consider it the act of a modest lady.'

Saskia's mouth fell open. After everything that had happened so far, the last thing she'd expected was for him to disparage her virtue at this stage of their mission. 'If you were so scandalised by me kissing you last night, why didn't you say so then?' she demanded, hurt and angry that he'd waited so long to criticise her.

'I wasn't scandalised,' he began. '*Surprised*, perhaps—'

'You have no right to cast judgement on me!'

'I'm not casting judgement.' He sounded exasperated. 'I do not hold you responsible for anything you did while you were asleep. I'm sure you thought you were lying beside your husband—'

'No, I didn't!'

He stared at her. Fire burned into Saskia's cheeks as she realised she'd just destroyed her last defence for what had happened.

'Who did you think I was?' he demanded.

'I was dreaming,' she prevaricated.

'Who were you dreaming about?' A hard, suspicious light suddenly gleamed in his eyes.

She glared at him. 'A gentleman wouldn't ask a lady that.'

'A gentleman who has been kissed in mistake for

another man does,' Harry said ruthlessly. 'Who were you dreaming about?'

'I knew it was you beside me,' she muttered, looking away.

'But who were you dreaming about?' She heard the underlying steel in his voice and knew he would persist until she had given a full answer.

'I dreamed you gave me a rose,' she said, glaring at him. 'So I thanked you.' There was no need to tell him that in her dream they'd been lying on the ground in a rose garden and he'd kissed her first.

'You dreamed I gave you a rose and you kissed me by way of thanks?'

'That's what I just said,' she pointed out crossly.

Harry stared at her. She scowled back at him, very disgruntled that he'd forced her to reveal her sleeping fantasy. Within seconds she saw heat, not disapproval, flare in his eyes.

'I was not commenting on your behaviour, but on how the situation might appear to someone who doesn't know you,' Harry said gruffly. 'It would be easier to say you sought my help because we're already acquainted. Not that you advertised for me in a coffee-house.'

'Oh, all right. Friend of the family.' Saskia nodded jerkily.

'Something like that.'

Saskia belatedly remembered she would be arriving at his friend's house in breeches. 'Perhaps, if it seems necessary, you should tell him that I'm your mistress,' she said brightly. She'd started the journey as the mistress of a nonexistent lover. It would make a far more convincing story if she pretended to be Harry's mistress. 'I don't suppose I'll ever visit Winchester again, so it wouldn't hurt my reputation.'

'What about my reputation?' For the first time Harry did sound disapproving. 'My friend would be offended—and furious—if he thought I'd brought my mistress to stay in his house and meet his wife.'

'You didn't tell me he was married,' Saskia said weakly. She'd assumed Harry's friend was also a bachelor, but of course Harry couldn't take even a pretend mistress into a respectable household. 'Perhaps it would be simplest if we stay at an inn,' she said.

'If Nicholson is not there, we may have to. But if he is there I want to call upon his help.'

'To go with us?' Saskia hadn't expected that.

'Not necessarily. But I would prefer to have more men at my command. At the very least, additional protection for you. All in all, I believe it will be acceptable for me to introduce you as my betrothed,' Harry declared.

Saskia stared at him. 'Your *betrothed*?' she repeated blankly.

'It was clever of you to pretend to be my wife when we stopped at the mill,' Harry said. 'It made me seem less threatening to the woman. Of course, Nicholson will not regard you as a threat, but it will make your presence seem less exceptional if I tell him we are betrothed.'

It took a moment before Saskia recovered sufficiently to find her voice. An image of herself as Harry's wife flashed into her mind. It should have appalled her—but it didn't. All her life she'd known her position in the world and when she'd married Pieter it had been with full awareness of his family background and the high status of the van Burens in Amsterdam. She knew nothing about Harry except that he'd been a factor in the Levant and his brother was a silent investor in a coffee-house.

He could be a fortune-hunter, taking advantage of her vulnerability to forge a financially advantageous marriage to her, but her instincts rejected that notion. Poor families could not afford to apprentice their sons into the Levant Company. She was sure Harry had been born a gentleman and, despite his vagabondish appearance, she was equally confident he had done well in his business ventures. He had proved himself to be brave—and far more honourable than she deserved, considering her behaviour in the night. And he kissed wonderfully. Of course, he hadn't asked her to marry him; he'd suggested they pretend to be betrothed.

'We could just…pretend to be married, as I claimed at the mill,' she said, and then flushed with embarrassment at her boldness. But after all, it was even less exceptional for a man to be travelling with his wife than with his fiancée.

'That would not be a good idea,' Harry said seriously.

Saskia wanted to curl up with mortification at his cool rejection of her suggestion. He'd said she'd been clever when she'd pretended to be his wife at the mill. Why had he changed his mind now?

'Unless you guarantee you are willing to marry me when this adventure is over,' he said.

'What?' Her gaze whipped to his face. '*Really* marry you?' Was he jesting?

'One of the reasons I returned to England was to find a wife,' he explained. 'It will hamper my search for a bride if everyone thinks I'm already married.'

Saskia felt as if a lead weight had suddenly settled in her stomach. His objection made perfect sense.

'That is the beauty of a betrothal,' Harry continued. 'If, at the end of this venture, you decide you do not wish to marry me, you can cry off.'

'And you'll be free to seek a preferable bride.' Saskia turned her head away. It was perfectly ridiculous to feel so devastated at the thought of him preferring another woman. She reminded herself sternly that she'd only known him a short while. Until they'd started this conversation, she'd never consciously considered marrying him.

Harry watched Saskia, uncertain of her mood, and feeling as if half a dozen rabbits had taken up residence in his stomach. 'I cannot imagine any lady who would be more suitable,' he said, keeping his voice very steady. 'But one must give practical consideration to the future. I would not wish to take dishonourable advantage of the situation in which you find yourself.'

Saskia turned to look at him again. From her expression Harry couldn't tell if she thought he was mad to suppose she'd marry him, or whether she was trying to come up with a courteous way of rejecting his proposal.

The rabbits inside him were kicking his ribs so energetically he was surprised the real rabbits in the field didn't hear and take alarm. He hadn't felt this nervous when he'd confronted the highwaymen—but he'd been confident of his ability to deal with that situation. The longer Saskia remained silent, the more he began to fear she would reject him. He still had doubts that any sensible woman would consider him a suitable husband. But he needed a wife, and Saskia was resourceful, strong and loyal to those she loved. Best of all, she wasn't scared of him or his kisses. She'd even dreamed of him kissing her! But she was taking too long to answer and he was assailed by terrible doubts.

She'd already taken off her coat. Now she took his borrowed hat off her head and dropped in on to the ground. Then she frowned and rubbed her hands vigorously through her hair until her curls were sticking up wildly all over her scalp. His heart and his hopes sank. This was surely not the way a woman behaved when she was pleased to receive a marriage proposal. He struggled to think of some way to make it easier for her, so she would not feel embarrassed to continue in his company. They would have to stay at an inn tonight, just as she'd suggested—

'Instead of pretending to be married, we are going to pretend to be betrothed?' Saskia interrupted his increasingly gloomy thoughts.

'I see no reason why the betrothal should be a pretence,' Harry said stiffly. 'Though if you do not wish to marry me after your brother is safe, I will not insist on it.'

Saskia rubbed her head again. Harry began to

feel irritated as well as depressed. He knew he wasn't the ideal husband, but she didn't have to make it so obvious the mere idea of marrying him gave her a headache. She could just say 'No, thank you'.

Saskia took a deep breath and stared straight at him. 'Did you just ask me to marry you?' she demanded.

Harry was certain he'd made his meaning perfectly clear. He opened his mouth to make a sharp response, but at the last moment thought better of it. A gentleman shouldn't snarl at the lady he'd just asked to be his wife. 'It occurred to me you might not object,' he said in a cold, stilted voice. 'I am sorry I misjudged.' He paused, eyeing her disordered hair, which he was starting to consider a silent insult to him. 'I still think you would be advised to allow me to introduce you as my fiancée to my friend and his wife,' he added, in an equally chilly tone. 'But the pretence can end at the earliest opportunity.'

'I did not say I objected to marrying you!' Saskia's shoulders rose as she took a deep breath. Her breasts pressed against the linen shirt. He could see the outline of her nipples. She wasn't wearing any kind of feminine undergarment! His thoughts and emotions spun into complete turmoil. He was torn between a compelling desire to step closer and touch her, and a possessive determination she must keep her coat on at all times until she'd changed into more modest attire.

'You have only known me a couple of days,' she said. 'In most unusual circumstances. How can you possibly have decided so quickly I would make you a suitable wife?'

For a few seconds Harry barely noticed she'd spoken. He made himself look away from her and focus on what she'd just said. Perhaps she wasn't flatly rejecting his proposal, but simply questioning the unconventional speed with which he'd declared himself. He relaxed very slightly. Questions implied a willingness to negotiate, and he was accustomed to tough bargaining.

'I am certain I already know more about you—that I know you better—than I would get to know any of the prospective brides my brother has in mind,' he said. 'During the marriage negotiations I would become better acquainted with her father or guardian than the lady herself.'

Saskia blinked, and then he saw a thoughtful expression appear in her eyes.

'Before we tie the knot, I would ensure an appropriate settlement is drawn up.' Harry pressed his advantage. 'You may be assured I have sufficient wealth to keep you in comfort.'

Saskia walked over to stand before him, all the

while gazing intently into his face. 'You mean it,' she whispered wonderingly. 'You really are asking me to marry me.'

She hadn't been rubbing her head because she didn't want to marry him, but because he'd asked her so ineptly she'd been confused! Harry felt a rush of mingled relief and fury at himself for handling the matter so badly.

'I was clumsy,' he said. 'I *am* asking you to marry me. But I have never proposed to a lady before. I am sorry I don't have an elegant speech for you.'

Saskia smiled tremulously. His heart gave a little, unaccustomed skip of hope. But when she did not immediately speak his anxiety returned. She took a deep breath, and he steeled himself to receive a kindly worded refusal.

'I do not need elegant speeches,' she said. 'But sometimes I need…words. I do not care if they are fluent—or brief and blunt. But sometimes I need words.' She paused, and he struggled to understand what words it was she needed. She started to tremble. Whatever she was trying to say was obviously very important to her, but Harry still didn't understand, and he began to fear he wouldn't be able to give her the words she needed.

'I cannot agree to marry you unless you promise you will never leave me in silence to wonder what you want,' she said in a rush. 'Wonder what you feel. Wonder what…you want from me.'

He looked down into her eyes, trying to control his own chaotic emotions so that he could better decipher Saskia's meaning. She didn't want him to leave her in silence to wonder what he wanted. Was that what her husband had done to her? Some people were comfortable living with a measure of uncertainty—others preferred decisions and negotiations to be laid out plainly. Everything he knew of Saskia suggested she liked things to be clear and straightforward.

He could tell she was having difficulty holding his gaze, but she didn't look away. She was bravely asking for what she needed to make their marriage a success. Her courage both aroused and pleased him. He felt a surge of optimism, because he was far more confident he could satisfy a woman who told him directly what she wanted, rather than one who demurely waited for him to work it out.

He put one hand on her shoulder and lifted his other hand to brush the side of his thumb across her mouth. Her lips parted a little at his touch and her eyes darkened. Was she already anticipating his kiss?

'I want the same promise from you,' he said, his voice a low growl.

'What?' Confusion flickered in her expression.

'You will not leave me to wonder,' he said. 'You will tell me in words what you want.'

He saw her swallow, and felt her sudden hesitancy.

'We will both promise to be direct and honest with the other,' he said. 'I will promise to tell you what I want, and not leave you wondering, if you make the same promise to me.' His hand tightened on her shoulder. 'Do you agree?'

'Yes.' Her voice was little more than a croak of acceptance.

'I want to kiss you,' he said. 'Do you want me to kiss you now?'

Chapter Seven

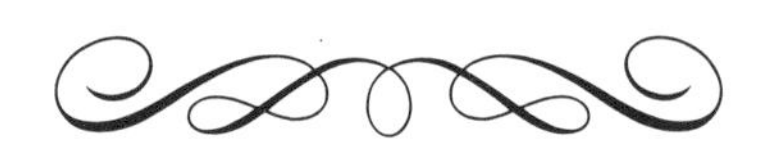

Saskia caught her breath, and then nodded. 'Yes,' she whispered, feeling the heat rise to her face.

A shiver of awareness rippled through her as his hand slipped down her back to circle her waist and pull her close for his kiss. Even after what they'd just promised each other, she still spent a few seconds worrying that Harry might pull back and make some disparaging comment about her brazen behaviour. But he didn't. He seemed to enjoy her willingness to be kissed, so she put her arms around him, and lost herself in the pleasure of being held by a man who wanted to hold and kiss her. Not just any man, but one who made her blood sing with desire. His tongue stroked against her lips. She parted for him and he pressed boldly inside. He tasted of danger, excitement and desire. He lifted his head a little and she instinctively pulled him down again. He made a sound low in his throat and less than a heartbeat later all her senses were overwhelmed in the most passionate kiss she had ever experienced.

When they finally drew apart she was dazed and panting, her heart racing and her legs weak with need. She rested her head on Harry's shoulder. She loved the way he made her feel and she loved the fact she could arouse such a potent response from him. She could still hardly credit she was truly betrothed to him. She did not normally make important decisions so impetuously. And even though he had said it was a genuine marriage proposal, she still half-wondered if her weariness after a full day's riding had somehow caused her to misunderstand their conversation. If it turned out it really was no more than a ruse to make her presence in his friend's house acceptable, she wouldn't be surprised. If he had meant it, they would have a great deal to think and talk about after Benjamin was safe.

It briefly occurred to her to wonder if Harry would be willing to move to Amsterdam. He was used to doing business away from England and, apart from his brother, he didn't seem to have any deep roots here. But those discussions were for the future. Right now she would not deny herself the pleasure of his attentions. He stroked her hair, his light caress sending a *frisson* of delight through her body.

'Now we've made our plan we should get moving,' he said, his voice husky. Despite his words it was another few moments before he released her and stepped back.

Saskia's body still yearned with unfulfilled arousal, but she didn't protest. Her mouth was tender and swollen. Her skin tingled from his whiskers. She sucked her lower lip between her teeth, relishing the lingering traces of his exotic taste and wondering when he would kiss her again. The image of his naked, muscular body pressed against hers—thrusting into her as he satisfied the throbbing need he'd aroused in her—brought another wave of heat to her skin. She pressed her hands against her damp cheeks and then explored her tangled hair. Between the warmth of the summer day and the fire of desire, she must look like an overheated scarecrow.

'I need my comb,' she said, taking refuge in the mundane activity. She went to fetch her bag from where it was strapped behind her saddle. 'I cannot present myself to your friend and his wife in such disarray.'

Two hours later Harry waited in Martin Nicholson's well-appointed parlour for Saskia to come to supper.

After their arrival and the initial greetings, Nicholson's wife, Dorothy, had carried Saskia off to make her comfortable and lend her a gown for the evening, while Harry had remained with Nicholson to offer a fuller explanation for their visit.

Harry suspected Saskia wasn't entirely at ease with the situation—perhaps she didn't like the idea of borrowing clothes from a stranger—but she'd been gracious in her thanks to their hostess. Harry was also wearing borrowed clothes, but his only discomfort arose from the fact that Nicholson was a shorter, weightier man. The brocade coat was too tight across Harry's shoulders and the shirt and breeches were somewhat too short in the limbs, while being much too spacious about the waist. Harry thought nostalgically of the Turkish costume he'd so often worn, and hoped his belt kept the breeches safely anchored.

'I'll give you any help I can,' Nicholson assured him, curiosity glinting in his eyes. 'You helped me many times in Turkey. I owe much of my current prosperity to your generosity.'

'It has always been a pleasure doing business with you,' Harry said. 'I am glad you've established yourself so successfully here in Winchester. It was always your aim.' He glanced around the parlour as he spoke. Signs of his host's prosperity were everywhere in the well-furnished room.

'A delicate situation in Mistress van Buren's family, you said?'

'A situation demanding discretion.' Harry injected a note of warning into his voice.

'Of course. You would not want any scandal surrounding your future wife's family,' said Nicholson.

'For Mistress van Buren's sake,' Harry said. 'It has been painful for her to discover that one of her relatives is…lacking proper family feeling.'

'Hmm.' Nicholson glanced sideways at Harry. 'Have you heard any news of Lord Hawkminster?'

'No.' Harry tensed, wondering if he was about to receive some. 'Have you?'

'Not within the past week. I understand he is very weak.'

Harry relaxed again. 'Mistress van Buren's brother is my first concern. It is only five days to his twenty-first birthday. I want to reach Cornwall well before that.'

'You'll have to ride hard. I can let you have several good men, including Woodruffe—you remember him from Smyrna? I would come with you, but…' Nicholson rubbed his jaw in a rueful gesture. 'You know I am not the best horseman.'

'I would rather you remained here and offered roof and protection to Mistress van Buren until I come to collect her,' said Harry.

Nicholson straightened slightly in his chair. 'I would be honoured,' he said.

'Make sure she doesn't leave the house and that no unfamiliar servants or tradesmen are allowed in while she is here,' Harry warned. He didn't like allowing Saskia out of his sight, but Nicholson was one of the few men he trusted. The merchant might not be an agile horseman, but he was a loyal friend, and well able to protect his own. 'It is particularly important not to allow any strangers into the house, because we believe Tancock may have poisoned Saskia's godfather, Sir Francis Middleton.'

Nicholson pressed his lips together. 'Until you return this house will become a discreet fortress,' he promised. 'Dorothy will be eager to show off her illustrious guest, but she'll understand the necessity for caution.'

'Thank you.' Normally Harry would have left it entirely up to Nicholson to speak to his wife, but for Saskia's sake he resolved to pay close attention to Mistress Nicholson's character and, if necessary, reinforce the need for discretion.

The door opened and the two women entered with a swish of silken skirts. Harry and Nicholson stood up. As soon as Harry set eyes on Saskia, every coherent thought dissolved. He vaguely heard his host offering a fluent compliment, but the words barely registered. He'd seen Saskia in the high-necked black dress in which she'd left London, and the men's clothes she'd worn on the ride to Winchester, but he'd never before seen her in a gown designed to emphasise her feminine beauty.

Her apricot-blonde curls had been tamed with a silk ribbon and brushed until they shone in the candlelight. The bodice of her borrowed gown was cut low on the shoulders and the tight lacing pushed up her slight breasts in a fashionably provocative way. He'd imagined female clothing would be more modest than the shirt she'd worn, but though he couldn't see the outline of her nipples, the gown was designed to entice a man. At that moment he was too dazzled to care. She was the most beautiful, desirable woman he'd ever seen. And she'd agreed to marry him. Joyful pride filled him as he gazed at her. Accompanied by an urge to hold her, kiss her and touch her.

Awareness that Nicholson could also see the seductive upper curve of her breasts and the elegant sweep of her bare shoulders abruptly swept over him. Such intimate charms should be seen only by a woman's husband. He took a step forward, meaning to cover her with his coat until he'd removed her from Nicholson's presence. Then he jerked to a halt. This was England. It was normal for ladies to go into mixed company in such attire. He would make a fool of himself and embarrass Saskia if he hustled her away.

His fingers flexed as he struggled with his conflicting impulses. He saw uncertainty, shading into anxiety, appear in Saskia's eyes as she watched him, and became aware that both Nicholson and his wife had fallen silent. The compulsion to reassure Saskia overcame all else and he moved forward with a good simulation of his normal grace to take her hand.

'You look very well,' he said. 'I hope you are feeling more rested.'

'Oh, yes.' A relieved smile lit up her face and he decided she must have been afraid he was going to mortify them both with his unsophisticated behaviour. 'Mistress Nicholson has been very kind and welcoming.'

Harry looked at Dorothy, who was also wearing a fashionably low neckline. He still thought the style was shockingly immodest, but he wasn't overcome with any desire to either touch or cover her. How his wife dressed was Nicholson's affair, but Harry made a mental note to have a private conversation with Saskia at the earliest appropriate opportunity about the style of her clothes. He was supposed to tell her what he wanted, and he didn't want her to expose her shoulders to other men's eyes. Then he remembered he should be grateful to Nicholson's wife, not silently criticising her choice of gowns.

'Thank you,' he said to Dorothy. 'I appreciate your help and kindness to my betrothed.' Despite his underlying sincerity, he couldn't prevent a degree of stiffness creeping into his tone.

'Supper is served,' said Nicholson cheerfully. 'Let us adjourn to the dining parlour.' He offered his arm to his wife.

Harry followed suit, offering his arm to Saskia. She put her hand on his sleeve, but she hung back slightly as the Nicholsons left the parlour. Harry glanced down and was immediately distracted by the stimulating view of her breasts afforded by such close proximity. She frowned and squeezed his arm and he started guiltily. She'd obviously guessed the inappropriate direction of his thoughts.

She leant closer and stood on tiptoe. 'What's your real name?' she asked in an urgent undervoice.

'What?' Harry was thoroughly disorientated.

'Is it Harry Dixon or not?' she demanded. 'I can't keep calling you "my betrothed". I sound like a noodle.'

'Ward. Harry Ward. I was christened Henry,' he added, trying to be helpful.

'I like Harry better. Come on, or they'll wonder

where we are.' She tugged on his arm. 'You look very fine and handsome,' she added.

'So do you.'

'Hmm.' Her free hand fluttered briefly across the base of her throat. 'I have never worn a bodice cut so low before. It feels very odd. But it is the fashion in England, so I must get used to it.'

'Not on my account,' Harry said quickly.

She glanced up at him, amusement glinting in her eyes. 'We'll have to make an effort to be less provincial in future,' she murmured.

'I may be a lost cause,' Harry admitted ruefully, and felt a stir of pleased satisfaction as she laughed softly in response.

'How did you meet?' Nicholson asked, looking curiously from Harry to Saskia.

Saskia smiled and made a small gesture to indicate she was deferring to Harry. She hadn't a clue how they were supposed to have met, and she was just as interested in hearing the answer as their host and hostess.

'We were introduced by my brother,' said Harry calmly.

Saskia nodded. 'It was a very happy introduction for me,' she said, smiling first at Harry and then at the Nicholsons. 'I first met Mr Ward—' she meant Harry's brother '—because I have also taken advantage of the new trading opportunities in coffee.'

Nicholson looked interested and his wife looked confused.

'Richard is a silent investor in a coffee-house,' Harry explained. 'Mistress van Buren was staying in London with friends when I arrived from Smyrna. Fortunately for me, her friends are also Richard's friends.' He smiled slightly. 'Richard has always had a gift for friendship.'

'Indeed he has,' said Nicholson. 'And a hard head for business.'

Saskia was convinced Harry's explanation must have left Nicholson with a lot of unanswered questions, but he didn't pursue the matter any further. She should have asked more questions about Harry's family, but so much of her focus had been on Benjamin. Even now, though she knew it was foolish, part of her wanted to jump up and insist they continue on their journey after they'd eaten.

The conversation between Nicholson and Harry moved on to their shared experience in Smyrna, but Saskia noticed that Harry did not seem fully at ease, despite the attempts of Nicholson and his wife to treat him as an honoured guest. As she watched and occasionally threw in a comment of her own, Saskia realised Harry was at his most studiedly formal whenever he spoke to Dorothy. After so long in Turkey he must have little experience of what, to most Englishmen, would be an everyday event—a family meal at which both men and women were present.

She cast around for something to say that might help Harry feel more comfortable. But then Harry asked about the Nicholsons' children. Nicholson responded briefly, though with obvious pride, but Dorothy was far more loquacious. Saskia observed, first with surprise, then with satisfaction, as Harry finally relaxed and became far less consciously formal in his manner. Within minutes it was Nicholson who seemed ill at ease and Harry who was comfortably discussing childhood milestones with his hostess.

Harry might not have had much experience in English society over the past fifteen years, but Saskia decided her betrothed was a clever man. She was almost certain he'd remembered how the mill woman had happily discussed her baby with him, and applied that lesson to talking to Dorothy. Saskia was proud of his versatility and she didn't mind at all that now she and Nicholson were the ones excluded from the conversation. She was grateful for the opportunity to lower her guard and rest. In fact, what she wanted more than anything else was to go to bed. Every now and then she had to blink because the candlelight was blurring before her eyes.

When they stood up to leave the table she discovered that, unlike her, Nicholson had been thoroughly disconcerted by Harry's conversation with his wife.

'Madam, I would not have you think there is anything weak or womanish about your betrothed because he indulged my wife with talk of our children,' Nicholson said in a low voice as he escorted her back to the parlour.

Saskia bit back a retort that being a woman didn't mean being weak. 'I know that, sir,' she said, smiling.

'I could tell you tales of his exploits. He is a brave and hardy man. He saved my life once.'

'Then we have something in common,' said Saskia. 'For he has also saved mine. Did he tell you we were attacked by highwaymen on the way to Guildford?'

'Yes.' Nicholson's face clouded. 'I am sorry you have been in danger, and to learn of your brother's plight. Harry has vowed to help him. I will do whatever I may to help.'

'Thank you.' Saskia knew Nicholson was most likely motivated by his sense of debt to Harry, but she still valued his act of friendship.

'You are tired,' he said. 'My wife will take you back to your room and make sure you have everything you need for the night.'

* * *

'Your betrothed is so handsome—and so knowledgeable about children,' said Dorothy as she led Saskia upstairs.

'Yes, he is.'

'There cannot be many earls who are so well informed.'

'I don't suppose so,' Saskia agreed, somewhat baffled by the relevance of the comment.

'Have you received any further news of old Lord Hawkminster's health?' asked Dorothy.

'I don't believe so,' said Saskia cautiously. Who was old Lord Hawkminster?

'I'm sorry. Martin told me not to mention it. But I have never had an earl and his future countess staying in my house before. I cannot help but be excited. And he was so gracious to talk to me about my children! I hope you will not think it impertinent if I say I think you are a lucky woman.'

'No, not at all impertinent,' Saskia said faintly. *An earl and his future countess?*

'I am so looking forward to helping you order your new gowns,' Dorothy continued. 'Martin says your betrothed does not wish you to leave the house, so of course the tradesmen will come here—and only those who are well known to us. You will be quite safe here.'

'Thank you,' Saskia said automatically, still trying to make sense of Dorothy's apparent description of her as a future countess. She suddenly caught up with the rest of what she'd just heard. 'Harry has said I will be staying here when he leaves?' she exclaimed.

'You are most welcome. We are very honoured,' Dorothy assured her.

Saskia forgot about earls and countesses in a rush of disbelieving anger that Harry intended to abandon her in Winchester without even discussing his decision with her. She turned on her heel, meaning to go straight back downstairs and confront him. As she did so she inadvertently met Dorothy's curious gaze and abruptly changed her mind. She would never consent to remain behind, but she didn't want to have a public argument with Harry.

'Thank you for your hospitality,' she said, doing her best not to let her temper show. 'I confess I am very tired after our journey today.'

'Of course. I'll send the maid to you at once.' Dorothy took the hint.

Saskia waited impatiently for the girl to arrive. She couldn't remove the back-laced bodice of her borrowed gown by herself, and she wanted that inconvenience taken care of so she could be left alone to think and plan. She had to speak to Harry at the first opportunity. She knew he'd been given the chamber next to hers. When the maid had gone she sat by the door, listening for his footsteps in the hall outside. But she was so tired her head kept nodding forward. Weariness blunted her anger at his high-handedness, but not her determination to continue the journey with him. She was terrified she might fall asleep in the chair and miss his return—and she knew he was an early riser. What if he left in the morning before she was awake?

She jumped to her feet in alarm at the prospect and grabbed the wall as the room spun dizzyingly. She had to sleep or she wouldn't be fit to continue with him tomorrow. She made her decision in an instant. Short of going downstairs and demanding to speak to Harry alone—which would be very embarrassing given that her host and hostess clearly knew far more about him than she did—there was only one practical solution to her dilemma.

She opened her door, checked there was no one about and then picked up her candle and slipped out of her room and into his. Once she was safely inside, she lifted the candle and glanced around to make doubly certain it was the right chamber. It would be mortifying if she'd made a mistake. But she saw Harry's sword lying on the oak chest at the end of the bed and her fears were allayed. She frowned as she considered her options, but the last thing she needed was a crick in her neck from sleeping at an awkward angle in a chair while she waited. It was bad enough she'd spent so many nights on the ground.

She put the candlestick on the nightstand, turned back the covers and got into bed. The night was far too warm to need anything more than a sheet. She drew it over her and sighed with relief at finally being able to relax her weary body. It didn't matter if she fell asleep before Harry came to bed because he would wake her up and then she would demand explanations and tell him categorically she wasn't remaining in Winchester, confined to the safety of Nicholson's house with no idea what was happening to the people she cared most about!

Harry liked Nicholson, but it was a relief to say goodnight to his old friend. There was still a lot he needed to do before leaving Winchester, but all of it could wait until morning. He'd been so focused on the need to make sure he could introduce Saskia to the Nicholsons without any potential hint of scandal, he'd forgotten there were other things he needed to tell Saskia herself. He grinned as he recalled how she'd reminded him of one of them with her hissed demand to know his name before they'd gone into supper. He was pleased with himself for finding a woman sensible enough to pay attention to such small but important details.

She was asleep now, so their next discussion would have to wait till morning. On past experience she wasn't going to be in a good mood if he woke her up early—but since he didn't think she was going to like what he said whenever he said it, the timing probably didn't matter too much, he decided ruefully. He closed the door and shrugged out of his borrowed coat. In a continuation of the same movement he reached up to unfasten the lace cravat as he walked towards the bed—and then he stopped dead, staring in disbelief. For an instant he thought he must have entered the wrong room by accident. But his sword was on the chest where he'd left it. Everything in the room looked the same—except for the woman in his bed.

'Saskia?' he said softly, but she didn't stir. He gazed down at her, a torrent of unfamiliar feelings washing over him. He liked finding her asleep in his bed. Waiting for him.

As he looked at her, he imagined her rolling towards him in her sleep, her head coming to rest on his shoulder, her legs entangling with his. Last night they'd both been fully clothed. Tonight she was only wearing a shift. His body hardened demandingly. His breath lodged in his throat. For a few seconds he could not move—then somehow he managed to start thinking again. He didn't fool himself he was at his quick-witted best, but he knew what he wanted to do. And it only took him another heartbeat to decide what he would settle for. He finished undressing, put on his borrowed nightshirt and slid into bed beside her.

Hawkminster Castle—late summer 1643

The priesthole had been made just large enough to hide one man lying flat on his back or his stomach—as long as he was neither fat nor broad-shouldered. When it had first been built into the castle wall more than half a century earlier, every joint had been seamless, hiding the occupant from Queen Elizabeth's officials, men who couldn't be denied entrance by a raised drawbridge or burning oil. But the wood had shrunk over the intervening years, and now there was a narrow crack in the panelling just where Harry could put his eye to get a view of most of the room.

'What's happening?' Richard whispered from the darkness behind him. Richard's head was by Harry's feet. Harry had already accidentally kicked his brother once, and now he was trying not to move. Such inactivity didn't come easily to either boy, although Harry had always been the most energetic.

'Nothing's happening.' Not that Harry could see,

anyway. The muffled sounds they'd been hearing in other parts of the castle were far more worrying.

'I want Father to come back and let us out.'

'So do I.' Harry swallowed, sick with fears he wouldn't repeat aloud. He'd always looked after his younger brother, and now he was even more acutely aware of his duty to protect Richard.

Father had put them into the priesthole before dawn. He'd given them bread and water and told them to be quiet and wait for him. Then they'd been left alone in the dark with the spiders and only the narrow crack of light. No one had come into the room for hours, but they'd heard the brutal sounds of the siege reaching its climax. Now it was quieter. Harry dreaded what that meant.

'Close your eyes and go to sleep,' he said. 'I will wake you up if anything happens.' He was glad Richard wasn't afraid of spiders. He felt as much as heard his brother move around behind him, trying to find a more comfortable position. Even though Richard was close by, Harry had never felt more alone or terrified in his life. If Father did not come for them, it would be because he was captured or dead. The possibility of losing Father filled Harry with clawing grief. But undercutting that fear was another, just as sharp.

There was no way to open the priesthole from the

inside. Father had told him so when he'd put the boys inside. And Harry, being Harry, had checked that fact hours ago. Not because he doubted his father's word, but because if Father didn't come back to release them they were trapped. Harry couldn't let Richard die of thirst and starvation in the priesthole. He'd divided his time between worrying over Father and plotting how to escape. He had his pocket knife. Perhaps he could whittle the narrow crack larger?

If Father didn't come back, it was because he and Hawkminster Castle were in the control of the enemy—Uncle Stephen. Father's older brother was leading the Royalist troops besieging the castle! Harry didn't understand how that could be. He was an older brother and he would never attack Richard with cannons and sharpshooters. The mere thought of his uncle attacking his father filled him with blind unrelenting fury at his uncle. Big brothers protected—they didn't hurt.

Harry scrubbed the back of his hand across his cheek. He couldn't remember that now. It made it too difficult to think clearly. And he had to think clearly to keep himself and Richard safe. If Father was a prisoner, he would have to rescue Father. If Father was dead… A sob rose in his throat, but he managed to suppress it so Richard wouldn't ask him what was wrong. Richard knew Uncle Stephen was with the enemy, but he didn't know about the conversation under truce when Father had begged Uncle Stephen to let the women and children out, and Uncle Stephen had laughed in scorn.

Running footsteps sounded. A few seconds later the door burst open. Heart racing, Harry put his eye to the crack. Martha, the nurse who had cared for him and Richard since the death of their mother, crashed into the room. For an instant Harry thought she must have come for them. He opened his mouth to call out to her, but she didn't look towards the priesthole—and he heard the pounding of heavier feet behind her. Martha was heading for the door on the other side of the room. Her dress was torn, her face stark with terror. The heavy oak table and chairs were in her way. Trying to dodge around them cost her precious seconds and the man behind her grabbed her hair, jerking her backwards. From the man's appearance Harry identified him as a German mercenary fighting for the Royalists.

Martha screamed and flailed at her attacker, but there was only cruel intent in the mercenary's face. He smashed her back against the wall—the one at right angles to the wall behind which Harry was hidden. The two of them were just within Harry's line of sight. The man trapped Martha between his body and the unforgiving wooden panels as he wrenched up her petticoats.

'Stop fighting or I'll stick you and take my pleasure after,' he warned in a harsh, guttural voice.

Harry and Martha saw the blade at the same time. Martha gave a shuddering gasp of fear. Harry clenched his fists against the wooden panel trapping him inside the priesthole. His mind froze in dreadful indecision. If he shouted he might distract the man from Martha—but what if the mercenary stabbed her before he dealt with the interruption?

And Richard? Harry would be revealing Richard's hiding place to a cruel, murderous enemy. Tears half-blinded him and blood filled his mouth as he unknowingly bit his tongue in his distress. The mercenary dragged Martha to the flagstone floor and unfastened his breeches. She made terrible, heart-wrenching sounds as the man covered her and began to pound savagely into her. The floor was so hard and Martha was soft and gentle. Harry knew Martha was being hurt worse every time the mercenary hammered into her, grinding her between the floor and his body. Harry closed his eyes because he couldn't stand to see Martha hurt, but he couldn't shut out the awful sounds. He opened his eyes again because he had to know what was happening.

It was because he could only keep his gaze on the

couple on the floor for an instant at a time that he saw a stranger suddenly appear in the doorway. Harry didn't know the man. The newcomer was tall with a lean, angular face. His cold expression didn't change as he gave one comprehensive glance around the room and closed the door. From his arrogant, confident bearing he had to be an officer. And since the Royalists must now control Hawkminster Castle, he had to be a Royalist. Harry wanted to scream at him. Didn't the officer care what his soldier was doing to Martha?

The stranger drew his sword. In one fluid movement he thrust it into the mercenary with his right hand and heaved the body away from Martha with his left hand. The dead man sprawled sightlessly on the floor beside her.

Martha stared up at the swordsman, her eyes dulled with pain, confusion and fear.

'Be silent and cover yourself,' the swordsman said in a clipped, unemotional voice. 'You will come to no harm at my hands as long as you do not betray me.' He looked around the room again, this time focusing unerringly on the panel that hid the priesthole. For a shocking moment Harry stared straight into arctic-blue eyes. Surely the man couldn't see him or know he was there? But the stranger walked towards him, cleaning the blood from his sword as he did so—

Chapter Eight

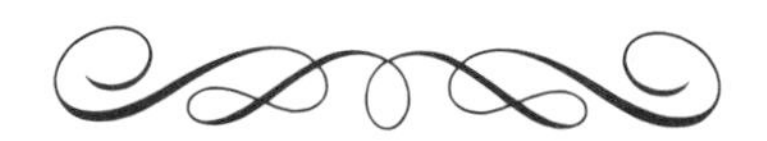

Harry jolted awake, his muscles rigid with ancient terror and rage, his forehead beaded with perspiration. It was years since he'd had that nightmare, but for a few moments the room at Hawkminster Castle still seemed more real than his present shadowy surroundings.

It took a few moments for him to notice there was a hand on his chest and someone speaking to him. His nightmare had primed him to respond violently to any unknown touch. His first instinct was to lock his hands around the intruder's throat—but though his muscles twitched, he didn't move. That soft, unexpectedly familiar voice triggered different, warmer emotions. Disorientated, he stared up at the bed canopy, and in a sudden burst of clarity knew it was Saskia lying beside him, touching him and speaking so soothingly. Hot shame seized him that she had seen him in the midst of his nightmare. He could hardly bring himself to look at her. He lay fighting for self-control, his hands unconsciously clenched into fists, but it was cowardly not to respond to her.

'Yes.' His voice was dry and cracked—he hardly recognised it as his own. He swallowed and tried again. 'Saskia?' He turned his head towards her, grateful that in the dim light she couldn't see him well.

She was propped up on her elbow, one hand resting on his shoulder.

'I think you were having a bad dream,' she said.

Unwilling to admit to such weakness, he made a wordless sound in his throat.

She moved closer, until he could feel her body all along his side, and began to stroke his chest. She probably thought she was comforting him, but his blood was still pounding from his nightmare. At the feel of her soft thigh against his leg, his hitherto ruthlessly controlled desire for her roared through his veins. Savage need seized his body. His erection was so hard it hurt. Every muscle in his body grew rigid with tension as he fought a battle with himself not to drag Saskia beneath him and find release for his ferocious arousal. The thought he could use her to slake his lust the way the mercenary had used Martha disgusted him. He didn't need to close his eyes to see Martha's body smashed between the flagstones and the mercenary's vicious thrusts, or hear again her sobs of fear and pain.

Harry gritted his teeth as he tried to blot out the memories and ignore Saskia's soft, feminine warmth.

'Don't you want me to touch you?' she said.

'Not…now.' He had to force the words out through his clenched jaw. He heard her breath catch and then she moved away from him. He pulled in a ragged breath and tried to unlock the tension gripping his body. They lay unspeaking in the darkness for long minutes as he sought some equilibrium. Eventually, as his own body became less racked with tension, he became aware of the tension emanating from Saskia. He felt a pang of regret. She'd been trying to soothe him and he'd rejected her without a word of thanks.

'Why not?' she said suddenly, her voice strained and almost belligerent.

'What?'

'I promised myself I would never let this happen again.'

'It hasn't happened before.' Harry was confused. This was the first time he'd had a nightmare in her presence.

'Lying beside a man who doesn't want me.' Her voice cracked. He could feel her trembling even though there were several inches between them. 'Touching him. Feeling him turn into a lump of cold rejection. Knowing he didn't want me, but not knowing why or what I can do to change things.' Her words got faster and faster until they disintegrated into a sob and she turned her face into the pillow.

Harry rolled on to his side to stare at her, the last remnants of his nightmare forgotten. He was stunned by the insight she'd just given him into her marriage. A few moments ago he'd assumed it was only his own lack of gratitude that had upset her. But there would be time to reflect on all the implications of what she'd revealed later. Now his overriding concern was to ease her distress.

'Saskia…I want you to touch me,' he said, putting his hand on her shoulder, then managing to get his other arm underneath her so he could pull her back to lie beside him. She resisted briefly, before ending up with her head on his shoulder and her palm once more on his chest.

'You didn't a few minutes ago,' she muttered.

'It wasn't…safe,' he said, trying to offer an explanation she'd accept, but which wouldn't frighten or disgust her.

'Safe?' She lifted her head to look at him, even though it was took dark to see his expression. 'What do you mean—not safe?'

'I'd just had a nightmare,' he reminded her. 'I am…I am accustomed to fight when I…ah…feel threatened.'

'Oh. Is that…was there a fight in your dream?'

'Yes.' He didn't want to tell her any more about it than that. He didn't even want to think about it. His old hurts and anger had no place in this conversation.

'Oh.' She settled down beside him again, tracing patterns on his chest through his nightshirt. By now the single sheet that had been covering them was tangled at the foot of the bed. If she let her hand drift lower, she would discover how powerfully his body responded to her touch. But Harry had regained his self-control. If she needed to snuggle in his arms he was glad to oblige her, even though there was a price to pay in discomfort.

'You'd been fighting after the highwaymen attacked us,' she said.

'Yes?' He didn't understand the connection.

'You didn't want to hold me then, either.'

'Ah…' He remembered the lust for her that had nearly overwhelmed him in the immediate aftermath of that incident. He couldn't explain that to her.

'You are a fighting man,' Saskia continued. 'I had not considered it before, but I suppose it is natural it should take a little time to adjust from being ready to fight to gentler feelings.'

'There is a feeling of extreme restlessness and irritation after combat,' Harry said, picking his words carefully.

'So it wasn't anything to do with me that you didn't want to hold me then or after your nightmare?' she said.

'No.' In truth he'd wanted to hold her too much, but he was ashamed of the violence of his desire and preferred not to admit it, even to himself.

'And you…like me touching you the rest of the time,' she said.

'Yes.'

'Good.' She sighed with what sounded like a mixture of relief and pleasure. Her thigh edged a little further over his and she continued to fondle his chest. Then she slid her hand up so that she could tug on the neck strings of his nightshirt and touch his naked skin. Even the slowest of men couldn't fail to notice the lady's hints, and Harry wasn't slow. He was also confident he was now in full control of himself.

Saskia's heart sang with happiness and relief. It was only because Harry had still been in the grip of fighting fever that he hadn't wanted to touch her. Perhaps he'd been afraid he might mistake her for the enemy and hurt her. Harry might be worried, but Saskia wasn't. To her mind, the very fact he'd been conscious of the risk meant there was no risk. A less considerate, less self-disciplined man would lash out without thinking and regret his actions later.

Now he'd recovered from his nightmare he seemed quite willing to be close to her. He was stroking her back with the lightest pressure of his fingertips, sending quivers of pleasure up and down her spine. Under her palm she could feel the firm contours of his muscles and his springy chest hairs through the fine linen nightshirt.

He cleared his throat. 'So…would you say that you enjoy touching me? My chest, for instance?'

'Yes.' She blushed and smiled in the darkness.

'And would you, perhaps, like the opportunity to touch me without a nightshirt in the way?'

She blushed even more furiously at that question, but she mustered all her courage and whispered, 'Yes.'

He moved her gently away from him, sat up, pulled the nightshirt over his head and tossed it aside. Then he put his arm around her and drew her down with him, so that she was lying half on top of him, though her hips and legs still rested on the mattress. He cupped her head in his hands as he kissed her, thoroughly claiming her with his lips and tongue until her body was liquid with tingling desire. When the kiss finally ended he murmured against her lips, 'You are so beautiful.'

She flushed with pleasure. 'You can't see me.'

'I've a good memory. You look beautiful—and you feel beautiful.' He skimmed his hand down the side of her body. 'You like me touching you?'

She nodded.

'Mmm?' His hum was a question and he moved his hand away.

She was suddenly afraid he might stop altogether if she didn't reply out loud, so once again she whispered, 'Yes.'

He put his hand back on her hip immediately, exploring her curves through the fabric of her shift before gently pulling it up so he could caress her naked skin. His hand lingered on her thigh, and then moved higher, over her hip to her waist. He let it rest there as he kissed her lips again. After a while he drew back and stroked delicately upwards until his fingers brushed against the underside of her breast. He paused and Saskia unconsciously held her breath as she waited for him to continue. He gently cupped her breast in his hand, holding it as if it were a rare and precious thing. As he stroked his thumb over her erect, sensitised nipple, a long sigh of pleasure escaped her lips.

He took his time discovering the shape and weight of each breast. Soon Saskia's whole body was glowing with arousal and wonderful anticipation. Never before had she felt so excited at the prospect of making love. She could barely stand to wait until he settled himself between her thighs.

She could tell from his own quickened breathing that he was fully engaged in their lovemaking. It thrilled her that she could rouse him to such passion. When he kissed her, his tongue thrust boldly past her lips in an unmistakable foretaste of how he would soon claim her body. They were both panting when he let his head fall back on the pillow. He gave her a little nudge so that he could put both hands on her waist beneath her shift. A second later he lifted her up and over to straddle him.

She gasped at her sudden change of position. She could feel his hard, ridged stomach against the backs of her thighs. Her legs were spread wide, her knees resting on the mattress on either side of his broad chest. Even though she was still wearing her shift she felt exposed and vulnerable—and very excited.

'If you do not wish for this—for anything—you must say "no",' he said, an unmistakable note of command in his husky voice.

She gasped and nodded, too dazed with anticipation to think or speak clearly. His hands tightened on her waist just enough to demand a response. 'Promise me.'

'Yes. Don't stop!' The plea emerged unbidden from her lips. If she hadn't been so overwhelmed by her feelings she would have been embarrassed by his low, rough laugh at her words.

He stroked his big hands down over her thighs and then back upwards, his thumbs brushing tantalisingly over the curls between her legs before sliding up over her stomach. She arched her back, unconsciously pushing her torso further forward as he devoted all his attention to her breasts.

'That's good?' he said, his voice so thick she hardly understood him.

'Mmm-hmm.'

'No more shift,' he decided. She helped as he pushed it over her head and threw it aside. He urged her to lean forward, lifting his head to take her breast into his mouth. The sensation of his tongue rasping against her hardened nipple sent a spasm of pleasure to the core of her body.

As she bent over him, her hips lifted. She wanted to kiss him again, and feel the firm planes of his chest against her breasts, so she began to edge down his body, her knees still on either side of him. Suddenly she felt the hot, hard tip of his erection against her most intimate flesh. She went quite still, her breath catching in her throat. Harry jerked beneath her, and then held himself absolutely motionless. She could feel the tension in his muscles, but it was not the immobility of rejection. Not when her slightest movement would bring his arousal into thrilling contact with her wet, throbbing centre. She rocked back, instinctively surrendering to her craving for another delicious caress. They both moaned. Harry's hands tightened on her upper arms.

'You want that?' he murmured against her cheek.

She nodded, too aroused to even pretend modesty, and then completely lost the ability to speak as he claimed her mouth in a passionately erotic kiss. 'Take it, then,' he said against her swollen lips when they were both gasping for breath.

For a few racing heartbeats she was too befuddled by glorious sensation to move. In all her previous, limited experience Pieter had been on top, directing every stage of the intimate embrace. It had never occurred to her to wonder whether Harry would do the same, so it took her a moment to adjust to the unfamiliar situation. But she wasn't going to reveal her naïvety or spoil the moment by telling Harry to get on top, so she continued to ease carefully back down his body until she could sit on his thighs. Now his jutting erection was completely exposed to her questing hands.

She felt him jerk as her fingers closed around him. His hips thrust upwards a few inches. She instinctively tightened her grip. He groaned and sank back into the mattress. His whole body was sheened with perspiration and trembling with his efforts to remain still for her. She half-wished she could see him—her virile, powerful lover who was so generously offering himself to her. But if she could see him, he would also be able to see her, and she was afraid she would be too shy to continue under those circumstances—and then she would lose all her newfound excitement in pleasuring her man. She explored his passion-primed body until he was shuddering with his efforts at self-control and she was flushed and urgent with desire.

'Now!' he ordered hoarsely. 'For God's sake, now!'

She lifted herself over his hips, positioning his blunt tip carefully at her feminine entrance. His hands clamped on her hips. As she began to sink down on to him he thrust upwards, his thick length surging into her, stretching and filling her with the most intimate caress of all. She cried out with a mixture of shock and delight at feeling him so suddenly deep within her.

His whole body locked rigid, the muscles in his arms became ropes of steel beneath her palms. 'Did I hurt you?' She barely recognised his voice.

'No. Oh, no.' She began to move against him, bracing herself against his supporting arms as she instinctively sought the most exquisite slide of his body against hers. He started to move with her, adjusting to her rhythm as the pressure within her built into a glorious crescendo. She hovered on the edge for long, anticipatory moments and then her body clenched in the ecstasy of release. Harry was still holding her hips. He began to thrust upwards more powerfully and with less control, and then she heard his rough groan and felt his own shuddering release deep inside her. She fell forward on to his chest, for several long moments hearing nothing but their quickened breathing and her own speeding heart. He was still inside her, though she could feel him beginning to soften. He put his arm around her shoulder, but it was an undemanding gesture. He was utterly relaxed beneath her. It wasn't the most comfortable position for her to rest in, but as long as Harry seemed content with it she didn't plan to move. He'd given her more pleasure than she'd ever dreamed of experiencing. Not only because he'd sated her yearning body beyond all her expectations, but because of his concern for her during their lovemaking.

Harry held Saskia in his arms as she relaxed on top of him. He had never before experienced such a glorious sense of fulfilled lassitude—yet at the same time part of him wanted to leap from the bed and shout out his joyful triumph. He stayed completely still because he was determined not to disturb Saskia, and because he wanted to prolong the great delight of remaining within her body. She was draped over him in a state of utterly boneless relaxation. He was awed and humbled that his lovemaking had brought her such deep physical contentment.

He'd always known it was a common human characteristic to find comfort in an affectionate touch or kind words, although many men might hide behind gruff words or a hearty slap on the back. It was those who'd been abused, like Martha, who shied from the gentlest contact. But he'd assumed a happy wife might accept the attentions of her husband as a sign of his affection for her. And that the thought of pleasing him, as well as her wish for children, would be her main source of pleasure in the marriage bed.

Saskia's anguished outburst when she'd described her husband's cold rejection of her had confirmed the first part of his assumption. His heart ached for her, even as he tried to imagine what it must have been like for Pieter, knowing he could no longer fulfil one of the primary duties of a husband. But Saskia hadn't only been denied children; she'd been denied the comfort of simple affectionate contact.

And after the way she'd responded to his lovemaking, he was questioning the second part of his assumption. She had taken pleasure in pleasing him—but he was sure she had claimed at least as much pleasure for herself. Until tonight he had never suspected a woman—a real woman, not a fantasy conjured in his daydreams—-would positively enjoy taking a man into her body. Now he had experienced the wondrous, life-changing revelation that, in some circumstances, she enjoyed it very much! Or at least, Saskia did, and she was the only woman he was interested in bedding, pleasing and learning about. He brushed his hand lightly over her tangled hair, profoundly grateful for the good fortune that had brought her into his life, and still somewhat amazed he was lying intimately entwined with her in the velvet darkness.

With her help he had finally achieved a rite of passage most men accomplished a decade or more earlier. Had she guessed she was his first? He hoped not. He knew how to use his body to maximum effect in every other physical activity he'd tried. Now he had pleased her once, he was confident he could please her again.

'Are you awake?' he murmured.

'Yes.' She didn't move.

'Are you comfortable?' He would have been content for her to lie on him all night, but he was concerned she might get cramp or pins and needles if she remained doubled up for too long.

'Am I too heavy?' She lifted her head.

'No.' He continued to hold her in a relaxed embrace.

'I am quite happy here, if you are,' she said.

He smiled. 'You can still put your head on my shoulder without being folded up like a frog.'

He heard her catch her breath and grimaced in the darkness as she levered herself up. He hadn't expressed that very well. 'A very pretty frog,' he said quickly. 'I just meant you would be more comfortable if you could straighten your legs.' But he could tell from the slight tension in her body his hasty explanation hadn't been entirely successful. He concluded it might take him longer to get the words right than it would the actions of lovemaking. He supported Saskia as she disentangled herself, and then reached down to pull the sheet over them. It was still a warm night, but the air was a little cooler, and he didn't want her to be chilled by a draught.

'Was this why you waited in my bed?' he asked, when they were settled again.

She stiffened. 'How brazen do you think I am?' she demanded.

'I'm sorry,' he apologised quickly. That hadn't been the right thing to say either. 'Of course I don't think you are brazen.'

'It was immodest and very forward,' she said frigidly. If his arm hadn't been wrapped around her shoulders she would have pulled away. Since he knew she only wanted to because of his clumsily worded question he had no compunction in keeping her close. 'I'm sure you disapprove,' she continued. 'Though in that case, you should not—'

He tipped her head up with a hand under her chin and kissed her. 'I have not said I disapproved, or that I disliked finding you here,' he said, once he'd coaxed her to relax against him. 'You could surely tell I enjoyed it very much.'

'It is perfectly possible for a man to take advantage of a woman, and then condemn her for surrendering to him,' Saskia said, obviously not entirely mollified.

'Has that ever happened to you?' Harry was ready to take offence on her behalf, even as a spike of jealousy twisted in his gut at the thought of her lying in another man's arms.

'No. But I have eyes and ears. I have seen what happens to foolish women who don't protect their honour.'

'Your honour is unsullied,' said Harry. 'You were already my betrothed when you came into my bed. For me that promise is as binding as the marriage vow.'

'I wanted to speak to you,' she said. 'I was afraid I'd fall asleep if I tried to listen for you in my own room. I thought you'd wake me up when you arrived.'

'You needed your sleep,' said Harry. 'You still do.'

'You are *not* leaving me behind!' Saskia said categorically, propping herself up on her elbow. 'Benjamin is my brother and I'm going with you.'

'Hmm,' said Harry.

'If you do not take me with you, I will simply follow after you,' she declared. 'You know I can.'

'I could always tell Nicholson to lock you in,' said Harry mildly.

'You would not!' she gasped. 'I would have the magistrate on you. You have no right—'

He put his hand over her mouth as her voice rose. 'Shush. No, I wouldn't. I will try reason instead.'

'Huh!'

'You will be safe here,' said Harry. 'Tancock won't look for you in Nicholson's home. To be absolutely safe, don't go outside or allow his wife to present you to her friends until I return to tell you Benjamin is well and the threat has been resolved.'

'No,' said Saskia. 'I feel safe with you—not Nicholson or his wife. And you have seen for yourself I am strong and resilient. I am going with you—and that is final.'

'Are you going to make all the decisions in our marriage as well?' Harry asked drily.

Her hand trembled against his chest. 'Are you angry?' she asked.

'No.' His main concern was to keep her safe.

And he wanted to spare her the rigours of any more hard riding.

'Aren't you going to say you travel faster alone?'

'I could,' he said slowly. 'In most cases it would be true—but maybe there is another way.'

'What?' she asked eagerly.

'Shush. I am thinking.'

'As long as you are thinking you won't leave me behind.'

He grinned. 'Persistent woman. Whatever I decide, I won't leave without speaking to you again. Go back to your own room now so you can sleep undisturbed until the maid comes in the morning.' If he was any judge, it wouldn't be long before the early dawn of high summer lightened the sky.

'I need my shift,' she said, sitting up. He thought she seemed reluctant to go back to her own room and hoped it was because she preferred to be beside him rather than because she didn't trust him not to leave without her. 'I don't know where it went. I cannot go naked into the hall.'

'Indeed not!' he exclaimed, and slipped out of bed to search for it. He'd not been paying attention to where they'd thrown their night garments at the height of their passion.

'Are you really an earl?' she asked suddenly, as he felt in the shadows beside the bed.

'Who told you that?' He looked up.

'Mistress Nicholson. Is it true?'

'Possibly,' he said shortly. 'It depends on whether my uncle is still alive.'

'So, if I marry you, I really will be a countess one day?' she said.

'Do you mind?' His hand closed on crumpled linen and he held it up, trying to decide if it was his borrowed night shift or hers. Then he realised she'd said 'if' she married him. Was she having doubts?

'Mind feeling like a fool because I know less about my betrothed than a woman who'd never met him before?' she said.

She'd just claimed him as her betrothed. The 'if' must have been a figure of speech of no significance—he hoped. 'I can see that must have been awkward,' he said. 'Is there anything else you feel you need to know about me before breakfast?'

'Not at this moment,' she said with dignity.

'This is yours.' Harry gave her the shift. 'And you *are* the future Lady Hawkminster. You will confer distinction on the title.' He pulled on his own night shift and then went to listen at the door to make sure it was safe to take Saskia back to her room. He might be out of touch with English customs, but he was sure a gentleman always escorted a lady to her door.

Tuesday, 18 June 1667

The next morning Saskia was back in the coach—this time on the way to Dorset. Harry was riding alongside with three men who usually worked for Nicholson. From what she'd overheard, it was clear Harry had known at least one of them, Woodruffe, in Smyrna, and Nicholson had vouched for the steady loyalty of the others. Saskia had offered to ride, but she'd submitted gracefully when Harry had insisted she travel in the coach. He'd said it was easier to protect her like that. Woodruffe was riding ahead to ensure changes of horses would be waiting for them, so they should make much better time than when they'd first left London.

But now Saskia had nothing to do but sit in the coach and think. The night she'd just spent with Harry was a vivid, wonderful memory. She was aware of aching muscles caused by the hard travelling they'd done yesterday, but that discomfort faded into insignificance compared to the afterglow of deep satisfaction lingering from Harry's lovemaking. For most of her marriage she had taught herself not to regret the loss of physical intimacy—but she'd never guessed it was possible to attain such a high peak of pleasure. Now she knew what it was like to share Harry's bed, she wanted to experience that ecstasy again.

And she wanted children. Harry could give her children, and she'd seen for herself when he'd picked up the miller's baby that he would be a good father. Now she knew Harry was going to inherit an earldom, she accepted there was no possibility he could move to Amsterdam, so she'd have to return to England. She'd lose the independence she'd gained as a widow, but she would gain a generous, compassionate husband and, with God's good grace, she'd have a family of her own.

She'd also be a countess. Saskia was the daughter of a baronet, but her aunt had married an earl. She had a good understanding of the privileges and hazards of marrying such a high-ranking nobleman, and she'd acquired self-assurance from her years in Amsterdam. She was neither daunted nor unduly impressed by the title Harry would inherit.

He was wearing a plain coat today, very like the clothes of their escorts. It fitted him better than Nicholson's coat, and she suspected he'd borrowed it from Woodruffe. Despite his ordinary clothes, he was easily distinguishable from other men by his air of command and the aura of latent power that always surrounded him. No, it wasn't Harry's future title that impressed her—it was Harry himself. He was the most charismatic, potently attractive man she'd ever met.

* * *

Harry rode beside the coach. He wasn't sure if he was making a mistake in allowing Saskia to continue with him, but after the previous night he wanted her close by. He'd meant to ride full pace the rest of the way to Cornwall, but he wasn't willing to push Saskia so hard. He'd made hasty alterations to his plans, and they were taking a diversion south through Dorset. Saskia had initially protested that it would make the journey take longer, but after Harry had explained his intentions she'd cast him a curious glance and fallen silent.

He couldn't stop thinking about the overwhelming delight of making love with Saskia. He'd relived every second in his mind until his body burned with the compulsion to make love to her again. Next time he wanted to be able to see her so that all his senses could contribute to his pleasure. He'd touched her naked breasts, her waist and legs, and felt the exquisite joy of being taken into her hot, welcoming body, but he'd had to imagine how she'd looked poised above him. He wondered if she would be embarrassed to make love to him in the light.

He felt light-hearted, excited, full of a frivolous joy and a sense of personal triumph that was surely inappropriate for a man of thirty-four. Not for anything would he have confessed his mood to the men escorting them. For the sake of his pride and Saskia's modesty he had put considerable effort into appearing his usual self with Nicholson and the other men. But it was hard to stop his gaze from straying to Saskia at every opportunity, and when he took her hand to help her into the coach her self-conscious blush thrilled him.

When they stopped for dinner he waited impatiently for Saskia to finish eating so he could suggest they take a short walk to stretch her legs before she climbed back into the coach. As soon as they were hidden from observers behind some trees, he pulled her into his arms.

She put her arms around his neck, her eyes sparkling up at him. 'Was this walk just a ruse so you can kiss me?' she asked.

'Yes.' He didn't waste any more time on words.

Saskia responded gladly to Harry's kisses. There was a lightness in him, a boyish happiness she had never seen before, that stirred a similarly joyous response in her. It was thrilling to be with a man who couldn't wait to get her alone so that he could kiss her. She also gained the sense that some unseen burden had been lifted from his shoulders. Was it the prospect of their marriage that had rendered such an overnight change in him? Or was it what had happened between them in his bed?

'Did Nicholson give you some good news this morning?' she asked a little while later, trying by indirect means to satisfy her curiosity.

'Only gossip about local merchants,' Harry said, looking momentarily confused. 'Ah no, I am sorry. I have not yet heard anything as to what has happened about the war between the Dutch and England.'

'Oh.' She'd all but forgotten the war, though only a few days ago it had caused her considerable inconvenience. 'I am glad to see you in such a good mood,' she said.

A slash of colour darkened his cheekbones. 'You may take the credit,' he said gruffly.

'Me?' It *was* the prospect of their marriage that had made him happy! And that made her feel happy and excited. She wanted to ask more, but he kissed her again before she could.

'We must go back to the coach now,' he announced, when he lifted his head. 'There is still a long way to go.'

Saskia let him lead her back to the others, though she was sure his haste was partly prompted by a desire to avoid her questions. It didn't matter. There was bound to be an opportunity for private conversation later.

* * *

As they neared their destination, Harry's good mood gradually evaporated. When they rode through Hawkminster village it disappeared completely. Most of the villagers were Hawkminster tenants, and it required only a cursory glance around to see that the cottages were in a poor state of repair. It was silent testimony that the current earl was not a good landlord. A few people came out to watch with impassive expressions as the coach and horsemen went by. Harry had left Hawkminster when he was ten years old and he doubted if any of them recognised him. Even if they did, they knew nothing of the man he had become, and had no reason to offer him a warm welcome.

Above the trees, the towers of Hawkminster Castle became visible. The south tower was a jagged shape against the sky, its top shattered by the pounding of canonballs twenty-four years ago. Hawkminster was not a true castle, but a fortified manor house with a moat, built several centuries ago by one of Harry's ancestors to protect against raids from lawless bandits and sea pirates. It had never been intended to withstand a prolonged siege by modern weapons. Harry's father had known from the first that if help didn't arrive quickly the outcome of the siege would be bloody, but he had vowed to hold the Castle for Parliament, and surrender had been unthinkable.

Harry's gut clenched. The serene, liquid song of a robin issuing from the leaf-laden branches of an oak seemed incongruous when in his mind he could hear the horrific sounds of warfare. He tried to shake off his memories. Common sense told him that violence had touched Hawkminster Castle only briefly during the centuries of its existence—and only a few days out of the thirty-four years of his life. But those few days had changed his world—and him—for ever.

The rutted road curved and he had his first full sight of the castle. Ivy grew on the side of the gatehouse. The moat was so overgrown with pondweed it was almost impossible to see the surface of the water, but a couple of ducks swam in the dark shadows close to the wall. There were people standing on the drawbridge, including Nicholson's man, Woodruffe, whom Harry had sent ahead.

Harry rode towards his childhood home, his back rigid, his heart thudding, not knowing if he was now Lord Hawkminster, or if the man he'd last seen twenty-three years ago was still alive. As he drew closer, the group on the bridge moved forward to stand on the path outside the moat. He could see none among them who looked like his uncle—but he hadn't expected to. He did see one face he recognised—his grandfather's steward, who had continued to serve the next Lord Hawkminster on his grandfather's death. Pryor, that was his name. After Harry and Richard had gone to live with their grandfather, Pryor had played chess with them and sometimes gone riding with them, but Harry hadn't seen the steward since his grandfather's funeral.

Harry reined to a halt a few feet away from the welcoming party. Immediately a lad ran forward to hold his horse. Harry swung his leg forward over the pommel and dropped lightly to the ground on the same side of his horse as the men watching him. An automatic action that meant they were never out of his sight. He heard the coach jolt to a halt on the uneven ground as he stepped forward.

'Master Harry?' said the steward hesitantly.

'Good evening, Pryor,' Harry replied, his voice sounding rusty in his ears.

'Master Harry!' Pryor rushed forward, seizing Harry's hand. 'Welcome home, sir. Welcome home!' Harry was astonished and moved to see tears in the older man's eyes. He had not expected anyone to remember him.

'How are you, Pryor?' he asked.

'Very well, sir. Very well. Only a touch of rheumatism, now and then.'

'My uncle is within?' said Harry. From the manner in which Pryor had addressed him, he was fairly sure his uncle was still alive.

'Yes, sir. He is very weak. He has not left his bed for weeks.'

'Is he conscious?'

'Yes, sir. He is expecting to see you.'

Harry nodded, knowing the confrontation he had avoided for more than two-thirds of his life was finally upon him. He was aware of the curious stares of the rest of the senior members of the household standing just behind Pryor. They were all strangers to him. He turned to the coach. Woodruffe had already assisted Saskia out, and Harry went to take her hand and place it on his arm. He escorted her over to the others.

'My betrothed, Mistress van Buren,' he said. 'This is Pryor, steward here?' He raised one eyebrow in silent question as to whether Pryor still held that role, and the other man nodded. 'Pryor, kindly introduce your companions to us.'

Chapter Nine

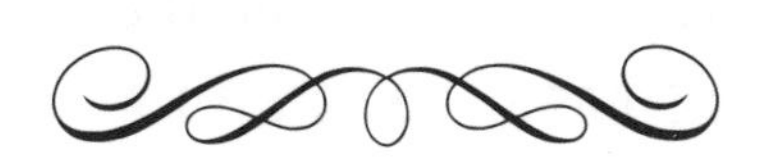

The chamber was over-hot and stank of decay. For a while the only sound that disturbed the oppressive silence was the buzzing of a couple of flies. The shutters were closed against the daylight. An elderly valet stood to one side in the shadows, his shoulders stooped as if he were worn out with his labours.

Harry stared down at the shrunken form of the dying man lying in the centre of the massive bed. It wasn't age that had brought Stephen Ward to his current state, but more than a decade of dissolute living. Harry had known his uncle's health was failing, but it was a shock to see his ravaged condition. In Harry's mind, Stephen was still the cruel, arrogant cavalier who'd mocked a boy's furious, heartbroken challenge.

'I'm not dead yet,' said Stephen. 'But what you and your father failed to accomplish, time will soon achieve.' His voice was thin and there were long pauses between his words, but the sneering tone Harry remembered was still evident.

Harry's hands balled into fists. He would listen in case Stephen said anything he needed to hear, but he had nothing he wanted to say to his uncle.

'You came closer to success than your father ever did, I'll grant you that.' Stephen's eyelids flickered like a weary snake's.

'Father never wanted to do you any harm,' Harry said tautly. 'He never *did* you any harm.' It was Stephen who had brought bloodshed and betrayal to Hawkminster Castle with his troop of mercenary soldiers.

'He betrayed his King.'

Harry shook his head. He had no interest in debating the politics of two and a half decades ago. As a child, knowing that both his grandfather and father supported Parliament, Harry had considered Stephen to be the one who'd betrayed his family. As a man he still did. Many counties had barely been touched by the devastation of the Civil War. And even at the height of the conflict it had been possible for some men to treat each other as honourable enemies. Stephen had never treated his younger brother as an honourable enemy.

Stephen stared at Harry through sunken eyes.

'You've grown,' he said, 'but you're a poor excuse for a man. Didn't have the guts to face me until I'm on my death bed. You sold your honour and your soul to the counting house.'

For the first time Harry was grateful he hadn't missed the opportunity for this final confrontation with Stephen. He would never have to lie awake at night in the future, wondering if his youthful judgement of his uncle had been wrong—or whether a meeting would have healed some of the old wounds.

'Have you anything to say apart from insults?' he asked.

'I've ruined you.' Stephen's eyes were opaque with encroaching death, but the venom in his voice was unmistakable.

'You have not that power,' Harry said coldly, but hidden behind his confident exterior his heart quickened with apprehension as well as anger. There was nothing Stephen could do to harm Harry himself, but what if he'd vented his malice on Richard? According to Richard, Stephen had ignored his existence, disdaining to acknowledge his merchant nephew—but that might have changed when Stephen realised he was dying.

'You'll find out.' Stephen was becoming breathless with the exertion of speaking. 'There's nothing but debts! By the time you've paid them there won't be a penny of your ill-begotten tradesman's fortune left! You'll be a broken man.'

Harry kept his face impassive, while a mixture of relief and disgust churned inside him. Stephen's spite had been directed at him, not Richard, but he wasn't his uncle's only victim.

'Have you bankrupted the estates?'

Stephen's mouth curved in a small, unpleasant smile of triumph. 'There's not even enough to pay the household wages.' For a moment satisfaction glowed in his eyes before they once more dulled.

Harry bit back a furious retort. He had lost control of his temper and his actions in Stephen's presence when he was eleven years old. He had no intention of doing so again. 'So, in your efforts to hurt me, you have ignored your responsibilities to those who depended on you,' he said contemptuously.

'Peasants,' Stephen hissed.

'Your dependants,' Harry said icily. 'But you showed your true colours when you incited mercenaries to kill Hawkminster men and rape the womenfolk to satisfy your petty jealousy.'

'The King. I supported the King,' Stephen panted.

'You betrayed your honour and your family.'

'It was *your* father who betrayed his honour. My mother must have played my father false. *Your* father was a bastard in all but name. *He* brought shame to our family. Soft. Cowardly. You've no Ward blood in your veins at all.'

Harry took a quick step forward before he managed to regain his composure. It wasn't the first time he'd heard Stephen make the false accusation that his father had not been his grandfather's true son, but it still had the power to enrage him. 'We have nothing further to discuss,' he said flatly, turning away. 'You will not see me again in this life.'

'Too scared to answer a nobleman's challenge?' Stephen taunted. By an effort of spiteful will he managed to raise his head from the pillow. 'No less than I'd expect of a baseborn brat turned common pedlar.'

Harry spun round, half-drawing his sword before he regained his self-control. His hand clenched convulsively, his muscles twitching as he fought for balance. He was disgusted with himself for responding to the malicious triumph glittering in Stephen's eyes. He slammed the sword back into its scabbard, turned on his heel and strode out of the room.

His temper was too volatile to tolerate company. He needed to be alone to master the storm seething within him. He went up to the roof of the gatehouse. The crenellated walls here were relatively undamaged. He could stride the width of the gatehouse unobstructed. Twenty-four years ago his father's men had squatted behind these battlements to defend the house from his uncle's troops. Today nothing disturbed the peaceful summer evening except the distant lowing of a cow. But there was no peace inside Harry.

He had known he would not be inheriting prosperous, well-managed estates, but he had not suspected that Stephen would deliberately run them into the ground. His hand clenched on the pommel of his sword as he considered what lay ahead. Depending on the extent of Stephen's debts and whether the estates had been mortgaged, it might well take most of Harry's existing fortune to set things right. He might even be compelled to go into debt himself to cover unavoidable expenses such as taxes. He ground out a low-voiced curse as he remembered Stephen's vicious promise that he'd be a broken man. He was not afraid of the future. He had made one fortune. He could make another and return the Hawkminster estates to prosperity. What filled him with deep, abiding fury and disgust was the callous wastefulness of Stephen's actions.

He looked out across the Dorset hills, bathed in the last of the evening light. Beyond them lay the sea and the next stage of his journey to Cornwall. That was his first concern now, not confronting his disastrous inheritance. In the morning they'd be gone from this place, and he had no intention of returning until he received news Stephen was dead. But before he left there was one more set of ghosts he had to confront and vanquish.

His muscles locked with renewed, irrational reluctance, he went back down the stone staircase and through the house to the west parlour. The shutters were closed, the chamber sunk in darkness, but by now dusk was falling outside. He lit a couple of candles and held one aloft to look around the room. Some of the furniture had changed, and all of it was covered with dust and cobwebs, but otherwise the chamber looked much the same as it had the last time he'd seen it. He almost expected to see the blood of the dead mercenary on the flagstones—but that stain had been removed long ago. He looked at the panelling, and then slowly walked over to stand immediately before the priesthole. He'd only seen it opened once, but the memory had burned into him because he'd spent so much of his time trapped within trying to devise ways of opening it from the inside.

He lifted his hand to the dark wood, his fingers searching until he heard the soft click. He pulled the panel open and stared inside. In his memory the hole had been small, but adequately spacious for two young boys. He gazed at the cramped space as a full-grown man and a rising tide of claustrophobia threatened to suffocate him. The hole wasn't even broad enough to accommodate his shoulders if he lay flat. He remembered again his terror that the house would burn while he and Richard were trapped inside the wall. He put the candle down inside and seized the lower edge of the hole with both hands as a door in his mind he'd fought to keep shut for so long slammed wide open.

Even before she'd alighted from the coach, Saskia had become increasingly uneasy about their destination for the night. The coach had been jolting uncomfortably over badly maintained roads for miles by the time she'd seen the dilapidated cottages of the small village. But it was the guarded, almost sullen expression of the villagers that made her most wary.

She'd been relieved to see Woodruffe's friendly face when he opened the coach door, and very glad to observe that at least one of the small party waiting to greet them remembered Harry. She felt better still when she realised that Pryor not only remembered Harry, but was overjoyed by his return.

Harry had taken care to present her to all the senior servants, and he had given unequivocal orders that her wishes should be attended to immediately. He'd also sent Woodruffe and a local man recommended by Pryor to hire a vessel to take them along the coast to Cornwall. But he had not remained with her. Saskia had been aware of his edgy, uncertain temper from the moment she'd stepped down from the coach. She could see it in the stiff way he held his shoulders, and hear it in his voice. She wasn't surprised when he announced he would see his uncle alone. From the set of his jaw, it wasn't a meeting he expected to enjoy.

'I understand Lord Hawkminster is very sick,' she said to Pryor as she ate the supper that had been hastily prepared for her.

'Yes, mistress,' he replied.

'It must be difficult for all of you to know that his suffering has been so prolonged,' she said, feeling her way.

Something flickered in Pryor's eyes, but his voice was expressionless when he repeated his previous answer, 'Yes, mistress.'

'I believe you knew my betrothed when he was a youth,' Saskia said, hoping Pryor would find the new topic of conversation more to his liking—and consequently be more forthcoming in his answers.

'I did.' Pryor smiled, suddenly appearing much younger. 'When he lived with his grandfather, the previous earl. A bold, brave youth he was. I knew he'd make his mark on the world.'

'And so he has,' Saskia agreed warmly, glad that

Harry had at least one firm supporter among the servants. Her limited observations suggested it was an unhappy and demoralised household. At first she'd thought it must be grief and the imminent loss of their present lord that overshadowed the mood of the Castle, but there was no warmth in the way any of them spoke of Harry's uncle. She did sense a wary curiosity directed to both Harry and herself, which was hardly surprising in the circumstances.

It was an awkward introduction to Hawkminster Castle, but she'd spent too long managing Pieter's affairs to be daunted by the situation in which she found herself. After she'd finished her meal, she asked Pryor to show her around. As he took her from room to room she saw most of the building had been left to fall into a shabby state. Dust lay thick in most of the rooms. Bed curtains were moth-eaten and brittle with lack of care.

As they continued, it was obvious Pryor was becoming increasingly mortified by the condition of the house, but he offered no explanations. Only at the end of the tour he suddenly said, 'We are looking forward to the bright future that awaits Hawkminster now that Master Harry has returned with such a lovely bride.'

'Thank you.' Saskia accepted the compliment with surprise and pleasure, momentarily distracted from the many questions she had chosen not to voice. 'Thank you very much. Do you know where he is now?'

'He went on to the roof after he'd finished speaking to Lord Hawkminster,' said Pryor. 'I believe he has now gone to the west parlour. I will show you.'

'There's no need,' Saskia said quickly. She wanted a chance to speak to Harry alone. 'You showed me that chamber at the beginning of our tour. If you would be kind enough to remind me how to get there from here, I am sure I will have no trouble.'

As Saskia approached the west parlour, she saw that the door was already ajar and a glow of candlelight came from within. After the gloomy mood induced by the tour of the house, her spirits lightened at the prospect of seeing Harry again. She quickened her pace, her soft-soled shoes making virtually no sound on the flagstones as she pushed the door wider and stepped inside.

She spotted Harry immediately. His back was towards her, his body bent forward in front of a candle. For a confused instant she thought he was praying at a shrine. The next instant he reared up, drawing his sword as he spun to face her. He moved so fast she couldn't track his actions—but in less than an eye blink she was staring at him along the length of his curved sword. Light glinted on the well-honed blade. His arm was drawn back in preparation to strike. His eyes burned with fighting fever. His face was taut with deadly intent.

Saskia froze, too stunned in the first moment of shock to be frightened. She had seen Harry in combat readiness before, after the highwaymen's attack. But this was unimaginably more terrifying. Tonight his expression was full of battle rage. This was the face his enemies saw just before they died.

Fear sluiced through her body.

Harry's expression changed. His eyes filled with recognition and horror. He snatched his hand even further back before lowering the point of the sword to the floor and releasing his grip on the handle. The sword clattered on to the flagstones.

Saskia's head jerked as she instinctively glanced in the direction of the brief, sharp sound, but she was shaking so badly she could hardly focus on the fallen sword. She looked up at Harry. His whole body was in the grip of shuddering tension, his face gaunt with distress. His eyes were wide with horror and regret. He took a backward step, shaking his head as if he could not believe what he'd done.

Hardly knowing what she was doing, Saskia crossed her arms in front of herself, clutching her elbows in an unconscious attempt to still her own trembling. She tried to speak, but her throat was locked tight. Her legs shook. The moment of threat had lasted less than a second, but it had been devastating. As her sluggish mind repeated what had happened, she realised there had never been a point at which Harry started to lunge towards her and then aborted his strike. He had turned to her with his arm drawn back, but he had not struck wildly without looking.

She dragged in an unsteady breath. She didn't know why Harry had instinctively expected to find an enemy at his back when she'd walked in, but she knew his anger hadn't been directed at her. His reaction now was proof enough of that.

'Harry…' she began. Her voice was little more than a croak. Her mouth was so dry she couldn't swallow. Before she could say anything else she heard running footsteps approaching the chamber, and a servant burst through the door.

'Sir, sir! Lord Hawkminster is dead!' The servant stared at Harry with round eyes, panting slightly, apparently oblivious to the tension in the room.

'Then by all means bury him!' Harry roared, making both the servant and Saskia jump. Saskia had never heard Harry use that voice before.

The servant stared in confusion until Harry shouted, 'Get out!' Then he backed out in clumsy haste.

Harry's gaze refocused on Saskia. 'Go!' he said hoarsely.

'Harry…' She took a step towards him, her hand outstretched.

'Leave.' His tone was as rough and unyielding as granite, his skin stretched taut across his angular features. He had never been more distant, his mood more impenetrable to her than now.

Her own emotions were in turmoil. Her heart was still racing, her muscles weak from the shock of staring down the blade of his sword into his furious eyes. She had an overwhelming desire to collapse on to the nearest seat, but Harry wasn't offering her comfort or reassurance. At that moment he wasn't offering her anything. She started to back away, still watching him, and suddenly realised she was treating him either as a circus freak or a dangerous animal, not trusting him enough to look away from him. She made herself turn around and walk calmly out of the room.

As she disappeared from his sight, Harry dropped on to his knees and covered his face with shaking hands. The fear in Saskia's eyes when he'd drawn his sword on her would haunt him for ever.

Saskia walked to the end of the corridor, then sank down on to the stairs and put her head in her hands.

Her momentary fear had passed, but she was far more profoundly disturbed than she'd been when she'd heard Lady Abergrave and Tancock plotting her murder. As soon as she'd understood the danger that evening in Cornwall, she'd had a straightforward goal and all her efforts had been directed to achieving it. Tonight she had no idea what to do. Doubt and shock overwhelmed her. For a few despairing moments she wished the whole nightmare would disappear. That Benjamin was safe in Trevithick House and she was back in Amsterdam, going about her familiar, well-ordered routine without threats of murder or violence. How could she give up her successful, comfortable life in Holland to become part of the dark, unhappy world Harry had introduced her to at Hawkminster?

But Benjamin's life was in danger more than a hundred miles away in Cornwall, and she was trapped in a decaying castle with a newly dead man upstairs, while downstairs the man who wanted to marry her had just threatened her with a sword. For a few more seconds she floundered in miserable, self-pitying thoughts, before her practical nature reasserted itself. She drew a hand across her eyes and decided that, since Harry had disowned all interest in his dead uncle, she'd better make dealing with the corpse her priority. As Harry's fiancée, she had gained at least some of the responsibilities of mistress to the Castle, and she could clearly imagine the confusion into which the household might descend if no one took command. She stood up, consciously relaxed her shoulders and set off to take stock of the situation.

'My lady.' Pryor met her on the stairs. 'Lord Hawkminster—the old Lord Hawkminster—is dead.'

'I heard,' she said calmly. 'Take me to him, please.'

'My lady?' He looked startled. It occurred to her he was already addressing her as if she was the new countess. Right now she wasn't sure it was a role she still wanted to fill, but that was a decision for later.

'I wish to pay my respects to my betrothed's uncle,' she said. And verify that he was indeed dead, although she didn't say so. It wasn't unknown for nervous attendants to mistake deep unconsciousness for death, and it would make an already difficult situation intolerable if the recently deceased interrupted the funeral preparations by waking up.

The grand bedchamber was stiflingly hot and smelt of decay and sickness. Saskia paused on the threshold and swallowed. 'Open the window,' she ordered.

'His lordship would not permit it—' one of the servants began.

Saskia glanced at him, raising her eyebrows. The old lord was not in a position to object any longer.

In the candlelight she saw the servant flush, and then he went to do her bidding. She approached the bed. She did not need to touch the body to be sure Lord Hawkminster was dead. Thin, greying hair straggled around a face so desiccated it appeared reptilian. She could hardly believe he had only just died.

'Was he conscious when my betrothed saw him?' she asked the elderly man standing near the bed.

'Yes, my lady.'

'Who are you?'

'I was his valet,' said the servant. He lifted his head proudly. 'I served the previous lord, Lord Harry's grandfather, for thirty years—and then I served him.' The valet nodded towards the bed as his shoulders slumped. 'Lord Harry will not want me.'

'The new lord won't want any of us,' the servant who'd opened the window burst out. 'Not after what *he* did.' *He* was indicated by another jerky nod towards the bed.

Saskia glanced between the two men and saw no grief, only deep anxiety in their expressions. She had many questions, but the first task was to make sure funeral arrangements were begun. The corpse could not be left to lie untended long in the summer heat.

'Come,' she said, and walked out of the foetid chamber. 'Where will Lord Hawkminster be buried?' she asked, crossing into the room opposite and reaching to open the window that overlooked the courtyard below. The younger servant immediately leapt to help her. As she felt the welcome night breeze on her face she took a deep breath. It was a relief to be in a less oppressive atmosphere.

The two servants glanced at each other and then at her, uncertainty in their expressions.

'The old Lord, *his* father, was buried in Yorkshire,' said the valet.

'Did *he* wish his body to be transported to Yorkshire?' Saskia asked, falling into the same pattern of referring to the dead man as *he*.

'I cannot recall him ever saying so,' the valet replied. 'I do not believe he would have wished that.'

'I'm sure he didn't,' said Pryor. 'Your ladyship.' He bowed respectfully to Saskia as he entered the room. 'He left the Yorkshire estate for London as soon as the King returned from exile. He never went back.'

'No doubt his coffin has already been prepared,' said Saskia. The coffins of the nobility were elaborate creations, often lead-lined to allow for the inevitable delay between death and burial caused by the lengthy arrangements needed for such grand funerals.

'There is no coffin,' said Pryor.

Saskia stared at him in astonishment. Lord Hawkminster hadn't been a young, fit man, killed in an unexpected accident. His death must have been anticipated for weeks, if not months. 'What preparations have been made for his funeral?' she asked.

'None,' said Pryor.

Saskia had already seen strong evidence that Hawkminster Castle wasn't in good order, but she was still startled by such brutal evidence of poor management and low morale amongst the household. It was clear none of these men had held Harry's uncle in high esteem while he was alive. And none of them had taken responsibility for protecting his dignity after his death, though they surely could have made discreet preparations to do so if they'd wished. A dozen questions whirled in Saskia's mind, but for now she limited herself to practicalities.

'Where will he be buried?'

The men looked at each other.

'In St Michael's graveyard, I dare say,' Pryor said after a moment. 'The church is in the nearby village,' he added.

'Send for the clergyman,' Saskia said briskly. 'Wait. Does the parish have a coffin?' Many parishes owned a wooden coffin in which the shrouded bodies of those too poor to afford their own coffin could lie during the funeral. When the service was over the corpse would be put into the ground in its shroud and the coffin used again for the next poor parishioner.

'Yes, my lady.'

'Ask the vicar to have it brought here,' said Saskia. She saw Pryor's eyes widen in surprise. She knew it was insulting to suggest an earl be treated like a pauper, but what alternative did they have? 'No doubt Har— I mean, the *new* Lord Hawkminster will order something more suitable by morning,' she said. 'But for now we must be practical. Do you have a shroud? Very well, then, he must be wrapped in a sheet. Rosemary? Do you have rosemary?'

'Yes, my lady,' said Pryor, sounding a little more energetic.

'Good.' The rosemary would be placed within the shroud. At least some of the due forms could be observed.

'I will ensure your commands are carried out promptly,' said Pryor, bowing again before he went out of the room, taking the younger manservant with him.

Saskia was left alone with the elderly valet, and a mild anxiety she had overstepped the mark. How would Harry feel when he discovered she'd given orders for the late Lord Hawkminster to be placed in the parish coffin? Then she remembered Harry's response when he'd received the news of his uncle's death. It appeared Harry had no more regard for the dead man than the household servants. And after the way he had summarily dismissed her from his presence, she decided she didn't care about his opinion anyway. As her initial shock receded, she further decided he could at least have apologised and explained who he'd mistaken her for before he had sent her away. He'd promised her he would always tell her what he was thinking—and as soon as she regained her equilibrium, she was going to hold him to that promise.

'Why are you afraid the new lord won't want you?' she asked the valet.

'I'm too old,' he said simply. 'And tainted by my service to him.' He twitched his head in the direction of the dead man's chamber. It was a shockingly disrespectful gesture, but there had been nothing disrespectful in the way the valet or Pryor had spoken to Saskia. Nor had they been exaggeratedly obsequious in an effort to curry the favour of their new mistress. Everything she had seen added weight to her suspicion that the dead man had been a bad master.

'I have always served Hawkminster,' said the valet. 'What else could I do? We waited for Lord Harry to come back—but now he won't want us.' Tears sprang into the old man's eyes.

'Sit down.' Saskia guided the valet to a nearby bench and sat beside him when he began to demur. His instinctive reluctance to sit in her presence was further proof that his resentment was directed only towards Harry's uncle. 'Why do you think Lord Harry won't want you?'

'Because the old lord has ruined him!' the valet exclaimed. 'I think he only stayed alive so he could taunt him with ruin. He never said another word after Master Harry—his lordship, I should say—left the chamber. He'd saved his last strength for that moment. He closed his eyes, and what was left of his black soul slithered away, like a shadow falling through the floorboards.'

Saskia shivered at the disturbing image conjured by the valet, then she recalled the first thing the valet had said and more urgent dread seized her. 'Ruined Harry how?' she demanded.

'Debt,' the valet whispered. 'He boasted of debt and ruin to the estates. None of us have received any wages since Christmas. He said all of Master Harry's new-made fortune would be swallowed by the debts. He said Master Harry would be a broken man. Master Harry will wash his hands of us. Maybe even Hawkminster itself. It's brought nothing but pain to him.'

'His uncle wanted to *break* Harry?' Saskia stared at the valet. For an instant she had a memory of Pieter's broken body on the street outside their house. But then she realised Harry's uncle had used the term more symbolically. He'd meant to ruin Harry financially and break his spirit. Every fibre of her being rebelled at the idea of a broken Harry. Unconsciously her hand closed into a fist. She would not permit it!

'Yes, my lady.' The valet nodded vigorously. 'But it was the insult to Master Harry's father that hurt him most, I believe. That's when Master Harry nearly drew his sword.'

'Harry drew his sword on his uncle?' For a wild moment Saskia wondered if a fatal sword wound was concealed beneath the sheet covering the dead man.

'He didn't use it,' the valet assured her quickly. 'He half-pulled it out of the scabbard, then slammed it back and walked away.'

'Dear God.' It couldn't have been very long after that when Saskia had startled him by coming up behind him unexpectedly in the west parlour. No wonder his instinct had been to treat her as a potential threat.

'We all—well, most of us—had such hopes for Master Harry's return,' said the valet. 'I remember him as a boy. He was strong. Resolute. I knew he'd make a success of himself. We had such hopes. Once Lord Hawkminster heard Pryor and me talking about the future—that things would be better when Master Harry was lord. I thought he would throw us out—but he didn't. Perhaps we're part of his revenge. We couldn't stop the ruin. We didn't dare do anything. Master Harry will hate the sight of us.'

'I don't hate you, Gatesby,' said Harry. He had entered the room so quietly that neither Saskia nor the valet knew he was there until he spoke.

Chapter Ten

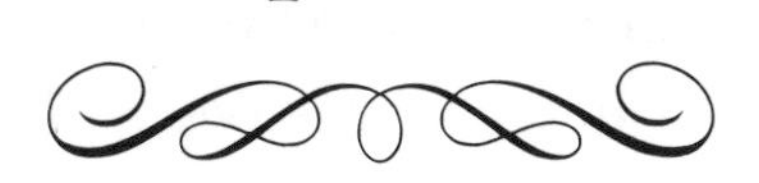

Saskia and Gatesby both started and the valet leapt to his feet.

Saskia stood up more slowly, searching Harry's face for indications of his mood, looking for any signs of despair. He seemed almost unnaturally calm. She had never seen such a bleak, desolate expression in his eyes.

'I do not recall everyone in the household, but I remember you and Pryor well from the years I spent with my grandfather in Yorkshire,' Harry said to the valet. 'I know you both served him with loyalty and affection. I expect you to give me the same service.' It was a command that, under other circumstances, would have been arrogant. No one could order affection. But Saskia took some comfort from it, because it meant Harry understood the two old servants had endured by clinging to their hopes for his future lordship. He was telling Gatesby that their faith would not be rejected. If he still cared about the feelings of men he hadn't seen for so many years, he couldn't yet have sunk into irretrievable despair.

'Yes, my lord.' The valet stared at Harry as if to make absolutely certain he'd heard correctly. Then he smiled tremulously and Saskia saw a tear on his lined cheek. 'Thank you, my lord. We will not fail you.'

'I know that,' said Harry. He looked at Saskia and she saw myriad emotions in his eyes, too complex for her to interpret. 'Thank you,' he said quietly. 'I understand you have already sent word to the vicar and ordered the parish coffin to be brought here.'

She nodded, wishing she could decipher his mood more clearly. 'In this heat it seemed best,' she said. 'If you have the means to cover the coffin with lead, there will be time to make plans for the funeral.'

Harry's expression didn't change. If anything, it became colder. 'I've sent additional orders for a grave to be dug immediately,' he said. 'There is no reason for delay.' He turned to Gatesby. 'I want to speak to the entire household in half an hour. Have everyone collect in the great hall.'

'Yes, my lord.' The valet bowed and hurried off.

Harry closed the door behind Gatesby and turned towards Saskia. In the candlelight his face seemed all hard angles and dark shadows. She could sense there were powerful emotions behind his rigidly controlled demeanour, yet at the same time he seemed to be icily remote from her. In that moment he had become a stranger, shrouded in the darkness of his past. Her heart thudded against her ribs as she waited for him to speak.

'I am sorry,' he said, his voice uncharacteristically harsh. 'No words are adequate restitution—but I am sorry.'

'Sorry?' she whispered. Then she realised Harry was referring to the moment he'd drawn his sword on her. For the past few minutes she'd been completely preoccupied with his uncle's terrible plan to break him.

She'd hired Harry in London partly because she'd needed a man capable of using his weapons to protect her and save Benjamin. She'd had one moment of panic-stricken doubt at the inn outside Guildford when she'd seen him talking to Selby, but since then she'd never expected his weapons or his temper to be turned against *her*. She knew—she'd known even in the parlour—that he hadn't raised his weapon against her. Given what she'd subsequently learned, she could even understand why he'd reacted the way he had to her silent approach. But none of that changed the fact that no one had held a sword to her breast before. She couldn't help imagining what might have happened if he hadn't recognised her so quickly. Or if he had struck blindly without looking—

'Do you always…make sure of your enemy before striking?' she asked, her voice rusty.

A muscle twitched in his jaw. 'I have never struck anyone I did not intend to strike,' he said. 'I would never—I would cut off my arm rather than deliberately cause you fear or distress.'

She nodded.

'I should not have brought you here,' he said.

'You said it would be quicker to take a boat along the coast.' She was suddenly terrified their journey would be delayed. 'Do not forget I am wealthy,' she continued quickly. 'With my fortune joined to yours, I am sure your uncle's plans to br—to ruin you can be thwarted. But we have to save Benjamin first.'

Harry's gaze snapped to her face. 'You think I'm going to break my promise?' He swore in a language she didn't understand. 'You think I have no honour at all?'

'No, no,' she stammered, daunted by the sudden anger blazing in his eyes.

'I came to tell you that I have received word a vessel has been hired for us. We can leave for Cornwall tomorrow morning.'

'Thank you.' Saskia took a deep, steadying breath,

telling herself it was a good thing her suggestion had infuriated Harry. His anger indicated he hadn't fallen into a despairing lethargy at finding himself the victim of such malice. 'I am sorry. I did not mean to question your honour.'

'You had every reason. An honourable man does not draw a sword on any woman—much less the woman who has agreed to marry him.' Harry stared at her. 'When your brother is safe, I will understand when you wish to end the betrothal.'

Saskia's gaze locked with his. She'd had some doubts about the wisdom of their marriage since she'd found Harry in the west parlour, yet her first instinct was to deny his assumption she wanted to end the betrothal. But was Harry telling her he too was having second thoughts? There was nothing about the stern-faced man before her that invited questions. And Saskia wasn't sufficiently certain of her own feelings to summon the resolution to ask them.

'The household will be waiting for you,' she said.

'Yes, I will escort you to your chamber first.'

'Thank you.' Saskia hesitated, then said, 'I am sure most of them are as deserving of your compassion as Gatesby and Pryor, but not all of them. When I was shown around I saw signs that advantage has been taken—-perhaps even with your uncle's connivance. Not all of them will be pleased at the thought of good order returning to Hawkminster.'

'I know.' Harry's lips pressed together for a moment. 'I mean to watch their faces as I speak. I may gauge something of their sentiments.'

'If I am present, I can watch also,' said Saskia. 'Unless…you would prefer me not to be there?'

Harry looked surprised, and then he searched her face for a few moments. Did he consider her offer an impertinence or potentially valuable help? As the silence lengthened Saskia almost wished she hadn't said anything.

Then he bowed very formally and offered her his arm. 'I would be glad of your observations,' he said.

She stepped forward and laid her hand on his sleeve. She felt his muscles flex beneath the cloth and suddenly wished they'd never come to Hawkminster, that they were alone beneath a tree or back in bed together at Nicholson's house. She'd been happy in that bed with Harry. But she wondered if it was a solitary moment of joy—never to be repeated now that the grim demands of Harry's life, as well as the need to rescue Benjamin, had intruded upon them.

He escorted her downstairs and took her out into the central courtyard. They could have reached the great hall without going outside, but she suspected

Harry wanted a couple of minutes in the open air before he addressed his new dependants. She was certainly grateful for the opportunity to breathe fresh air. As she glanced up at the stars above she heard a church bell start ringing. The sound carried across the dark fields to where they stood in the courtyard. The message about old Lord Hawkminster's death had reached the vicar. Soon everyone in the area would know there was a new master at Hawkminster Castle.

Early morning, Wednesday, 19 June 1667

Harry stood with the vicar by the hastily dug grave. The grass was damp with dew, the graveyard striped with the long shadows of early morning. Some of the servants watched from a short distance, but few villagers had roused themselves to attend the funeral arranged for their late lord with such unseemly haste. Harry was grimly aware he was not the only one who felt no grief at Stephen Ward's passing.

Stephen was laid in the ground in the parish coffin. Harry had already given the vicar the funds to replace it. He glanced around, instinctively comparing this funeral with that of his grandfather. Mark Ward had been determined to protect the dignity of his title, family name and his person, and he had made careful preparations for his own approaching death. He had arranged in good time for Swiftbourne to become the guardian of his grandsons, and for their future beyond the range of Stephen's possibly vengeful reach. He had made provision for the dole, the old-fashioned custom of distributing charity to the local poor in the form of food and drink, and he had specified most of the details of his funeral procession. The ceremony had taken place at night, as was common with the funeral of a high-ranking man, and Harry could still remember the flickering torchlight that had added to the drama and significance of the occasion.

Harry and Richard had already been apprenticed to one of the wealthiest members of the Levant Company for three years at the time of their grandfather's death. They'd spent most of those years in London, learning book-keeping and how to buy and pack merchandise for the market in Turkey. Their grandfather had appointed Lord Swiftbourne their guardian, but Harry had been nearly nineteen years old by then, and his future course already set. He and Richard had gone north for the funeral, but within days they'd returned to London. A few weeks later they'd set off for Aleppo in one of the Levant Company ships. As well as the goods they were to sell on their master's behalf, they'd also had the stock of merchandise left to them in their grandfather's will, which they were able to sell on their own account. It was that original stock which Harry had grown into his present fortune. Stephen had returned from exile in France to claim his inheritance three months after Harry and Richard had left England.

After Harry had spoken to the household and escorted Saskia to her bedchamber he'd spent the rest of the night going through his uncle's papers. By the time he followed the coffin to the graveyard, he knew he faced weeks untangling the debt-ridden chaos he'd inherited. He had already written letters to Richard, Nicholson and Swiftbourne. Before he left Hawkminster he would give the letters to one of Nicholson's men to ensure that they were received in a timely fashion.

'You arrived most opportunely, my lord,' said the vicar.

'Hmm.' Harry twirled the piece of rosemary Pryor had thrust into his hand as the makeshift procession had carried Stephen Ward over Hawkminster drawbridge for the last time.

'Were you able to speak with your uncle before his demise?'

Harry looked at the vicar, noting his expression was guarded rather than pruriently curious. Was he an honest man of God who'd disapproved of Stephen's conduct and now feared the new lord would be equally dissolute? Or had he taken advantage of Stephen's lack of interest to prey upon his parishioners? Harry was bitterly aware it would take him months to track all the threads of Stephen's spite and begin to unpick them.

'I spoke to him,' Harry said curtly. He flicked the piece of rosemary to one side. 'He is dead. I am lord here now.'

The vicar bowed his head in acknowledgement of Harry's claim.

'I have existing obligations that require me to leave Hawkminster immediately,' said Harry, 'but I will return at the earliest opportunity.' He saw a flicker of scepticism behind the vicar's bland expression and his eyes narrowed. 'What I say I will do—I do,' he said coldly.

'The previous lord spent no time here until his health broke down completely,' said the vicar.

Harry turned to look across the fields to the Castle. He could see the cannon-damaged top of the south tower through a gap in the trees. 'I prefer to build, not destroy,' he said. But even as he made his harsh claim, he recalled what had happened in the west parlour the previous evening. His fear he had destroyed all Saskia's trust in him tormented him far more than Stephen's malice. She had not raged at him for his unforgivable action, but she had been politely withdrawn when he'd spoken to her later. He could not imagine she would ever again trust him to kiss her or to make love to her. Why would any woman be willing to accept a husband who reacted to the shadows of the past in such an undisciplined, potentially lethal way?

Not only that, if she became his wife, she'd have to live with him in Hawkminster Castle for much of the year. Harry could not look at the place without experiencing a spasm of revulsion. He couldn't believe Saskia felt any more favourably disposed to spending time here than he did. He was bitterly afraid that when he returned to Hawkminster, Saskia would not be with him.

The boat sailed out of Poole harbour under a high, arcing dome of blue sky. The glare of sunlight on the sea was strong enough to make Saskia squint, but a brisk wind filled the sails and whipped her skirts around her legs and her hair across her cheeks. She kept one hand on the rail and turned into the wind so that her hair was blown back from her face. For a few hours at least she could allow her driving need to press the journey forward to ease. She was on her way to Cornwall by the fastest means possible and, until they arrived, there was nothing further she could do to expedite matters. She could only trust in the skill of the crew and that the weather would continue to favour them.

She saw movement from the corner of her eye and looked up as Harry came to stand beside her. All morning he'd been treating her with very careful, formal courtesy. They'd discussed only the arrangements for continuing their journey, and even those conversations had been stilted. It was hard to believe that the boyishly good-humoured man who'd teased her yesterday during their break for dinner had ever existed.

She wondered if she was a fool, because it wasn't the memory of Harry's naked blade that made her most doubt her future with him—it was his withdrawal into remote, uncommunicative courtesy. She knew he had the capacity for violence, but he had always been gentle with her. She didn't believe he would ever physically hurt her. After what she had seen and heard at Hawkminster, she knew there had been bitter divisions within his family, but she wasn't afraid of sharing his pain and trying to offer him comfort. It was the prospect of living with another man who excluded her from his deepest hurts that chilled her soul. She had known Harry for such a short time. How could she be sure that the good-humoured man she'd first met was the real Harry, and that the grim-faced, distant mood currently claiming him was only a temporary response to the circumstances of his succession?

'You should rest,' he said. 'Quarters are cramped, but I have arranged with the captain for you to have privacy and as much comfort as possible while we are aboard.'

Saskia didn't want to rest. She wanted Harry to talk to her rather than send her off to be alone with her thoughts. But she couldn't help feeling reassured that he was still trying to make her journey as pleasant as possible.

'Thank you. You have made my journey back to Cornwall much easier than my journey to London.' She smiled at him, but her smile faded as she received no answering smile in return. Harry's expression barely changed, but she thought she saw a flicker of distress in his dark eyes before he turned his head to look out at the horizon.

'I will show you to your quarters—'

'Not yet,' she interrupted. The glimpse of raw emotion she'd spotted in his expression suddenly made her desperate to continue the conversation. 'I will rest later,' she said, when he looked at her. 'But just now I am enjoying standing on deck. We are making good progress, aren't we?'

'Yes, we are.' Harry glanced briefly at the sails, stretched taut by the wind. 'You want to stay here for a little while. Yes, you can see how quickly we are moving,' he said, almost as if he was explaining to himself why she might want to do so. 'Is there anything I can do for you?' he addressed her directly. 'Would you like a warmer coat to wear?'

Saskia shook her head. For a moment her throat was too tight with emotion to let her speak. The stiff breeze in the English Channel meant she was cooler than she would have been inland, but she didn't need any more clothes. Was Harry's question a sign that he too was trying to break through the barriers that had arisen between them since she'd startled him in the west parlour?

'I…only wish for your company,' she said.

Something flashed in his eyes, gone too quickly for her to interpret.

'As you wish.' He moved a couple of paces so that he too could rest a hand on the ship's rail. Now his body provided her with a shield against the worst of the wind. For several minutes neither of them said anything, but Saskia was acutely aware of Harry standing so close beside her. Though he balanced easily on the shifting deck, he was not relaxed. They'd shared a bed and she'd experienced ecstasy in his arms, but now there was an ocean of uncertainty between them.

She watched the swell of the waves, her own

tension growing as the silence between them lengthened. She was the one who had demanded Harry's company. He was accommodating her wishes. Perhaps that meant it was up to her to initiate the conversation they had to have before they could move forward.

Harry gripped the rail with both hands, trying to find the resolution to speak. But he was afraid. He didn't want to begin because he feared that, by the end of their conversation, the dreams he had briefly held for his future would all be over. From their first meeting Saskia had never hesitated to speak her mind to him. Now that had changed. Whatever she was thinking was hidden behind a composed, self-contained politeness. He had encountered such behaviour among other well-bred ladies since he'd returned to England, and he hated it. He had learned how to decipher the unspoken signals of the men he knew and the children he'd cared for, but women were surely different. He did not understand what Saskia's reticence signified. He would rather she raged questions or accusations at him, than treat him so politely. At least then he'd have some idea of how he stood in her regard—perhaps he'd even be able to try to win back her trust and affection. But overnight her manner had become so guarded he was increasingly convinced she was regretting her acceptance of his proposal. No doubt the only reason she hadn't already told him she couldn't marry him was because she didn't want to do anything to interfere with the rescue of Benjamin.

The possibility that she might be sacrificing herself for Benjamin's sake was intolerable. 'I will save your brother, no matter what,' he said.

'Why was your uncle so bitter?' she asked simultaneously.

He hadn't expected that question. He was still tormented by the memory of drawing his sword on her. He realigned his thoughts, his lips twisting in a self-derisive, humourless smile as he recalled his last conversation with Stephen.

'You mean—why did he hate me so much?'

'Well…yes.' Her gaze was fixed on his face.

Harry drew in a breath as he considered how best to answer. He rarely spoke of his childhood, but Saskia had more right than anyone to know about his family's past.

'It began before I was born,' he said after a moment. 'The rift in the family. At least, from what I have heard. Uncle Stephen was the older son, my father the younger. But Stephen believed my father was the favourite. I have no idea if that was true, but later, after my father's death, my grandfather never spoke to Stephen again, even though he was the heir. I do not believe that was simply because they had taken different sides in the Civil Wars. Not all families allowed such differences of opinion to rend them irretrievably apart.'

Harry did not say, but he had often wondered whether Stephen had chosen to support the King to spite his father and younger brother.

'There was a siege,' said Saskia. 'I saw the damage to the tower—and the bullet scars in one of the rooms.'

'Father was holding Hawkminster for Parliament. Stephen laid siege with German mercenaries from Prince Maurice's army,' Harry said.

'Your uncle and father *fought* each other?' Saskia sounded aghast.

'I don't believe they drew weapons on each other, but they commanded men who fought and killed each other,' said Harry. His hands clenched the rail. He paused, glancing away at the horizon as he struggled to maintain his composure. Even now he could not remember his father's death without pain. 'My father died at the hands of one of Stephen's mercenaries. I did not know then, but I've heard since that some of the worst cruelties did not happen when Englishman fought Englishman, but when professional soldiers from the continent were involved. The continental mercenaries were used to more brutal customs of war.'

'I am so sorry.' Saskia reached out to lay her hand on one of his.

He looked down, startled, but not disturbed by her touch though at that moment his emotions were too volatile to allow him to respond. She pulled away almost immediately. Her withdrawal was a minor wound that hurt more than he knew it should.

'I understand why you would hate Stephen,' she said. 'But I don't understand why he hated you.'

Harry's chest expanded as he dragged in a deep breath of salty air. This was the hardest part of the story. He steeled himself against the horror he was afraid he'd see in Saskia's face at his answer, but he was too proud to evade the question.

'I tried to kill him.'

'What?' Saskia's eyes widened in shock. 'When? During the siege?'

'No, not then. Later.'

Silence hung between them for several seconds. Harry waited for Saskia's reaction, tension in every muscle.

'Were you in the castle during the siege?' she asked.

'Yes.' Harry tried to speak and had to swallow before he could continue. 'During the last day we were hidden in a priesthole—'

'We?'

'Richard and I. I was afraid we would be trapped

if Father didn't return…but Swiftbourne had come out of friendship to Grandfather.' Harry recalled the moment Swiftbourne had walked towards the priesthole after killing the German mercenary. 'When he headed straight for our hiding place, sword in his hand, I thought the enemy had found us. I thought if I burst fighting from the hole when he opened it, Richard would have a chance to escape.' For a few moments Harry was completely lost in the past. 'But Swiftbourne spoke to us before he operated the mechanism. Told us he was Grandfather's friend. I wasn't sure I should trust him—but he knew the secret of the priesthole. I found out later Grandfather had shared it with my father, but not Stephen. Perhaps Stephen was right—he did not have Grandfather's favour.'

Harry caught sight of Saskia's appalled expression and, with an effort, pulled himself back to the present. 'By then the castle was overrun with victorious mercenaries,' he said. 'But with his usual cool efficiency, Swiftbourne managed to smuggle the three of us out of the castle and deliver us safely to Grandfather.'

'Three of you?' Saskia looked puzzled.

'My nurse was with us,' Harry said shortly. Swiftbourne would have left her, but Harry had insisted she went with them. He still flinched inwardly whenever he remembered how Swiftbourne had turned the full force of his cold personality on the terrified, weeping Martha to ensure her silent obedience. He understood why Swiftbourne had been so brutal. As a man, Harry knew if he found himself in a similar situation he was capable of giving equally ruthless commands. Sometimes inflicting the lesser hurt was necessary to avoid a greater threat. But it scarred his heart whenever he was forced to make such a choice.

'Didn't anyone challenge him?' Saskia said. To Harry's relief she didn't ask any questions about his nurse. 'What about your uncle?'

'Swiftbourne shed a little blood along the way.' Harry smiled grimly at the thought of the dead mercenary. 'But Stephen never knew Swiftbourne had been there till we were long gone. Even now, Swiftbourne can command all eyes when he wants to—but when he doesn't, he has a knack for avoiding attention.'

'He thinks I'm a Dutch agent,' said Saskia, reminding Harry that even though she'd never met the Earl of Swiftbourne, his influence had touched her.

'He doesn't any more,' Harry said quickly. Glad he could at least reassure her on that point. 'I sent him a letter from Winchester and another one from Hawkminster.'

She nodded. 'So when did you try to kill Stephen?' she asked, her tone too neutral for him to guess at her feelings. She could have been a magistrate questioning a witness. He suddenly remembered all the years she'd taken an active part in her late husband's business. Most successful merchants learned how to conceal their emotions when they chose. Saskia had clearly made herself mistress of that skill.

'Later,' he said. 'I ran away from my grandfather, trekked across the country to find Stephen. When I did, I challenged him to a duel. I considered myself a man of honour, even if he wasn't.'

'What did he do?'

'He laughed at me.' Even now the memory had the power to fill Harry with frustrated outrage. 'So I abandoned my notions of honour. Drew my knife and attacked him,' he finished harshly.

The wind was too strong for him to hear Saskia catch her breath, but he sensed the small jerk of her body at his revelation. Was she recalling the moment he'd drawn his sword on her last night? Did she think his first instinct was to solve all his problems with a sharpened steel blade?

'How old were you?' she asked.

'Eleven. His companions pulled me away. One of them had known my father in happier times. He carried me away before Stephen could exact immediate revenge.'

Saskia stared up at him. Her eyes were stormy. He couldn't doubt his story had stirred a powerful response in her. He braced himself for her condemnation. Even his grandfather, who'd grieved deeply for the death of his younger son, had beaten Harry soundly for his undisciplined quest for vengeance.

Chapter Eleven

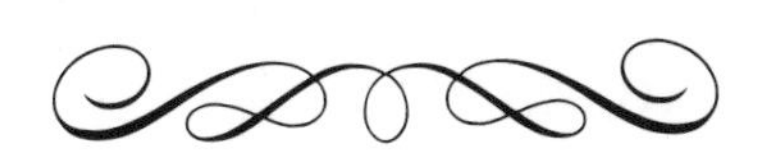

'But it was *Stephen* who'd attacked Hawkminster Castle!' Saskia said furiously. 'He was responsible for the loss that drove you to such extremity. I do not understand...how can a man bring an army to attack his own brother? His family home!'

Her outrage at Stephen soothed Harry. 'History tells us that murderous rivalry is a common pastime of kings,' he said. 'Perhaps it is not so surprising to discover similar lack of restraint in lesser families.'

'Stephen was not a king,' Saskia retorted. 'And he was already the heir. When your grandfather died, he became the next Earl. He didn't need to fight and kill to take control of Hawkminster Castle.'

'There were a few years when it seemed he might have lost everything,' Harry said scrupulously. 'After Parliament seized control of England, he went into exile with other Royalists—but he slipped back into the country to claim his inheritance after Grandfather died. Richard and I were already on our way to Aleppo by then.'

'So, do you mean… Was yesterday the first time you'd seen Stephen since you tried—since you were eleven?' Saskia asked.

'Yes.'

'My God! No wonder it wasn't a pleasant meeting!' she exclaimed. 'Did you stay in Turkey so long because you were afraid if you came back to England you'd try to kill him again?'

'No!' Harry said, more sharply than he'd intended. 'As a man I have greater control over my baser instincts than I had at eleven,' he continued in a more even tone. He did not want her to believe that all that had stood between him and Stephen's untimely death were one and a half thousand miles of land and sea.

'Of course you have.' Saskia flushed. 'I should not have made such an outrageous suggestion.'

'I was successful in the Levant,' said Harry, a little less stiffly. 'When I first sent Richard back to England I was worried Stephen might seek him out to cause him harm, but Cromwell was still in power and Stephen lay low in Yorkshire, well away from London—and Richard. Later, after the King was restored, Stephen spent most of his time in London, but he only moved in Court circles and ignored Richard. But Richard wasn't his heir—nor was I until his only surviving son died at the age of three. A few months later his wife fled back to her family, and by the time she died Stephen was already too sick to father any more children, even if he'd found another wife. So…' Harry shrugged in acceptance of his fate '…here I stand, fifth Earl of Hawkminster. For all that Stephen brought shame to his name, I am not ashamed of my heritage. All those who bore the title before Stephen were honourable men.'

'And now you must make right all the wrong that Stephen did. It is not fair!' Saskia hit the heel of her clenched fist against the rail. Harry thought her flash of temper on his behalf was the most reassuring thing she'd said or done all morning.

'Will it truly take all the fortune you have earned to salvage Hawkminster?' she asked.

'I don't know. The documents at the castle were in deliberate chaos. I have no idea how the Yorkshire estate stands, but Stephen never cared for it. Once he no longer needed to avoid the attention of Parliamentarian authority he never returned. There were many signs of his destructive meddling in the affairs of Hawkminster, though as far as I could tell they only date from after the death of his son. Before then he was a negligent lord, but not actively destructive of his inheritance. The Yorkshire estate may…*may*…have fared better, simply because he had less interest in it.'

'It is a criminal shame.'

Harry gave a twisted smile. 'It is certainly a shame,' he agreed. 'But I will set the estates to rights. Though it may take years rather than months.'

'I am sure you will.' Saskia sounded absolutely confident of his ability to do so. She looked up at him searchingly. 'I think you should rest first,' she said suddenly. 'You cannot have slept at all last night—and it will be hours before we reach Cornwall.'

Harry was deeply relieved Saskia apparently didn't feel any revulsion towards him after hearing his story, but he didn't want to be sent to bed in the middle of the day on his own. He wanted to know if she was still willing to marry him. He almost asked her, but his circumstances had drastically changed since he'd proposed outside Winchester. Then he'd been a wealthy, independent merchant and he'd believed the title he'd soon inherit would be an asset in the eyes of any future bride. Now his future was tied to a ravaged inheritance and, after what she'd seen at Hawkminster and he'd told her today, Saskia must surely consider his family to be tainted.

'I will take your advice,' he said, because he knew it was essential he was fully alert when they reached

Cornwall. Saskia was devoted to her brother. Harry was bleakly certain that if he did not succeed in saving Benjamin, he would have no hope of redeeming himself with her. 'Though I do not need much sleep to refresh me,' he added. 'Woodruffe will attend to you while I am resting.'

Woodruffe supplied Saskia with a simple but adequate meal, and then she decided that it would be sensible if she too rested. Though she'd gone to bed the previous night, she'd spent very little of that time asleep. She didn't expect to sleep on the boat either but, to her surprise, she did.

When she woke, she lay contemplating the things Harry had told her. She was disturbed and angered by his story, but she was also profoundly relieved he'd shared his family history with her. She knew he'd found it difficult. Perhaps he would never willingly discuss it again, but the mere fact he'd talked to her about it once gave her hope for the future.

Neither of them had referred to the moment he'd drawn his sword in the west parlour, but he'd told her about the priesthole. Saskia had learned a lot about stomach-cramping fear since she'd overheard her aunt and Tancock plotting her death. It wasn't hard for her to imagine how terrifying it must have been for Harry to be trapped while fighting raged through the castle. And how overwhelming those memories would have been when he'd looked into the priesthole. She wondered how long it would be before he stopped associating Hawkminster Castle with death and violence. Probably a very long time, she thought sadly, especially since he would be confronting the evidence of Stephen's spite on a daily basis as he tried to restore the estate to prosperity.

Before she went back on deck she changed into her male clothes. The breeches would be more comfortable and modest on the windswept boat than her skirts. She didn't think Harry would have any serious objections—and how Benjamin would stare when he saw her in such attire! Without warning, her anxieties for her brother returned tenfold. She was finally within reach of him, and her fear she might be too late intensified until she felt physically sick.

She stumbled on to the deck. They'd rarely sailed far out of sight of the south coast, and she stared shorewards, trying to locate their position. They hadn't reached Plymouth yet. She gripped one of the shrouds and wished she could give the boat wings. They were almost sailing towards the sun as it dipped lower across the western sky. It was still a few hours to sunset, and Saskia prayed the wind didn't slacken with the approaching evening.

'Tell me about Trevithick House,' Harry said, joining her by the shrouds.

Saskia looked up at him. His expression was serious, but he seemed less tense than he'd been earlier. For a moment she was startled that he should be calmer just at the point when her own anxiety had become so acute she could barely hold herself upright. But of course Harry was used to dangerous adventure. It was adjusting to mundane, everyday life he often seemed to find perplexing.

She liked the idea that he probably considered rescuing Benjamin a straightforward task. It gave her confidence that everything would go smoothly. Though she did not anticipate much adventure would be involved now they had Nicholson's servants and Harry's elevated status to add weight to their cause. Her worst fear was generated by the possibility they were already too late.

'Trevithick House is situated on the west bank of the river,' she said. 'The land is steeply sloped and the house is much higher than the river.'

'Can you draw a plan of the house and grounds for me?' Harry said. 'I particularly need to know the location of your brother's bedroom.'

'Why?' Saskia frowned in confusion. 'When I

believed I was going to rescue him with a nameless adventurer I thought we'd have to break him out of the house unnoticed. But you don't need to sneak anywhere. You're the Earl of Hawkminster! We can just walk in with Woodruffe and Glover at our backs and you can demand Benjamin.'

'I can, and I will,' said Harry. 'I'd have done that even when I was a nameless adventurer,' he added drily, and she realised he would have done. He didn't derive his personal authority from his newly acquired title. He'd always possessed it. 'But first we make sure your brother can't be hurt if your aunt refuses to give up without a fight.'

Saskia stared at him. The idea that their arrival at Trevithick House might precipitate the very disaster they wanted to avoid horrified her. She was shaken she hadn't considered the risk herself.

'You're right,' she whispered. 'We still have to save Benjamin first.'

'Not we,' Harry replied. 'You will remain here on this boat until the house is under my control and it is safe for you to enter it.'

'No!' The protest burst instinctively from Saskia. Then she saw the uncompromising set of Harry's face and knew he had already made his decision without consulting her. 'You have no right to confine me!' Her temper flared.

'It is a matter of common sense, not rights.' His tone and the expression in his eyes became even more inflexible. 'Benjamin's well-being is your priority. Do not forget you fled from Trevithick House in the first place because your own death would put your brother at great immediate risk.'

Saskia ignored the hair whipping across her face as she confronted the truth of his words.

'The situation has changed,' she said at last. 'You're here now.'

'I am here, and you have charged me with rescuing your brother. I can do that best if I am not also worried about your safety.'

Saskia took a deep breath. She had no logical argument to dissuade him, only her fierce need to see Benjamin at the first opportunity. She had to assure her brother she'd not abandoned him when she'd fled Cornwall—and see for herself that he was unharmed.

'What do you intend to do?' she asked at last. She hadn't given up the notion of going with Harry, but after years of managing Pieter's business affairs she'd learned that sometimes the best way to win an argument was to approach it indirectly. She wasn't Harry's prisoner, but if he'd decided she wasn't to leave the boat until he gave his permission she doubted she'd be able to persuade the other men to disobey him. It was Harry's mind she had to change.

'Enter the house unobserved. Find your brother. Tell him who I am and that you are well. Since his leg will still be splinted, I doubt it will be possible to get him out of the house unobserved, but I will leave Woodruffe to protect him. After that—' Harry's eyes narrowed thoughtfully. 'What I do next will depend on the situation I find. Your aunt and her supporters need to be confined so they can be brought to justice. Tancock is most likely still searching for you—but when your aunt has been dealt with I'll hunt him down too.'

'Oh God, Tancock!' So much had happened since they'd left London Saskia had almost forgotten him. 'How will you ever find him?'

'Perhaps he'll come to me,' said Harry grimly. 'If this business can be carried off without raising a great stir in the neighbourhood, Tancock may return expecting to continue plotting with your aunt. And then I'll have him.'

Saskia looked into Harry's fierce eyes and knew without doubt that he was ruthlessly determined to exact justice on her behalf. But she still wanted to be there when he found Benjamin.

'I am no good at drawing plans,' she said. 'It will be quicker and more efficient if I go with you to show you the way through the house.'

'No,' he said flatly, his expression becoming shuttered.

'*Yes*. Listen, I must think.' She knew instinctively that ranting at him would not make any difference. But he had demonstrated on more than one occasion he was willing to change his mind if he found her suggestions logical or practical. The wind blew her hair across her eyes, nearly blinding her, and she tossed her head in irritation.

Harry stepped a little closer, braced his body against the side of the boat and gently cupped her face with his big hands. He pushed them back over her temples and the crown of her head, holding her tangled hair away from her face.

'There must be a way of controlling your hair so it doesn't bother you in the wind,' he said.

'If I was wearing a hat it would be long gone,' she replied, a little breathlessly. His expression was still guarded, but his touch was tender and considerate—-just as it had been when they'd made love.

'A scarf, perhaps?' he suggested. 'You could tie it on. I have not previously had occasion to study female attire. Perhaps I will have to pay more attention.'

'As long as it's *my* attire you're attending to,' she retorted, before she considered her words.

His eyes widened, then took on a warmer glow. He'd liked her brief flash of jealousy, but she suddenly felt shy and uncertain. Though the connection between them was still strong, she wasn't ready to trust herself to it entirely. But with his hands still holding her head in a gentle grip she could not easily evade his gaze.

'If I had short hair like you it would not be a problem,' she said. He'd suffered no inconvenience from being bare-headed throughout the sea voyage.

'No.' His response was immediate and definite. 'Your hair is beautiful. Glorious. You will not cut it. But you may cover it when you find yourself travelling among strangers,' he added. 'So you do not inadvertently entice them.'

'I've never inadvertently enticed *anyone*,' she said, mildly indignant.

'So it was all deliberate?'

'What? Oh.' Understanding washed over her in waves of self-conscious awareness. He meant she had enticed him—and he'd proved at Winchester that he wanted her. From his expression he still did.

He moved one hand slightly, so that he could stroke her cheek with the side of his thumb. 'Do I…still entice *you*?' he asked in a low voice.

She swallowed past the emotion constricting her throat. 'Yes,' she whispered.

'Despite what you know of me now?'

'Yes.' She laid her palm on his chest and felt him

draw in a deep ragged breath. She was amazed and humbled to realise he had feared she would give him a different answer.

The boat tacked and Saskia only managed to keep her footing because she was still holding on to the shroud. Harry kept his balance better, but even he staggered a little. A trace of wry humour flickered in his eyes. 'Even a man of my limited experience can tell these aren't ideal conditions for gentle conversations.'

'You mean kissing me?' Saskia teased him, suddenly feeling amazingly light-hearted all things considered. 'Is that a gentle conversation?'

'Hmm.' He hesitated a moment. 'I can speak four languages fluently, but my vocabulary is limited in this area. If you do not object to calling a kiss a kiss, I dare say I can bring myself to be equally bluntly spoken.'

Saskia gave a small choke of laughter, born as much from relief that their humour was tentatively re-forging the bonds of intimacy between them, as from amusement. 'Which languages can you speak?'

'English, French, Turkish and Greek. Turn into the wind,' he commanded.

'Why?'

'I've had an idea.'

'That's not an informative answer.' But she did as he'd requested, and a moment later she felt him lift her hair from the nape of her neck and slide a strip of fabric underneath. She gripped the rail and focused on every small caress of his fingers against her skin and hair as he drew one end over the top of her head and tied the two ends just behind her ear.

'Is that tight enough?'

'A little tighter.' In his efforts not to pull her hair or hurt her he was being too gentle. His light touch was stirring such a wonderful sensual response through the rest of her body she was reluctant for it to end—but if he persisted in tying the fabric so loosely his idea wasn't going to work.

'You hold my hair back. I'll tie it,' she said, her natural practicality asserting itself. Their hands briefly tangled together and the small, co-operative effort to make her more comfortable on the windy boat suddenly felt very significant. This was the essence of Harry. A man who noticed and tried to alleviate the distress of others, even when that distress was nothing more serious than her hair blowing into her eyes or a waking baby crying because he was temporarily bereft of his mother.

Stephen had wanted to break Harry. He wasn't going to break. Saskia had known that from the first, but she'd been afraid he would retreat into a dark, austere mood where she could not reach him. But only a day after he'd received the punishing blow to his future, his good humour was resurfacing—and he'd never lost his consideration for others. Almost his first words to Gatesby had been a reassurance the valet still had a home at Hawkminster.

A great warmth unfurled within her, like rays of golden sunshine. The feeling was so strong it brought tears to her eyes. She fumbled and dropped one of the ends. Harry caught it for her and put it back between her fingers.

She loved him. She loved Harry. It wasn't just that he excited her senses beyond her previous experience, or that she found his company so stimulating and satisfying. She loved the whole of him. In good times and bad times. She wasn't the uncertain young wife she'd been six years ago in Amsterdam. If Harry ever retreated into uncommunicative silence, she would not politely accept the situation. She would find a way to break down the barriers between them again. Full of resolution and hope, she pulled the strip of cloth tight.

'Put your finger on the knot,' she ordered huskily, and then tied another knot.

She turned to face him, seeing him for the first time with the eyes of self-acknowledged love. She was aware of the challenges in his future, but he was everything she wanted. Nothing and no one, including his own internal demons, was going to take him away from her.

He must have sensed her changed mood, because a question appeared in his dark eyes. She wasn't quite ready to put her feelings into words, so she cast around for something else to say to ease the tension growing between them.

'You gave me your cravat for my hair,' she exclaimed, as she noticed his bare throat.

'It's of more use to you than me,' he replied, his gaze fixed on her face. Her lips. He was looking at her lips. Did he want to kiss her as much as she wanted to kiss him?

She half-lifted her hand to put it on his shoulder. And then the movement of one of the crew working on the rigging caught her eye. She froze. The germ of an idea spun into a fully formed plan in a few seconds.

'I know how we're going to break into Trevithick House!' she exclaimed.

'You're not coming,' he responded instantly.

'Yes, I am.' She put both hands on his chest. Now she had a workable plan she was perfectly willing to use his desire for her to add persuasion to her argument. 'Harry, I am safer with you than with any other man on this boat.' She slid her arms coaxingly around his neck. 'Besides, no one will be expecting us the way I have in mind. And it will be quicker and safer if I guide you, rather than you relying on my badly drawn plans to find your way through a dark, unfamiliar house.'

She could see his eyes darken with arousal, yet his gaze was oddly inscrutable as he looked down at her. She wished she could tell what he was thinking.

'Tell me your plan,' he said abruptly. 'If I do not judge it safe for you, I will not let you come, no matter how you try to tempt me into changing my mind,' he warned. 'Richard raged at me for days when I decided he must return to England, but I did not change my mind. I would rather endure his resentment or even hatred than watch him die of fever in Aleppo. I will be equally guided by my own judgement in the matter of your safety in Cornwall.'

It was an arrogantly unequivocal statement, but the expression in his eyes was bleak, not triumphant. Saskia instinctively knew Harry had paid a high price for making the decision he'd considered best for his brother. It gave her a moment's pause, but she wasn't a fever-weakened lad, and she didn't intend either of them to suffer as a result of Harry agreeing to her scheme.

Saskia waited with Woodruffe and Glover in the shadows of a box hedge as they watched Harry climb the wall of Trevithick House. In the starlight, in dark clothes, he was little more than a shadow rising up the ivy-clad brickwork. She was here, and she was determined to do nothing to make Harry regret his decision to include her in the rescue. But most of all she was filled with a sickening mixture of hope and dread over what they would find when they sought Benjamin.

Harry reached the top of the parapeted roof. She saw him outlined briefly against the paler sky and then he vanished from view. It seemed a very long time before his head and shoulders reappeared a little further along the parapet, away from the thickest part of the ivy. She knew the delay was because he'd been checking there was no one else already on the roof walkway. She gave a shaky sigh of relief when he raised a hand, and then began to lower the rope he'd carried coiled on his shoulder. That was the signal for Woodruffe to move forward and tie the end of the lowered rope to the top rung of a rope ladder. Harry hauled it up, leaning out to make sure the rope ladder didn't become snagged on any of the trailing tendrils of ivy. Only when Harry silently indicated it was secure did Saskia leave the shadows of the hedge to run across the grass to the foot of the wall.

As she reached up to grab a wooden rung she briefly wondered why Harry hadn't questioned her ability to climb a rope ladder, when he'd questioned every other part of her plan. Of course, she hadn't admitted she'd never done it before. And Harry had proved on more than one occasion he didn't prejudge her physical abilities. She'd said she could ride a horse all day and he'd trusted her to do so. She'd said she could climb a rope ladder and he accepted her claim. An image of Pieter's shattered body briefly flashed into her mind before she blocked it out. Pieter hadn't fallen. He'd been the victim of an accident when the rope had broken. She knew Harry had checked their equipment thoroughly before they left the fishing boat. All the same, her legs were shaking from tension rather than effort by the time she reached the top of the parapet.

Harry helped her over and then pulled up the rope ladder and left it still secured, but rolled up in the shadows of the parapet. If they had to, they could leave the same way they'd entered the house. He recoiled the rope he'd originally lowered and put it across his shoulder again. Saskia led the way to the door that opened on to the stairway down into the house. Relief filled her when she discovered that it still wasn't locked.

There were windows in the stairwell on each flight, but it would still be dark inside. She took a moment to orientate herself and calm her racing heart.

'I'll go first,' Harry said in a low voice. She was very aware of him standing poised and alert beside her. She sensed he was completely attuned to his surroundings.

'We must go down four flights,' she murmured. 'We take the first door after the second window.'

They descended cautiously. The stone steps were narrow and it would be easy to slip in the deep shadows. Haste was less important than remaining undiscovered. Harry paused when they reached the door that led on to the first floor. He put his ear to it, listening for any sound on the other side. Saskia's heart thudded nauseatingly against her ribs. It seemed ridiculous that she was afraid of entering the house in which she'd grown up. She was suddenly blindingly furious with her aunt for causing so much pain and terror. Rage burned away her fear and she almost charged through the door to find and confront her aunt.

She must have made some small sound or movement that gave her feelings away. Harry swiftly straightened, turned and pulled her into his arms. 'Justice later,' he murmured in her ear. 'First we protect Benjamin.'

She leant against him, ignoring the uncomfortable ridges of the rope across his chest as she drew upon his resolute strength to regain her composure. 'How did you know?' she whispered. She was surprised and pleased by his correct interpretation of her unspoken feelings.

'I have been so angry I lost sight of everything except the cause of my fury.' His voice was so low she had to strain to hear him. 'Are you ready? No more talking now.'

He eased open the door. Saskia winced as the hinges creaked, but Harry only pushed it wide enough to let them slip through. He pulled it closed behind them and listened intently to the sleeping house. There were no sounds to suggest anyone was coming to investigate the noise. Saskia touched Harry's shoulder and pointed in the correct direction. He went first, staying in the middle of the corridor because if they got too close to the walls there was a risk of bumping into pieces of furniture in the gloom. Saskia kept close behind him. When a floorboard groaned beneath her foot it sounded shockingly loud in the heavy silence. Saskia froze, terrified the noise would alert Lady Abergrave and her henchmen to their presence.

But there was no indication they'd been heard. She tried to control her nerves and followed after Harry as he prowled forward. He was in his element now. A dangerous man who had survived many situations far more potentially lethal than this one. But if Benjamin was already dead, none of Harry's skills would bring him back. As they drew closer to her brother's chamber, Saskia's anxiety became almost suffocating. Hardly realising what she was doing, her thoughts became a repetitive prayer: *Please let him be safe.*

Harry put his arm back to stop her. She looked past him and gasped when she saw Benjamin's door was half-open. She tried to push forward, but Harry's grip on her arm tightened. With his other hand he gently pushed the door wider. It swung inwards without a sound. Keeping Saskia behind him, Harry stepped over the threshold, swiftly scanning every part of the room.

'He's not here,' Saskia breathed. Even though she was so afraid for Benjamin, it was almost impossible to accept the reality of his empty bedchamber. 'She'll tell me where he is!' Fury and desperate terror overwhelmed her. She swung around, intent on challenging her aunt, but she had only taken a single step before Harry's arms closed around her in an unyielding cage.

'Steady,' he murmured against her ear. 'We have not finished our reconnaissance.'

'But—'

'Hush.' He didn't relax his grip. 'The bedclothes are untidy and there's something on the floor. Someone got into bed and then got up again.'

'Benjamin?' Saskia forced herself to study the

room more carefully. The window was uncovered, and though there wasn't much light she could see the rumpled state of the bedding.

'Perhaps. Don't move.' Harry released her and bent down. A moment later she saw he was holding up a nightshirt.

'What does it mean?' Had Benjamin already made his escape alone?

'Let's see. Very cautiously,' Harry added softly. 'Now we know we may not be the only ones creeping about the house. It may not be your brother.'

'He will be on crutches.' Saskia took a steadying breath. Her nerves were overstretched and raw. She wanted to scream from the tension and marvelled at Harry's focused self-control.

They went back to the door. This time Harry took the lead. There was no point in returning the way they had come, so he continued along the gallery. Saskia tugged at his sleeve. He stopped and she stood on tiptoe to murmur, 'Anne's chamber is at the end of the next corridor.'

He nodded and continued moving soundlessly through the shadows. But though she and Harry made no betraying noise, Saskia became aware the rest of the house was no longer so silent. A harsh, rhythmic sound intruded upon her consciousness, getting louder as they proceeded.

Her imagination conjured a large beast, growling as it lay in wait for them to come within reach. There hadn't been any dogs in the household the night she'd left, but what if her aunt had brought one since? She was sure Harry could deal with a menacing dog—but the noise would rouse everyone. They'd be trapped before they'd saved Benjamin. At every step forward she expected a monstrous hound to leap at them. As they neared the end of the corridor she saw a dark shape rising from the floor.

The dog crouched to attack! Her heart almost stopped—and then her vision cleared and she saw it was a man's body. Fear stabbed at her. Was it Benjamin? Was he dead? But dead men didn't snore—she had belatedly realised what she'd mistaken for a dog's growling was really a man snoring. Still half-fearful it was her brother, she edged nearer, aware of Harry close beside her.

'Not Benjamin,' she whispered in relief. His face was in shadow, but she didn't need to see it. 'Too fat and no splint.'

Harry nodded. He put his finger over her lips and pointed to Anne's door. Saskia saw that it was open. Harry signed to her to remain where she was and eased around the snoring man to check inside the room. He returned immediately and led her back down the corridor a few paces. 'Empty. Let's try the main stairs.'

Saskia hurried to show the way. Had Benjamin and Anne already made their escape unaided? Somehow they must have given the snoring man a sleeping draught. But where were they now?

Saskia began down the first flight of the main stairs. Harry put his hand on her arm to slow her down. She nearly shook it off, because she was so desperate to find Benjamin, but after a moment she obeyed his silent command. She had originally hired Harry for his skill in hazardous situations, and she would be failing her part of the bargain they'd made on the boat if she did not let his experience guide them now.

As she stopped and listened she became aware of a faint, uneven tapping sound from lower down the stairwell. She frowned, unable to identify it, and cautious of leaping to any more false conclusions. Harry moved in front of her and they continued downwards. At least there was no risk of the stone treads creaking.

A woman's scream shattered the brooding darkness.

'Anne!' It was Benjamin's desperate shout.

If Saskia hadn't already been so shaken from the scream, she would have cried out herself at the sound of his voice.

'Selby has a knife. If you do anything foolish, he will cut the girl.' Tancock's words echoed up from the shadows below.

Chapter Twelve

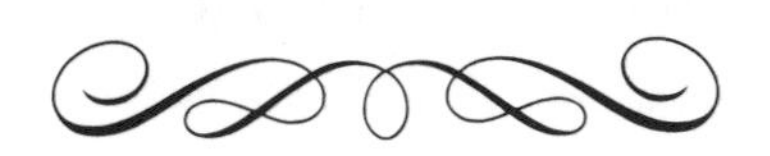

Saskia's legs almost gave way. She gripped the stone balustrade of the stairs for support. From the direction of their voices, Benjamin was on the next flight down, hidden from view by the bend in the stairs, and Tancock was lower still, probably in the front entrance hall.

She felt Harry's hand on her upper arm as he reached back to her. 'Tancock,' she breathed in horror, leaning close to him.

'Anne?' Benjamin said sharply.

'I…I'm all right,' Anne replied. It sounded as if she was below Benjamin, perhaps on the same level as Tancock, but her voice was so unsteady it was hardly recognisable.

'And she will remain so as long as you co-operate. Continue down the stairs,' Tancock ordered.

'Where's Saskia?' Benjamin demanded. Saskia

heard the same fear in his voice for her that she'd felt for him for so long. She wanted to tell him she was safe, but that would betray them to Tancock and lose Harry the advantage of surprise.

'On her way here, no doubt,' said Tancock. 'Hurry up. You were making faster progress before.'

'She's still alive?' Desperate hope throbbed in Benjamin's voice.

'If she was dead, you'd be at the foot of the stairs with a broken neck,' said Tancock. 'And I'd be on my way to being master here.'

'Not you,' Benjamin said. 'My aunt would own it all.'

'She would have made me a good wife—for a while, at least,' said Tancock. 'But your bitch of a sister spoiled that plan—'

Benjamin gave a snarl of fury and Saskia heard the clatter of wood against stone.

'Careful,' Tancock warned. 'No one will hear you, and if you and your sister co-operate you will both survive this adventure. A better deal than your aunt offered you.'

'Why won't they hear?' Benjamin asked. 'Have you drugged them? Is that why Fenwick was asleep—instead of bringing Anne to me as he promised?'

'Just a precaution,' said Tancock. 'I did think of giving everyone including you a sleeping draught and leaving the girl behind—but then we'd have had to carry you. It's easier if you carry yourself. Though I had no idea you'd get this far on your own.'

'If you're not working for my aunt any more, why take me anywhere?'

'Ransom,' said Tancock. 'Your sister is wealthy and so will you be on Saturday. And I'll earn a fortune of my own when you both pay me for your freedom. Now pick up the crutch and continue down the stairs. And remember—if you make any more stupid moves, it will be Lady Anne who suffers.'

'Let her go. I'll come with you if you let her go.'

'No. She's my guarantee that you'll behave. And you're my guarantee that Saskia will co-operate when she eventually arrives. Pick up the crutch.'

'I can't see it, damn you.'

Light suddenly glowed faintly up through the stairwell. Saskia was momentarily confused, until she realised Tancock must have uncovered an already lit lantern.

Saskia heard Benjamin's soft curse and awkward scraping sounds, and then the tap-tap she'd heard earlier resumed. Now she knew it was Benjamin making his way downstairs on his crutches.

Harry was still reaching back to hold her firmly behind him. She wanted to ask him what he was going to do, but she didn't dare speak. This was Harry's kind of business. She would do whatever he told her.

'Stay.' His order was no more than a breath against her ear. Then he moved into the darkest shadows of the broad stairway, avoiding the dim glow of rising light, and went down the next flight of stairs like a cat.

Saskia stood absolutely still. According to Tancock—and he should know—the rest of the household was asleep. There was little danger anyone would attack her from behind, though she couldn't help listening out for any threatening sound from the shadows above. As her first panic gradually cleared, she realised that the greatest danger was currently to Anne. Tancock would inherit nothing if she and Benjamin died. He had to keep them alive at least until they had signed the documents that would give him access to their fortunes. And her fortune, based as it was in the financial markets of Amsterdam, was both larger and more portable than the wealth embedded in Benjamin's estates. A few days ago Tancock had wanted her dead. Now her continued good health was crucial to the success of his plans.

Saskia was in no state to appreciate the irony of the changed situation. She did appreciate that it was more important than ever she didn't fall into his grasp. Not only for her own sake, but also for

Anne's. If Tancock ever had both Saskia and Benjamin in his power, he could use threats to each of them to ensure the other's co-operation. He would no longer need Anne to control Benjamin.

The tap-tap of Benjamin's crutches paused.

'Where are you taking us?' His voice was more distant. Saskia guessed he was by the front door.

'That's my business,' Tancock replied. 'Take Lady Anne across the garden, Selby. Sir Benjamin and I will follow. Bear in mind I have a pistol, my lady,' he added casually. 'If by some unimaginable chance you should escape Selby, I will shoot you.'

Saskia bit her lip so hard she tasted blood. She prayed Anne would not panic. Then she remembered Woodruffe and Glover, still waiting in the grounds, and ice ran through her veins. Glover was watching the wall where they'd climbed the rope ladder; Woodruffe was watching the window of Benjamin's bedchamber. If all had gone according to plan, Harry would have let down the rope he still carried and given a signal for Woodruffe to climb up to the chamber to guard Benjamin and Saskia while Harry captured Lady Abergrave.

As long as the two men were still where they were supposed to be, they wouldn't see Tancock and the others leaving by the front door. But what if they'd moved? What if they thought everything was all right when they saw the small party leaving the house and revealed themselves? Tancock would have no hesitation shooting them out of hand.

Uncertainty paralysed her. Should she go back up to the roof and climb down to warn them? If she moved Harry wouldn't know where she was, and that might spoil his plans. She saw movement, felt a clutch of fear and then Harry was beside her again.

'Come down, soft as you can.' He didn't waste any unnecessary words.

She'd been up and down those stairs countless times during her childhood. As long as she kept one hand on the balustrade she could do it by feel in the darkness. Harry was a few steps below her, giving her enough room to move, though his body partially protected her from anyone below. As they reached the bottom flight she felt the night breeze and saw the front door had been left standing open.

Harry turned briefly to face her. 'Keep to the side. We need to get to the door without moving across it.'

As they slipped quickly into the shadows to one side of the door she caught a glimpse of four figures moving down the gravel path. Tancock was silhouetted by the lantern light. Benjamin was just inside the circle of light, while Selby and Anne were dark figures ahead. None of them were likely to spot movement in the shadows of the unlit house, but Saskia had no quarrel with Harry's caution.

'We're going out through the right side of the door into the shadows of the holly tree,' he said in her ear. 'Tread lightly.'

Saskia swallowed nervously and nodded. She knew that in the moonless night they were more likely to betray their presence by sound than by being seen. Harry took her arm and then moved like a fluid ghost through the door, keeping close to the door jamb. She didn't hear a sound from him as he crossed the gravel. She could not achieve such silence, but she didn't believe Tancock and the others had noticed the small shift of tiny pebbles beneath her feet. Between the scrape of Benjamin's crutches, Anne's suppressed sobs and Tancock's impatient orders, their own progress was not particularly quiet. The fact that Tancock was so unconcerned at the noise was another confirmation he didn't expect anyone to investigate. Saskia supposed Lady Abergrave had kept Benjamin and Anne apart from the rest of the household, and Tancock had put the sleeping draught in the food or drink everyone else had had for supper. She shuddered as she thought of the time she'd spent in Tancock's company, completely oblivious of how dangerous he could be.

Harry put his lips close to her ear once again. 'When I let go your arm, stay still exactly where you are.'

She didn't understand, but she nodded. She was sure she'd find out what he meant when the time came. He started across the garden and she quickly realised they were staying in the shadows of the trees and shrubbery that bordered the path. When he tugged on her arm to bend double, she went low with him. She stopped trying to think and just tried to be as silent and ghostlike as Harry. They reached an old willow tree with wide spreading branches that fountained all the way to the ground. Harry carefully drew back the fronds and led her beneath the branches. Once they were inside she wasn't surprised when he released her arm. As a child she had often played beneath this tree. In the daytime it was an imperfect hiding place, but at night it was unlikely anyone would spot her as long as she remained still and close to the trunk. Harry disappeared through the fronds the same side they'd entered. Saskia gripped her hands together and wondered what he meant to do.

Without Saskia to slow his progress, Harry quickly drew level with Tancock. It was one of the shortest nights of the year. The first hint of dawn was already beginning to show in the sky, but it had not yet lightened the landscape and Harry took care not to lose his night vision by looking directly at the lantern. He had a good idea where they were going. When they'd first arrived, he'd left Saskia with Woodruffe and Glover while he'd made a quick tour around the garden. Between what he'd seen for himself earlier and what Saskia had described while they were on their way up river, he had a fairly clear picture of their surroundings.

The steps from the garden to the path below curved round in a half-circle, following the bend in the retaining wall. Even during the daytime, no one at the bottom could see someone at the top and Harry had already noted that Tancock was staying well out of reach of Benjamin's crutches. A long piece of wood could always be turned into a weapon, no matter what its intended original use.

Selby and Anne reached the gate first.

'Take care not to trip on your way down, Lady Anne,' Tancock said almost genially. 'Selby's knife might slip.'

Anne gave a little sob of fear and Harry gritted his teeth against a spike of rage at Tancock's cruelty.

'Don't worry, Anne, we'll get out of this safely,' Benjamin said. His breathing sounded laboured. Harry couldn't tell whether it was from the effort of moving on his crutches or trying to control his emotions, but the respect he already felt for Saskia's brother increased. Benjamin evidently hadn't been tamely waiting for rescue; he'd engineered his own escape attempt.

'That's right. Everyone will come out of this safely when I have my fortune,' said Tancock.

Selby and Anne started down the stairs. Harry waited, silent as a ghost, to see if Tancock would do as he expected. If he didn't, Harry would have to adjust his plans.

'Now you, Sir Benjamin.' Tancock managed to inject a sneer into his use of the title. He waved his pistol in encouragement, but didn't step closer to Benjamin.

Benjamin manoeuvred closer to the gate and began downwards. The narrow, uneven steps strewn with occasional loose stones were more difficult to negotiate than the broad main stairs of the house and his progress was slower. As Benjamin disappeared from view, Tancock moved forward, his attention focused entirely on the top of the steps.

Harry rose up behind Tancock, swift and deadly as a striking panther. He clamped one large hand around the back of Tancock's neck. With the other he reached for the wrist of Tancock's pistol hand. With Anne's life still in the balance Harry could not afford to hesitate and he didn't. One sharp, deadly jerk and Tancock died before he even knew his life was in danger. Harry carefully lowered his body to the ground, grateful Tancock's pistol hadn't fired. He'd bought himself a little time.

The steps curved to the left, in the same direction as the quay. Harry threw a loop of the rope he'd been carrying over the stone gatepost on the right and went straight down the wall. Even though pre-drawn light was beginning to illuminate the garden, it was still dark on the path below, overshadowed as it was by the wall on one side and trees on the other.

Harry crossed the path and went flat on the grass beneath the trees. He moved forward on his elbows and knees until the others came into view. Selby and Anne were a large silhouette, standing locked together as they had been ever since he'd grabbed her in the house. Benjamin was a little way apart from them. None of them had moved far from the bottom of the steps.

'Tancock! Tancock! Hurry up with the lantern!' Selby shouted. 'It's dark down here.'

Silence answered him.

Harry edged further into position. He had to make sure that, when he jumped Selby, Anne wasn't accidentally stabbed in the struggle.

'Tancock! Where are you, man?' Selby was starting to sound uneasy. As he turned to peer back up the steps he moved further away from Harry. Harry mentally cursed, but remained still. Selby had no reason to hurt Anne without Tancock's order, but if he panicked he'd stop thinking straight. He'd strike wildly at any threat and Anne was likely to be the innocent victim.

'Tancock! Tancock!'

Harry remained silent, watching for the tell-tale signs that in his distraction Selby had loosened his grip on Anne.

'Selby. It's Saskia.' Saskia's voice echoed clearly down from the garden above.

'Saskia?' Benjamin shouted.

'Saskia?' Selby sounded stunned. 'Saskia? Where's Tancock?'

'He had an accident,' Saskia called in the same kind of tone she might have said Tancock had fallen and scraped his knee.

'What kind of accident? What are you doing here?' Selby demanded.

'I expect he'll explain later,' Saskia replied. 'The good news for you is you can deal directly with me.' Despite the dangerous situation, Harry couldn't help feeling a flicker of amusement at her perky tone.

'I can?' Selby's wary response suggested he was both confused and suspicious.

'Yes, indeed,' Saskia declared. Even though her

voice was carrying clearly, Harry was glad to see her head wasn't visible over the top of the wall. 'Everyone who knows me says what a pleasure it is to do business with me. Now you can have one hundred percent of the profits.'

After his first shout of astonishment, Benjamin had fallen silent. Selby was looking upwards, his face pale against the darker wall behind him. His grip on Anne had slackened. He'd all but forgotten her in his uncertainty at this new turn of events.

Harry sprang. He whirled Anne well out of Selby's reach before he closed with his prey. This time there was a brief struggle. Selby was a larger, more powerful man than Tancock, and less afraid of getting hurt in a fight, but he was already bewildered by the reversal of the situation. By the time he'd realised he was fighting for his life and freedom, it was too late.

'Saskia!' Harry shouted. 'Unhook the rope from the right gatepost and throw it over the wall.'

'Selby's not dead, then?' Her voice receded slightly. She was obviously hurrying to do as he'd ordered. 'Is everyone else all right?'

'Selby's not dead.' Selby's cheek was currently pressed to the stony path with his arm twisted up behind him and Harry's knee in his back. 'Did he cut you, my lady?' Harry asked Anne in a gentler voice. 'Are you hurt?'

'N-no.' She shook her head and stumbled, weeping, towards Benjamin. Benjamin let his crutches fall with a clatter and leant against the wall as he embraced her. Footsteps sounded on the steps.

'We're coming down,' Saskia called. Woodruffe appeared with the rope and a lantern, Saskia close behind him. 'Glover stayed in the garden to protect our rear,' she assured Harry earnestly, before turning immediately to her brother. 'Benjamin, you're safe!'

'We're all safe,' he said unsteadily. He was still holding Anne tight in one arm, but he opened his other arm to Saskia. 'God, I'm so glad you're safe!' His voice was hoarse with emotion. 'I was so afraid for you.'

Harry finished roping Selby and stood up. He drew in a deep breath and allowed himself to relax into a less intense state of alertness. The crisis was over, and they'd all come through unhurt, though not necessarily unscathed. He was afraid that Anne, at least, would have nightmares about this night's adventure. He couldn't predict how Saskia would fare. So far she'd been remarkably resilient. But perhaps now the danger was over and she no longer had to force herself to act, she would feel bad in retrospect. He hoped she didn't have nightmares. Lady Abergrave deserved to be tormented by nightmares for the damage she'd caused, but Harry wanted the dreams of those he loved to be happy and peaceful.

And he did love Saskia.

He'd acknowledged that truth to himself on the boat when he'd allowed her to persuade him to let her come on this rescue mission. Fourteen years ago he'd sent Richard back to England, trusting that the brotherly love that had bound them together for all of Richard's life would withstand Richard's anger at his decision. But Harry had been afraid his new-budding relationship with Saskia was too fragile to survive if he thwarted her on a matter of such profound importance to her. He wanted her to be part of his future so much he couldn't bear to earn her resentment. Even so, he would have held out against her arguments if he'd believed there was any serious physical risk to her. When they'd discovered Benjamin's chamber was empty he'd cursed himself for permitting her to come with him, but by then it was too late.

Now he was full of pride in her. She'd kept her head—and when Selby's failure to elicit a response from Tancock had made the situation perilous for Anne, Saskia had provided the distraction Harry had needed to finish the business.

He knew she was the perfect wife for him. But why would Saskia want him, with his dark family history and blighted future, now her brother was safe and she could go back to her orderly, prosperous life in Amsterdam? He jerked in a sharp breath because the thought of losing her hurt as painfully as a physical injury. He'd lost or been separated from those he loved before. He knew how long it took for the wounds to mend. Sometimes they never truly healed.

He gazed at Saskia. She was still hugging Benjamin, and the longer she remained clinging to her brother, the more Harry's hopes faded. He didn't begrudge her the reunion with her brother. But the uncomplicated, devoted affection in her manner as she cried, asked questions and even occasionally laughed as she gave an incoherent account of her own actions caused Harry a pang. He wanted her to share such easy confidences with him.

Just as he was sure Saskia had completely forgotten him, she disengaged herself from Benjamin and came over to him. 'Thank you,' she said. She put her arms around him and rested her head on his shoulder.

A fierce surge of relief and hope overtook him as he enclosed her in his embrace. She felt perfect in his arms, as if she belonged there, her body warm and yielding against his. But almost immediately she stiffened and let her arms drop. 'I'm sorry, I forgot,' she whispered, stepping away from him.

Her withdrawal after that brief moment of

intimacy was almost more painful than if she hadn't hugged him at all. Something tore inside Harry. He wanted to pull her back in to his arms or, at the very least, demand an explanation for why she suddenly didn't want to touch him.

But Woodruffe was standing by his side. Selby was trussed up a few feet away. And Lady Abergrave and her henchmen still slept inside the house. After all the grief and fear Saskia, Benjamin and Anne had suffered during the past few days, Harry was not prepared to let the situation slip out of his control at this late stage. But with his anxiety about Saskia's behaviour gnawing at him, it took a severe effort of self-discipline to focus on the practical demands of their situation.

He glanced at Woodruffe, wondering how the other man had met up with Saskia.

'Glover and I heard them leave the house and came round to investigate,' Woodruffe said, responding to Harry's silent query. 'We didn't know what was going on, so we held back. Mistress van Buren saw us as we crossed the garden. Gave me a hell of a start when she suddenly appeared at my elbow. She's very good at stealthy action,' he said admiringly.

'Yes,' said Harry. He hoped Saskia would never have to employ stealthy tactics again, but he was proud and relieved she'd acquitted herself so well.

'When Selby started shouting, it was her idea to distract him until you could deal with him,' said Woodruffe.

Despite his pessimistic mood, Harry smiled faintly. 'I was already sure of that. Go down to the river and fetch up the rest of our men,' he ordered. The house still had to be secured, and Lady Abergrave and all the servants of questionable loyalty confined under guard. If that meant lugging them into the cellars in their sleep, so be it. Harry wasn't inclined to be gentle with any of those who had contributed to the suffering of Saskia and her family.

'She's dead.' Harry stared down at Lady Abergrave. At first they'd thought she was in an even deeper sleep than the rest of the household, but Harry had quickly realised she would never wake again. There was no evidence her death had been painful. In the dawn light from the window he could see she'd still been a physically attractive woman. From what Saskia had told him, her aunt had not hesitated to use her feminine appeal to influence the men around her. Had she believed Tancock was so fascinated by her he would not betray her?

If that was the case, she'd been fatally mistaken. All the household servants they'd found had been sleeping as soundly as Fenwick, the man who'd been snoring outside Anne's door. Only Lady Abergrave was dead. Harry wondered if she had reacted badly to the same sleeping draught everyone else had taken—or whether Tancock had deliberately prepared a deadly dose for her. Tancock couldn't answer his question, and Harry doubted if Selby knew the answer. All he'd been able to reveal was that, after losing Saskia and Harry at the inn, Tancock had decided to continue to Portsmouth. He'd hoped to overtake Saskia on the way but, when that failed, he and Selby had hired a boat to take them to Plymouth.

'Watch the door,' Harry ordered Woodruffe. He didn't want Saskia, Benjamin or Anne to stumble across Lady Abergrave's body before he'd told them she was dead.

Woodruffe nodded, and Harry went off to deliver his news.

Friday, 21 June 1667

'Unbelievable villainy!' Sir William Boscawen said vehemently.

'Certainly villainous,' Harry agreed with the magistrate.

'After the murder of her mother and her own dreadful experiences last night, I am not surprised Lady Anne is too overset to speak to me,' said Sir William.

'Stepmother,' Harry corrected softly. 'Lady

Abergrave was Lady Anne's stepmother,' he clarified as the magistrate looked at him questioningly. 'Yes, what Lady Anne endured last night was sufficient to terrify even the most battle-hardened of men—let alone a gentle lady.' It was also the case that the fading bruises on Anne's face would have been hard to explain in terms of an attempted abduction that had taken place only a few hours ago.

'It is a tragedy Lady Abergrave should all unknowingly have harboured such a villain as Tancock in her household,' said Sir William.

'Sir Benjamin's household,' Harry said, though he kept his irritation out of his voice. He'd had a hasty discussion with Saskia, Benjamin and Anne before the magistrate's arrival. None of them wanted their family to be the subject of any more gossip than necessary, and they'd all decided that they did not want Lady Abergrave's murderous plans to become public knowledge. Sir William's assumption of Lady Abergrave's innocence fitted with their plans, but it still annoyed Harry. 'Lady Abegrave and her retinue were long-staying guests here,' he said evenly.

'I remember her as a girl,' said Sir William, paying no attention to Harry's comment. 'I was one of her suitors—but she chose Abergrave…' His voice faded as he seemed to be looking into the past.

They weren't trying to hide Tancock's crime, but

Harry had anticipated it might require some degree of subtle manipulation to get the magistrate to focus only on those aspects of the situation he chose. As it happened, Sir William's rose-coloured memories of Lady Abergrave, and barely concealed grief at her death, were making Harry's task easier. The magistrate's questioning about the details of what had happened was desultory at best.

Harry and Benjamin had agreed they would tell the tale as if it had begun that same night, with no mention of the threat Benjamin and Anne had been living under for so many days. They'd said that Tancock had forced Benjamin and Anne from their beds at pistol point with the intention of demanding a ransom from Saskia for their safe return. They'd not revealed that Harry and Saskia had already been in the house, hidden on the stairs, when Tancock made his move.

'It was fortunate indeed that you and Mistress van Buren were arriving at Trevithick just as Sir Benjamin and Lady Anne were being abducted,' said Sir William. 'Although dawn is an odd hour for a social call,' he added, with a puzzled frown.

'Perhaps under other circumstances,' Harry replied smoothly. 'But Mistress van Buren was eager to be reunited with her brother. It is his twenty-first birthday tomorrow.'

'It his hard to believe he is so old. I can remember when he was a babe in arms!'

'Now he is a man,' said Harry.

'Tall lad. Just like his father.' Sir William momentarily roused himself from the lethargic manner he'd fallen into after viewing Lady Abergrave's body. 'Pity he managed to break his leg, but I dare say he'll be back on two feet soon. Selby had a knife pressed to Lady Anne's side, you say, and Tancock was covering Sir Benjamin with a pistol?' The magistrate's voice sharpened.

'That's right. While Tancock and Selby had full sight of each other there was little I could do without endangering Sir Benjamin and Lady Anne,' said Harry. 'My opportunity arose when Selby and Lady Anne went down the garden steps first.'

'Selby will be held for trial at the July assizes,' said Sir William. 'By God, I wish Tancock was still alive to suffer the full punishment of the law for treacherously turning against his mistress!' he added savagely.

The law did consider it treason if a servant killed their employer, but Harry wondered if Sir William's idealised image of Lady Abergrave would have allowed him to accept she'd invited Tancock into her bed as well as paying his wages.

'My first concern was that Selby would not

overhear anything that might startle him into hurting Lady Anne,' said Harry. 'Acting alone, I could not take any chances.' He heard a slight sound and glanced round to see Saskia coming quietly into the room. The sight of her filled him with pleasure, even as he searched her face for any signs of distress or weariness. And any hint of how she felt towards him now their quest was nearly over.

Sir William didn't notice her. 'It must have been terrible for Mistress van Buren to arrive at such a time. I am surprised she did not faint from the shock.'

'It was terrible,' said Saskia, 'but I did not faint.'

Sir William started, while Harry suppressed a proud smile. His Saskia did not faint.

The magistrate turned hurriedly and bowed. 'Mistress van Buren! I did not see you there. I trust you are recovered from your ordeal?'

'Yes, thank you.' Saskia went to stand beside Harry. She was wearing one of her own grey silk gowns in place of her male breeches, so now she appeared the model of a prosperous, modest Dutch widow. It was the first time Harry had seen her in such a guise. She'd been the mysterious, masked agent in the coffee-house, an adventurous tomboy in her male clothes and an inadvertent seductress in the low-necked gown she'd borrowed from Dorothy Nicholson. Now she was a respectable Amsterdam matron. The perfect image of a woman who lived in a very well-ordered world. Would she really be willing to leave that world behind to help Harry face his own untidy future?

'But if Lord Hawkminster had not been here, I don't know how things would have turned out,' Saskia said, laying her hand on Harry's arm. 'I am sure I owe Benjamin's life to him.'

Harry's whole body responded to her small gesture. He was suddenly very tired of the magistrate and eager to be rid of him.

'Lord Hawkminster. Yes, indeed.' For a moment Sir William appeared flustered. Harry couldn't understand why until he realised the magistrate had obviously forgotten he was in the presence of an earl. Since Harry was not accustomed to thinking of himself as such, he had not noticed any lack of appropriate deference. 'All of Sir Benjamin's friends must be very grateful for your intervention, my lord,' Sir William said stiffly.

'I am glad I was here and able to take action,' Harry replied. 'Is there any further information you require, Sir William?'

'No…no. You will inform me of the time of Lady Abergrave's funeral?' said the magistrate. 'I would wish to pay my last respects to her.' His eyes glistened a little more brightly than before.

'Yes, of course,' said Saskia.

'I wish I had Tancock in my grasp now!' Sir William burst out furiously, his hands clenching into fists. 'But what is done is done.' He deflated sadly. 'I will take my leave of you, my lord… mistress.' He bowed to each of them in turn.

'He is grieving for my aunt,' said Saskia quietly when she and Harry were alone.

He looked down at her. 'Do you feel any grief?' he asked, thinking of his own reaction to his uncle's death. He did not grieve for Stephen. It was possible he would never lose the residual anger he felt towards his uncle. But he did regret there had been such a lack of harmony within his family.

'I don't know what I feel,' Saskia admitted. 'I cannot pretend it is not a relief that she is dead. I don't suppose I will ever be able to forgive her for what she planned to do. It is horrible to know there was such a deep rift in my family.'

'There is no rift in your family,' said Harry firmly. 'There is no rift between you and Benjamin. And though Anne is no blood kin of yours—which is a good thing I suspect,' he added, remembering how Anne and Benjamin had clung to each other, 'this has not caused a rift with her, either.'

'No.' Saskia smiled briefly, but then her manner became businesslike. 'All the servants have to go,' she said briskly. 'My aunt brought them with her when she moved here with Benjamin and Anne. Benjamin says he has no certain idea which ones may have been aware of Aunt's plotting—and all of them took their orders from her rather than him. We'll give them all a generous payment and send them back to Gloucestershire. That's where the Abergrave estates are, and the county most of them came from.'

Harry hesitated, and then he nodded. 'I'll take care of it,' he said. It was obvious Saskia's mind was full of the immediate problems that had to be dealt with at Trevithick House. He would wait until she was no longer so preoccupied with Benjamin's concerns before he discussed their future.

'Except for Fenwick,' said Saskia. 'Benjamin persuaded Fenwick to help him and Anne. Yesterday evening Fenwick hid the crutches in Benjamin's chamber and promised to come back later with Anne. We don't know whether Fenwick would have kept his word if he hadn't fallen victim to Tancock's sleeping draught, but without the crutches Benjamin would not have been able to leave his room. He wants Fenwick to receive the reward he was promised.'

'I'll speak to Benjamin before I do anything about Fenwick,' said Harry.

'We'll need new servants,' said Saskia. 'I want to go to see Rebecca Marsh. I must thank her for what she did for me when I was escaping, and I am sure she will know all the gossip about who might be suitable. There has been a long tradition of service at Trevithick House among local families. No doubt there are many people who would be willing to serve here once the others are gone. I must also send a message to Johanna that all is well, and to thank her again for her help. You did ask Lord Swiftbourne to check on my godfather's health in the message you sent him from Winchester, didn't you?' she added anxiously.

'Yes, I did,' said Harry. 'And I will dispatch another letter to Swiftbourne this morning. We'll send for Rebecca Marsh,' he continued, 'but there is no need for you to rush from pillar to post to solve all these problems in the space of one day.'

'It is Benjamin's birthday tomorrow,' said Saskia. 'I want everything sorted out and comfortable by then. And we still have to arrange the funeral of my aunt.'

'Benjamin might want some say in who serves him,' Harry said mildly.

'Well, of course,' said Saskia. 'But he has never appointed servants before. It is only right that I should help him.' She paused just before she reached the door. 'I keep thinking that if I'd gone to Sir William for help, he'd have believed my aunt, not me,' she said. For a moment her expression was stark and she crossed her arms in front of herself. 'It was so lucky I didn't.'

'It wasn't luck. It was your own common sense and strength of mind,' said Harry gruffly.

'It was lucky I found you. Or at least, it is lucky Lord Swiftbourne thought I might be a spy and sent you to investigate me,' she retorted. Her smile wavered and Harry saw her brush a tear from the corner of her eye. He reached towards her, but she'd already turned and whisked out of the room.

Chapter Thirteen

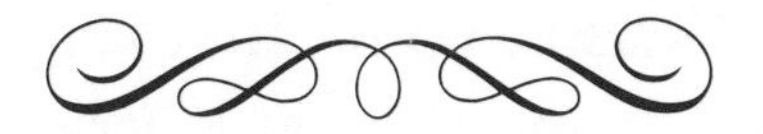

Saturday, 22 June 1667

'Happy birthday, Benjamin!' Saskia smiled across the table at her brother. They were celebrating Benjamin's twenty-first birthday over a quiet dinner which had been prepared under Saskia's close supervision by the newly hired servants. The idea of eating or drinking anything Tancock might have tampered with haunted her, and she'd insisted on new food being brought into the house and watching every stage of its preparation.

The small party didn't seem enough for such significant a birthday, but none of them were in the mood for grander festivities. In any case, they were officially in mourning for Lady Abergrave. The funeral was planned for Monday, since there was no need for the degree of unseemly haste that had attended Stephen Ward's burial.

'Happy birthday.' Anne and Harry echoed Saskia's words as they drank a toast to Benjamin.

'Thank you.' Benjamin took a sip of his wine and then looked around the parlour as if he'd never seen it before. Saskia was afraid there must have been times when he'd wondered if he'd ever live to celebrate this day. 'Thank you...for everything,' he said, looking at Saskia and then at Harry.

There was so much emotion in her brother's eyes, Saskia felt like crying. He'd been very brisk and matter of fact since the threat from Lady Abergrave and Tancock had been lifted, but she was sure he wasn't so calm inside. After their initial reunion he'd become ill at ease with her attempts to fuss over him, so she'd concentrated all her fidgety, restless energy on rearranging the household and worrying about her future. She understood why Benjamin didn't want to talk about what had just happened, but why was there such a strangely grave expression in Harry's eyes whenever he looked at her? And why hadn't he made any attempt to discuss his plans with her? She knew he would soon be obliged to leave Trevithick to fulfil his own obligations, yet he'd said nothing to her. For all the deceptive calm of those around her, she felt as if she was on the brink of a thunderstorm.

'It was my fault!' Benjamin burst out, his voice so harsh and abrupt that both Saskia and Anne jumped.

'What?' Saskia stared at him in confusion and then disbelief. 'Of course it wasn't! Aunt—'

'No.' Benjamin clenched his fist as it lay on the table, as if he was restraining the urge to hit something. 'It is *my* fault because it is *my* house and I should have done something to stop it.'

'But you could not have guessed that she and Tancock would be so iniquitous! I beg your pardon, Anne.' Saskia belatedly remembered Lady Abergrave had been Anne's stepmother.

'There is no need to apologise,' Anne replied quickly. 'She never cared for me—nor I for her.'

'You cannot blame yourself,' Saskia said earnestly to Benjamin, horrified that he should do so. Instinctively she looked to Harry for support.

Instead of joining in her protestations, Harry studied Benjamin thoughtfully. 'Why do you consider it your fault?' he asked.

Saskia opened her mouth—and then closed it again as Harry flickered a brief warning glance in her direction. She bit her lip, worried and angry at the direction of the conversation. How could Benjamin blame himself? And how could Harry possibly consider there might be any truth in the notion?

'I did not act when I should have done—when there was still time,' Benjamin said jerkily. 'As soon as I reached my majority I was going to give her a suitable pension and ask her…tell her…to find her own house. I should have acted sooner, but I knew it would cause a scandal. And she would have taken Anne with her,' he added in a low voice.

'Wasn't she your guardian?' Harry asked, in a neutral voice.

'Lord Abergrave, her husband, was named my guardian in Father's will,' said Benjamin. 'Aunt was not named. She assumed the role by custom. I believe I would have had grounds to contest her claim.'

'Hmm.' Harry frowned. 'You could have done so. But if the majority of your most influential neighbours were as entranced by Lady Abergrave as Sir William appears to have been, you might have found allies hard to come by. You had been away from Trevithick for some years before you moved back here with Lady Abergrave. Your neighbours would still have been thinking of you as the boy who left, not the man who returned.'

'Nevertheless, if I had acted in time, Anne would not have been abused and terrified, and Saskia's life would never have been in danger,' Benjamin replied, barely controlled anguish and self-condemnation in his voice.

Harry studied Benjamin, obviously weighing his claim. 'I understand how you feel,' he said at last. 'I would feel the same.'

To Saskia's surprise, she saw a hint of relaxation in Benjamin's posture. Perhaps Harry had been right not to dismiss out of hand her brother's feelings of guilt.

'And I agree that every honourable man is obliged to act to protect those who depend on him,' Harry continued. 'But it is not profitable to judge our actions in the past according to the knowledge we possess in the present.' He smiled faintly. 'Some might even consider such an assumption of responsibility to be arrogant. At least, so I was once told by a friend. Did you suspect your aunt of plotting your death?'

'Good God, no!' Benjamin exclaimed.

'What *did* you suspect?'

'I thought she was most likely milking the estate.'

'And you also believed that soon you would gain control and be able to deal with her in a discreet manner that would not embroil the family in public scandal,' said Harry.

'Well...yes.'

'But she wouldn't have been satisfied.' Saskia suddenly remembered the conversation she'd overheard between her aunt and Tancock. 'She would still have wanted it all, not just a widow's portion. Until I'd come to England she'd been plotting to kill you *after* your twenty-first birthday, when she'd either have coerced you into writing a will in her favour, or perhaps she'd simply have forged one.' Saskia abruptly pressed her fingers to her lips, feeling too sick to continue.

Anne caught her breath in a gasping sob.

'Fortunately the Lady Abergraves of this world are few and far between,' Harry said. 'I doubt if any of us will meet another one. And it is over now. It will take a little while before the vividness of the memories fade, but there are no unwelcome encounters ahead of you. Your future is unblemished. You may walk into it and claim it with confidence, knowing that you acquitted yourself in this test with great courage and resourcefulness.' He spoke directly to Benjamin, with so much quiet conviction in his voice that Saskia was sure he meant what he said. Tears pricked her eyes at Harry's generous attempt to ease her brother's turmoil.

For a few moments Benjamin did not respond, but then the rigid set of his shoulders relaxed completely. 'Half the time I was terrified,' he confessed, 'and the other half I was so enraged I could barely think straight.'

'But you almost succeeded in escaping on your own,' Harry pointed out. 'And you dealt very coolly with Tancock while he held you hostage.'

'I cannot believe we all ended up on the stairs at the same time on the same day,' Saskia said, trying to give a lighter note to the conversation. 'Even though Tancock never knew we were listening.'

'It's not so surprising,' Harry said. 'Benjamin was trying to escape before his birthday. We were trying to rescue him before his birthday. And once Tancock decided to ransom Benjamin, he must have been equally eager to get you out of Lady Abergrave's reach before you turned twenty-one,' he said to Benjamin. 'Thursday night was the last whole, clear night any of us had left to act to be absolutely sure you were away from Trevithick well before your birthday.'

'This is supposed to be a celebration!' Saskia exclaimed. 'Harry is right. It is over. We should all be happy!'

'We are happy,' said Anne. 'We're just…reflecting.'

'A few good nights' sleep will also help,' Harry said. 'I have experienced enough adventures in my life to know that victory is also sweeter when you're sufficiently well rested to appreciate it.' He continued with an anecdote about an occasion when he had dared a couple of other young factors to go out on the Bay of Izmir at night. They had gone to watch the sailors on a Turkish galley spear fish by the light of flares hung from the galley bows. But of course they hadn't been content to just watch. Whether by accident or design—though Saskia suspected it was design—there was no danger and a great deal of humour in the tale.

She rested her chin on her hand and listened. She felt a wave of deep pride in him. Pride and love. He was a good, honourable man. Well able to defend those under his protection, but also compassionate and gentle when his fiercer qualities were not required. Perhaps it was wrong and selfish of her to want him to talk about their marriage so soon after rescuing Benjamin. She wouldn't be able to truly relax until everything was settled between them, but perhaps Harry didn't want to divert attention away from Benjamin on this important day. Surely after all they'd shared he knew she was the right woman for him?

He was sitting in a shaft of mid-afternoon sunlight that streamed in through the parlour window, the lean, angular lines of his handsome face clearly revealed in the shaft of light. It was easy to imagine him boldly adventuring in distant lands, and he had a way of telling a story that drew his audience in until they almost felt part of it. When Saskia glanced at Benjamin and Anne, she saw they were both lost in the tale. Benjamin even smiled with genuine amusement at something Harry said. Anne didn't smile, but Saskia was surprised to see how intently she was watching Harry. There was something almost calculating in Anne's expression. Saskia felt a stir of uneasiness. Why was Anne looking at Harry in such a determined, almost possessive way?

They did not remain at the dinner table much longer because it was uncomfortable for Benjamin. They'd sent the servants away so they could talk freely over the meal, and Saskia went to give orders for the table to be cleared. When she went back to join the others she discovered only Benjamin.

'Where are Harry and Anne?' she asked.

'They went for a walk.' Benjamin sounded disgruntled.

'What?' Saskia instinctively glanced out of the window, though she could see no sign of anyone outside.

'Anne invited Lord Hawkminster to escort her about the garden,' said Benjamin. 'She said she knew I'd want to rest my leg.'

'Anne invited Harry into the garden—and he went?' Saskia said, surprised into indiscretion. 'But he doesn't like being alone with women he doesn't know.'

'He seemed perfectly cheerful about being alone with Anne.' Benjamin scowled.

'Good heavens.' But Saskia uneasily remembered the intent way Anne had watched Harry over dinner. 'She hasn't even got any children.'

'What's that got to do with anything?'

'Never mind.' Saskia felt just as ill-tempered as Benjamin sounded with this unwelcome turn of events. She spun on her heel, intending to go and find out just why Anne had dragged off another woman's fiancé for a tête-à-tête. Then she looked at Benjamin's stormy face and changed her mind. Her brother had endured enough. She wasn't going to create a scene on his birthday.

'I am sure Anne is just being a conscientious hostess,' she said weakly, as she sat down.

'He's an earl. And he saved her life.' Benjamin plucked irritably at the strapping holding his splint in place. 'It's easy to see why he has dazzled her.'

'He hasn't dazzled her,' Saskia said firmly. She didn't want to admit, even to herself, that she was more worried that Anne might have dazzled Harry. He'd had so little to do with women that Saskia was half-afraid he might be flattered by the hero-worship of a younger, prettier girl. Anne had never done anything so unfeminine as wear breeches and sleep under a hedge at night. What if Harry had decided that now he was an earl he needed a more conventional wife?

Harry found Saskia in the pantry. He tracked her by the sound of smashing stoneware. Her manner towards him had been distinctly cool during supper, and then she'd disappeared in the direction of the kitchen and he hadn't seen her again.

He stopped in the doorway and watched her pitch a stoneware pot into a barrel. The scent of bottled quince filled the air. 'What are you doing?' he asked.

Saskia straightened up, wiped the back of her hand across her damp forehead and glared at him. The pantry was lit by the flickering light of a lantern. 'I'm throwing out all the old food,' she said belligerently.

'Why?'

'In case Tancock poisoned it.'

'I see.' Harry eyed the jar she'd just picked up. It was still sealed and covered with a thick layer of dust. But there was something about the way she was weighing it in her hand that suggested she might throw it at him if he pointed out that it was unlikely Tancock had troubled to poison the contents, reseal it and hide it at the back of a shelf.

He'd been feeling increasingly pessimistic about the prospects of their marriage all evening, but his spirits began to rise at the hint he could still provoke a strong reaction from her. He didn't want that reaction to take the form of a pot lobbed at his head though, so he held his tongue. After a few moments she tossed it into the barrel with an air of dissatisfaction.

'I would like to talk to you,' Harry said, now she didn't have a missile in her hand. 'If it would be convenient to you.'

'Why? Doesn't Anne want to give you a tour of the house, now you've seen the gardens?' Saskia turned away to pick up another pot.

She was jealous! The startling suspicion momentarily locked Harry's muscles. Never in his life before had a woman been jealous of him, but surely that had to be the reason for Saskia's comment? And if she was jealous, it meant she still had strong feelings for him.

New energy galvanised him. He stepped forward and seized her hand just before her outstretched fingers touched the pot. Her eyes widened in surprise.

'I had a pleasant conversation with Lady Anne.' Harry picked up the lantern and tugged firmly on Saskia's hand, compelling her to follow him. 'Now I would like to talk to you.'

She pulled in the opposite direction—but it was only a token resistance—before she let him lead her out of the kitchen. 'I don't like being an afterthought,' she said coldly.

Harry kept his head turned away because he couldn't suppress a small grin of relief at her revealing words.

'Besides, it was not courteous of you and Anne to abandon Benjamin on his birthday,' she said.

'That's why you left him in the parlour after supper while you came down to the kitchen,' Harry said.

'I was trying to make sure he isn't accidentally poisoned!' she retorted indignantly. 'Are you taking *me* into the garden now?'

Harry paused in the main hall. He hadn't intended to take her into the garden, but he did glance consideringly at the front door for a few seconds before he began to tow her up the first flight of stairs. 'No.' Benjamin and Anne had already retired for the night, but he wanted to make sure his conversation with Saskia wasn't interrupted—and that it took place in a comfortable location.

'You have no business dragging me around like this,' she protested, but she caught her skirts in her free hand and went with him.

A few days ago, Harry would have been unable to imagine treating a woman with even such limited forcefulness. But he was confident that if Saskia really didn't want to go with him she'd have objected in a far more determined way. It was a liberating thought.

He pulled her into the bedchamber he'd been assigned and closed the door behind them. That was something else he wouldn't have considered doing before he met Saskia. But she'd proved more than once she wasn't scandalised at finding herself alone with him in a room that contained a bed.

As soon as he released her, she put both hands on her hips and glowered at him. 'Why did you go out in the garden with Anne?' she demanded.

'She wanted to persuade me to stay here at Trevithick House,' Harry said, and watched the turbulent emotions swirl in Saskia's eyes.

'She… *Why?* I thought Anne was devoted to Benjamin.'

'She is,' said Harry. He was glad to know Saskia had such a strong reaction to him talking to another woman, but he didn't want to torment her with misleading information. 'Lady Anne wants me to stay at least until your brother is back on both feet. I believe Lady Anne views me as a particularly effective guard dog,' he added, with a brief, twisted grin. Whatever Saskia feared, he was certain Anne saw him as no more than proven protection for Benjamin.

Saskia's eyes widened in surprised comprehension. '*That's* why she insisted on taking you in the garden? So she could ask you to protect Benjamin?'

'She didn't want to wound your brother's manly pride by begging me in front of him,' said Harry. 'She assured me he is a brave man—which I already knew. And that he has many other excellent, admirable qualities. But she wants me to remain for a while in case sudden danger threatens again.'

'Oh.' Saskia crossed her arms in front of her waist. She looked momentarily at a loss—and as if she was in need of comfort. Harry's heart contracted with the need to hold and reassure her. But she hadn't reached out to him, or given any sign that she wanted him to touch her. He was still haunted by the memory of her stiffening and moving out of his embrace after only a few seconds when he'd held her after rescuing Anne and Benjamin.

'But you can't linger here,' she said. 'You have to go back to Hawkminster—to sort everything out there.'

Harry looked at Saskia, and then turned to look out of the window at the shadows patterning the gardens as he gathered his thoughts about his inheritance. He sensed Saskia's small, abrupt movement behind him and instantly turned back to her. In the lantern light her face seemed pale. 'Are you all right?' he asked, concerned.

'Yes, of course.' But her light laugh sounded false to Harry's attentive ears. 'I was just thinking how glad I am we are not dashing from the cover of one tree to another tonight.'

He nodded. There were already a couple of moths fluttering around the lantern, so he closed the shutters against the encroaching darkness and lit several more candles. He understood very well how sights or sounds could recall distressing memories and he didn't want any painful associations to intrude upon this conversation. He took a deep breath, bracing himself to ask the most important question he'd every spoken. His future happiness depended on Saskia's answer.

'I do have to return to Hawkminster soon,' he said. 'And I need to know. After all that happened, can *you* bear to go back there? Could you ever bear to live at Hawkminster Castle?'

Saskia stared at him. Try as he might, he could not interpret the expression in her eyes. 'It's your home now,' she said.

'It's one of them.' Harry's throat tightened. He'd conducted many delicate negotiations in his life, but none had meant as much to him as this. 'Grandfather spent the last nine years of his life at the Yorkshire estate. I will have to spend part of every year at Hawkminster. If I am to restore my inheritance as quickly as possible, it is likely I'll end up travelling frequently between Yorkshire, London and Dorset.' He didn't know if she would consider that an advantage or not. She might prefer a husband who was absent for several months a year, though he didn't relish the idea of being separated from her for long periods. 'However much Stephen decried my activities as a merchant, it will be profits from my ventures in the City that will bolster Hawkminster's revival,' he said.

Even though it was a warm evening, Saskia was still hugging herself. 'Won't your brother protect your interests in London, just as you protected his interests when you thought I might bring his coffee-house into disrepute when you believed I was a Dutch agent?' she asked.

'I am sure he will,' Harry said, wishing he knew what lay behind her question. 'Instead of corresponding with me in Aleppo or Smyrna, he will correspond with me in Dorset.'

'You would rather be closer to him.'

'I would rather be closer to you!' Harry exploded fiercely, no longer able to pretend this was just another business negotiation. 'Why did you step away from me so quickly after Selby was restrained?'

'What?' Saskia gaped at him.

'You hugged Benjamin for long minutes—but you stepped out of my arms within seconds.' He was sure he sounded like a fool, measuring the seconds she'd spent in his embrace, but he set his jaw resolutely and pinned her with a hard-eyed stare.

After a dumbfounded silence, Saskia exclaimed, 'You don't like being hugged after you've been fighting! You've made it plain on more than one occasion—I am not to touch you at such moments!'

she continued with growing indignation. She stopped wrapping her arms around herself and put her hands back on her hips. 'For an instant I forgot. But then I remembered. You cannot blame me for respecting your wishes.' By the time she'd finished speaking, fire blazed in her eyes.

Harry's mind went blank. That was the last thing he'd expected her to say. 'You stopped hugging me because you thought I didn't want you to touch me?'

'Yes!' Her voice rose dangerously. 'It is outrageous of you to berate me for trying to accommodate your foolish sensibilities. I cannot see any reason why you should object to me hugging you when you've just saved my life.'

'But I didn't mind.' Harry understood now why Saskia had moved away from him so quickly. He wasn't surprised she was incensed with him. He was more amazed at the change in himself—and the fact he hadn't been aware of it. 'I did mind on previous occasions,' he said, 'but not then. I didn't even think of it. I wanted you to hug me.'

For an instant Saskia looked nearly as disconcerted as Harry felt, but she recovered quickly. And she wasn't mollified by his revelation. 'If you didn't mind, and you wanted to be hugged, you shouldn't have let me go. *You* should have hugged *me*. It is ridiculous to blame me for abiding by your old wishes if you haven't made your new wishes clear.'

'It's not my wishes that concern me right now. I know what I want,' Harry shot back. 'I want to know if you can bear to live at Hawkminster. I want to know if you can bear to live with me?' he finished in a lower voice.

'Of course I can!' Saskia shouted at him. 'Good God, you are enough to try the patience of a saint.' She began to pace up and down, her skirts swishing with the speed of her turns. 'One minute you don't want to be hugged. The next minute you do. How am I possibly supposed to know what you want if you don't tell me? You're *supposed* to tell me. You promised you would. I've been rushing through all the arrangements here so I'll be ready to leave with you—and now apparently we're not going anywhere.' She threw up her hands in exasperation.

By the time she'd finished, the small ember of hope in Harry had blazed into a full, glorious flame. He loved watching the energy in her movements, hearing the passion in her voice and seeing the flash of temper in her eyes. And for the first time since he'd met her he felt confident all her emotions were fully focused on him. Always before he'd been aware that no matter what else was happening, some portion of her mind and heart had been here in

Cornwall with Benjamin. But Benjamin was safe now, and Saskia had been rushing through the reorganisation of Trevithick House so she'd be ready to leave with him!

But Harry wanted everything cut and dried so he could be completely confident about the future.

'Will you marry me, Saskia?' Even though her exasperated rant had come close to a declaration of her wishes, his stomach still knotted with tension as he waited for her to give him an unambiguous answer.

She drew in a deep breath of her own and exhaled in a long sigh. 'Yes,' she said.

He covered the gap between them in two strides and pulled her against him. She wrapped her arms around his neck, returning his kisses with all the passion he'd imagined during the long, sleepless hours of the previous night.

Chapter Fourteen

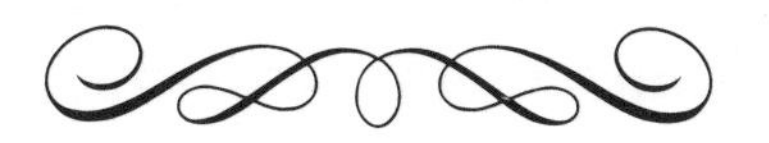

After a little while, when they were both breathless, Saskia eased back slightly to rest her head against Harry's shoulder. Every fibre of her being glowed with happiness. When she'd set off to rescue Benjamin she'd believed when her brother was finally safe her world would right itself again. But it hadn't happened. For the past two days she'd felt tense and sometimes even on the brink of tears. It was only now that she was in Harry's arms, their marriage confirmed, that her world finally balanced again.

Harry wanted her. He wanted to hold her. He wanted to marry her. And as his hands began to roam over her back and hips, pressing her more tightly against him, she became very aware that his virile body was ready to make love to her. An answering heat flowed through her veins. When his fingers started to track up and down her sides, she realised he was following the seams of the bones in the bodice of her formal gown.

She lifted her head to look at him, torn between shyness and amusement as she saw the intent, slightly frustrated expression in his eyes.

'I cannot take it off without help,' she said. 'The points are at the back.'

He frowned, momentarily distracted. 'That's not practical.'

She smiled. 'Fashion and practicality have little to do with each other. And though this gown is not as daring as the one I borrowed in Winchester, it is still the height of fashion in Amsterdam.'

'It is very modest.' His fingers trailed down from her shoulder to rest on the grey silk covering her breast. Her breathing quickened as she imagined how it would feel when he touched her bare skin. Suddenly she couldn't wait, and she turned her back on him.

She heard his sharp intake of breath. For a dreadful instant she was afraid he'd either misinterpreted her action, or that her brazenness had repelled him. Then he gave a husky laugh and his arms closed around her from behind. He pulled her back against his chest and all the strength melted from her bones as he kissed her neck below her ear. She let her head fall to the side, closing her eyes at the delicious sensation of his lips caressing her tender skin.

She was flushed with arousal and getting hotter by the second. Her breasts ached for the touch of his fingers and her tightly laced bodice felt unbearably restrictive. Her clothes had become a frustrating barrier to enjoying the full pleasure of Harry's questing hands. A soft moan of mingled pleasure and frustration escaped her throat.

Harry froze. 'Am I hurting you?'

'No!' She was mortified as soon as the emphatic denial left her lips. But surely he would hurry up and undo her laces before she tried to rip off her clothes herself.

To her relief she felt his hands start to work on the points. From his fumbling efforts it was clear he hadn't unlaced many ladies, but eventually between them they managed to extricate her from her bodice.

'I will become more efficient with practice,' he assured her somewhat ruefully.

'I know you will.' She sensed he was a little embarrassed by his clumsiness, yet it had been largely caused by his obvious determination not to cause her the smallest discomfort. She stood on tiptoe and brushed her lips against his. At once he took control of the kiss, claiming her mouth so thoroughly that she was giddy by the time he lifted his head.

He was wearing too many clothes. She pushed at the front of his coat until he shrugged it off his shoulders and let it fall on the floor behind him. Then she tugged at his shirt until it came free of his breeches. She put her hands underneath the fine linen and explored the smooth, firm muscles of his back.

'Saskia.' It was his turn to groan as he shuddered in response to her touch. 'Wait a little. I have to take off your skirts.'

She started to laugh with pure happiness. 'I have to take off your breeches.'

'Not yet.' He held her away from him. 'Where does your skirt fasten?' he demanded, a hint of sensual desperation in his voice.

'Here.' Her petticoats were easier to be rid of, and soon she was standing in a pool of grey silk, clad in nothing but her shift and her stockings.

'Oh, my lady,' he breathed, his eyes dark with desire as he looked at her in the candlelight. The appreciation in his expression and the near reverence in his tone filled her with joy. She could not possibly doubt that he wanted her. Her body tingled with need and anticipation, but she also felt a hint of shyness because she wasn't used to being the focus of such intense masculine attention.

To cover her momentary awkwardness she began to untie his cravat. He took advantage of her nearness to stroke his hands up and down her back and kiss her temple. She managed to get his cravat off and dragged his shirt up. He paused in his exploration of her curves to pull it over his head.

She put her hands on his chest, glorying in the firm muscles beneath her palms. Even when he was standing still he radiated masculine energy. His muscles flexed beneath her touch, and the heat in his eyes blazed even hotter.

'I want to see you,' he said, his voice a low, sensual growl. 'Will you take off your shift?'

She was briefly surprised he didn't finish undressing her himself, yet she discovered there was something excitingly erotic about uncovering herself to his burning gaze. As she let her shift fall he caught her hand. She had a brief fantasy that he might sweep her up into his arms and carry her to the bed, but instead he bent to press a kiss against her knuckles before leading her to the four-poster. He pulled back the covers with his free hand and with an oddly courtly gesture invited her to get in.

She sat on the edge of the mattress, her heart racing with anticipation as she watched Harry pull off his boots and stockings, and then unfasten his breeches. Her breath caught as his erection thrust into view. There was no doubting that he was fully aroused, despite the control he was exerting over his movements.

She expected him to push her back on to the

mattress and position himself above her. She felt a surge of excitement, tinged with a small portion of nervousness, because this was only the second time they'd made love, and everything was so much more intense with Harry than it had been with Pieter.

But instead of going to her, Harry went around to the other side of the bed. A moment later he was stretched full length behind her. She twisted round to look at him as he reached out to catch her round the waist and pull her close. She tumbled backwards until she was sprawled over him.

'Harry!' she gasped.

'Mmm.' He cupped the back of her head and kissed her.

Sensation overwhelmed her. Everywhere they touched Harry's body was hot and hard beneath hers. He was driving her wild with his lips and tongue, and she was thrillingly aware of his erection against her thigh. She was already swollen and damp in readiness for him. His breathing was quick and excited. She could feel the rapid thud of his heart beneath her palm. His muscles were taut with the urgency of his arousal, but his touch was gentle and controlled as he stroked his hand over her hip and down her thigh. When he reached the top of her stocking he hesitated, almost as if he was confused to encounter the knitted silk rather than her skin, and then began to explore her garter with his fingers.

'I should have taken off your stockings,' he murmured against her mouth.

'Take them off later.' Saskia was throbbing with the desperate, exquisite need to feel him inside her. She'd never dreamed she could reach such a peak of arousal so quickly. She tugged at his shoulder, trying to reverse their positions so he was on top. But he was stronger and more adept. His muscles bunched and in one smooth movement she found she was fully astride his stomach, just as she had been in Winchester. The speed and unexpectedness of his action briefly distracted her from the sensual urgency that gripped her.

'Do you always prefer your women on top?' she gasped, without thinking what she was saying.

He went quite still beneath her. There was a subtle but unmistakable change in the quality of the tension in his lean body.

She sat upright, pushed her hair back from her face and looked down to meet his dark eyes.

'You are my only woman,' he said.

'I should hope so! We're about to be married,' she exclaimed.

His hands had come to rest on her hips. She felt them tighten for a few seconds before his grasp loosed again.

'Ever,' he said.

'Ever?' She stared at him in bewilderment, which gradually transformed to comprehension. 'You mean in Winchester it was your first time?'

He nodded very slightly, his gaze fixed on her face, his tension palpable. 'I have always been quick to learn new skills,' he said gruffly. 'It will not take me long to master the art of pleasing you.'

'But—' Saskia swallowed back her questions. Now was not the moment to ask why an obviously virile man had chosen to remain a virgin until his thirties. Not when he was watching so closely for her reaction, and she could hear a hint of vulnerability beneath his confident statement that he would learn quickly. Love and tenderness filled her as she put her hands on his chest and stroked slowly upwards to his shoulders. 'You already please me very much,' she said, smiling mistily. 'I cannot imagine how you could please me more.'

She felt the wary tension in his body ease. His eyes gleamed. 'Is that a challenge?' He cupped her breast, and then began to toy with her nipple, watching her all the while. She caught her breath as delicious sensations arrowed from her sensitive breast to the throbbing place between her legs.

'If it is, I know you're equal to it,' she said unsteadily.

'But you don't want to be on top?' He slid his other

arm around her to draw her down until she could feel the dark hair on his chest teasing her breasts.

'It is wonderful on top. I expect you would like it too,' she added, just managing to remain coherent. Between his hand stroking her back, his other hand still playing devastatingly with her nipple and the feel of his lean, muscular waist between her thighs, she was rapidly losing the power of intelligent thought.

His caresses paused. 'You would not mind being trapped between my body and the bed?'

'It would be exciting.'

'You would *like* it if I was on top?'

'Yes.' Her affirmation had barely left her lips before he reversed their positions. She gasped at the speed of his action, clutching his biceps as he laid her gently back on to the mattress. He was still between her thighs, but now he was poised above her, his weight braced on his arms.

'You are sure you like it?' His muscles were twitching with coiled tension, but he held himself completely still as he looked down at her.

'I like it,' she assured him huskily. She did not waste any time wondering why the matter was of such concern to him, she simply acted on instinct. She cradled his hips between her bent legs and reached down to take him in her hand. He jerked convulsively as her fingers closed around his rigid length. His body was damp with perspiration, his gaze locked with hers. She was sure he could see her soul as she guided his erection to her hot, damp entrance. She quivered with delight and anticipation as his blunt tip stroked across her swollen, sensitised flesh. Then he was in position and she instinctively lifted her hips in a silent, eager invitation. He thrust into her. A groan tore from his throat. She was so overwhelmed by the intensity of the sensation of him filling her she didn't hear her own moan of pleasure. He began to move carefully within her. After a few thrusts he found an exquisite rhythm.

She wrapped her legs around him, surrendering utterly to the taut anticipation spiralling outward from the delicious slide of his erection within her body. Her fingers dug into his arms, her heels pressed against the backs of his legs as she climbed with him towards the peak. She hovered on the brink—and then her inner muscles clenched around him as pleasure burst through her from the place where their bodies were joined. Through her haze of delight she felt him shudder and heard him groan as he continued to move urgently while waves of ecstasy surged through her until even her fingers and toes were tingling.

She clung to him, dazed and gasping for breath as he began to thrust faster. To her surprise she felt another coil of anticipation building quickly inside her. She closed her eyes as her second climax rocked through her at almost the same moment Harry found his release. He groaned and shook with the power of it, until at last he came to rest above her. He leant his weight on his elbows, letting his head fall forward as his chest heaved.

It took a while for Saskia's pulse and breathing to return to normal, and longer for her to summon even the small effort needed to open her eyes. When she did, she found that Harry was watching her. He was still inside her, and still making sure she did not have to bear the full weight of his body on hers. He shifted his balance slightly and lifted one hand to touch her lips with a gentle finger.

'You look happy,' he murmured. 'Peaceful and happy.'

'I feel happy.' She smiled.

'Good.' He scanned her face before his gaze focused once more on her lips. 'You are my miracle,' he said, and kissed her gently.

She wrapped her arms around him, so stunned and moved by his assertion she could hardly speak. 'I've never been a miracle before,' she said unsteadily.

'You are mine.' He eased carefully and, she thought, reluctantly, out of her, and rolled them both over so her head was resting on his shoulder.

She relaxed against him, still overwhelmed by what he'd just told her. She could feel his fingers playing idly with her hair. His other hand rested possessively on her waist. She was his miracle. He'd told her so, and she knew it was true because he did not make such assertions lightly. She was coming to understand he was honest in a way that went far beyond not telling deliberate lies. And his courage was far greater than a mere willingness to face physical danger. She knew he was justifiably confident in his general physical prowess, and he had assured her he would be quick to learn how to make love to her—but even so it could not have been easy to admit his lack of experience to a woman who had been already been married once.

She stroked his chest, delighting in the firm contours of the muscles that flexed beneath her exploring fingers. He made a soft sound deep in his throat, almost as if he was purring. She turned her head slightly to kiss his shoulder, and then relaxed again. Such moments of shared happy contentment were a rare gift in life and she didn't want to spoil this one with questions.

She must have dozed for a while, because when she became fully aware of her surroundings again a couple of the candles had burned out. But she knew Harry was still awake because his fingers were moving in a delicate, circular caress on her hip. She wondered if he'd slept at all. She was more alert now and she raised herself on to her elbow to look down at him.

'Harry?'

He turned his head to meet her eyes in the muted light. His expression was calm, perhaps a little rueful. 'You want to know why you're my first?' He reached up to brush his fingertips across her cheek and push a lock of hair behind her ear.

'You don't have to tell me,' she said quickly. She desperately wanted to know, but she didn't want to spoil the precious harmony they shared. 'The present is more important than the past.'

'Yes.' He smiled suddenly, unmistakable amusement in his eyes. 'But that doesn't mean you won't imagine all kinds of explanations of your own if I don't tell you.'

'I wouldn't nag you,' she said, feeling slightly indignant.

'I don't mind if you nag me,' he said, sounding unexpectedly cheerful about it. 'Much better than you being cool and polite. I can't make head or tail of what you want when you're too proper.'

'Oh.' She thought about it for a moment. 'Like me saying I want you to tell me what you're thinking and feeling, and not leaving me guessing?'

'Just like that.' He disentangled them and moved so they were more than a foot apart. Then he pulled up the sheet and settled it over her so that she was covered from her shoulders down.

'I'm not cold,' she protested, not pleased with the distance he had put between them.

'It's not that.' He draped the sheet over his hips so he too was modestly concealed.

Her pulse fluttered as she realised this was part of his preparation for talking to her. She'd been afraid he wouldn't want to touch her in the aftermath of rescuing Benjamin and Anne and her fears hadn't been warranted. But it seemed his former reluctance to be touched in certain situations still applied to this conversation. She felt a flicker of anxiety at what she was about to hear, but she tried not to let it show in her expression. 'Can I put my arms on top of the sheet?'

'Of course. Just—' He broke off.

'It's all right. I know.' She extricated her arms and turned on to her side, making sure the sheet remained tucked demurely over her breasts. She folded her hands together and rested her cheek on them as she waited for him to speak.

'Perhaps you'll think I'm a fool—'

'I would never think that,' she interrupted. 'You are the bravest, least foolish man I've ever met.'

His gaze flew to her face. He gazed at her for several long moments, and then she sensed his tension ease slightly.

'It was when we were in the priesthole,' he said abruptly. 'I did not tell you what happened when we were trapped inside.'

He kept the story brief, and gave little in the way of detail, but Saskia's hands clenched into fists as he described how his nurse had been chased down and raped before his horrified eyes. 'Then Swiftbourne arrived and killed the mercenary,' he concluded.

Saskia wanted to reach out to Harry, but she forced herself to remain unmoving. She could tell from his expression that his inner gaze was focused on the violence of the past. 'What happened to your nurse?' she asked, struggling to keep her voice even.

'Swiftbourne took her with us. She went to live with us at the Yorkshire estate. She died six months before I was apprenticed. But she was...broken.' Harry's eyes were clouded with remembered grief and pain. 'The mercenary broke her. Martha had always been light-hearted. Readier to laugh than to scold. But she changed. She hardly ever laughed. She became bitter and suspicious of men. Even with me. She'd known me since I was a babe. I remember her better than my own mother. But when I grew taller than her and my voice broke, she started to watch me as if she were afraid of me…'

'Oh, Harry.' Saskia clutched the sheet in an effort not to reach for him.

He shook his head in a sharp movement, not looking at her. 'I know it was the mercenary who hurt her, not me,' he said. 'I know that in Grandfather's house there was no one to give her the gentle care she needed—but it was hard to watch her spirit twist in pain from what had been done to her. Later Richard and I went to London. Many apprentices learn to wench with abandon, but I…did not choose to do so. And then I went to the Levant. Richard came back to England, but I stayed there. It wouldn't have been impossible to take a mistress, or I could have visited a brothel. I understand there are some exotic opportunities in Istanbul, and I visited the city more than once. But I never went to the brothels.'

One candle was still burning, and he met her eyes in the dim light.

'You waited for marriage, as an honourable man should,' said Saskia.

His lips twisted in a wry acknowledgement of her comment. 'Did your first husband come untried to your marriage bed?' he asked.

'No. He did not directly boast of his previous experience,' she added quickly, 'but I knew I wasn't his first woman.'

'Did you truly not know you were mine until I told you?'

'I truly didn't know,' she assured him. 'I never would have known if you hadn't told me. You are so…I mean, I never felt so…happy and content afterwards…before,' she finished incoherently. She did not think it was fair or honourable to make a direct comparison between Pieter and Harry, but Pieter's lovemaking had never excited her so much, nor had he given so much of his attention to her enjoyment.

Harry released a long breath. 'I told you I learn quickly. We will practise as often as you please, and you will tell me which caresses make you most happy and contented.'

Saskia felt a glow of anticipation at his words. 'You must tell me what pleases you most too,' she said, because it seemed to her that he was still putting her wishes well ahead of his own needs.

There would be time later to ponder what he'd told her, but she already understood how much of his treatment of her had been influenced by his memories of what had happened to his nurse, together with all the years when he'd had little opportunity to meet any women. She remembered how she'd tried to escape from him at the inn after they'd been attacked by the highwaymen. She'd flailed at him with her knife. She'd always known he could have subdued her far more ruthlessly than he had done. She'd even taunted him with looking more afraid than she felt, but it was only now she understood why he'd turned them so his back was against the stable wall and she had the open fields behind her. Even when he'd still half-suspected she was a Dutch agent, he'd done all he could to make sure she did not fear he would use his larger, more powerful body to rape or abuse her.

'Everything you do pleases me,' Harry said, his words recalling her to the present.

'Can I touch you yet?'

He nodded and she let go of the sheet and reached for him. 'I'm sorry,' she whispered against his cheek. 'I'm sorry for what happened to your nurse, and that you saw it. I am sorry you were both hurt so badly. But I am not sorry I am the first woman you made love to. I'm glad. Because if you'd ever made love to any other woman the way you make love to me, she would never have let you go. But now you belong to me, and I am never going to let you go.'

His arms closed tightly around her. 'I'm not going to let you go either. It's too late to change your mind. You're going to be my wife as soon as I can make it so.'

'Yes, yes.'

He kissed her and she felt passion flare between them. Without taking his mouth from hers he rolled them both over until she was underneath him again. She opened her legs so that he could settle between them and he lifted his head to look down at her.

His eyes were dark with arousal, but she also saw a gleam of humour in his expression as he smiled at her. 'I like being on top,' he said.

'Of course.' She threaded her fingers through his hair as she returned his smile. 'It is in your nature to take command of every situation. You do it wonderfully well.'

'You can be on top next time,' he promised. 'We will also experiment with a more leisurely pace. I would like to take all night to explore every inch of your beautiful body. It's just…I am not feeling leisurely at the moment. I am feeling…in great, urgent need of you.'

The idea of him spending a whole night exploring her body sent a thrill of anticipation through Saskia. She glided her hands down his sides. 'I'm feeling in great, urgent need of you too,' she said huskily.

His muscles flexed as he carefully positioned

himself, and then thrust into her. She closed her eyes and surrendered completely to their lovemaking.

Hawkminster Castle—one year later

Saskia stood on top of the gatehouse, watching the road for their guests while she mentally reviewed all her preparations, making sure she hadn't forgotten anything. There had been many changes at Hawkminster over the past year. The village cottages were now all in a good state of repair, and the farmland was being well tended. As long as the weather continued to favour them they had hopes of a good harvest.

Even the castle looked different. Harry's initial priority had been unravelling and resolving the debts he'd inherited, but Saskia had persuaded him to have the South Tower repaired. Now the building work was complete, only the different colour of the stone work was a reminder of the violence Hawkminster had endured during the Civil War.

She heard footsteps and turned to smile up at Harry as he joined her. He'd allowed his hair to grow fashionably long, and he was dressed in the silk velvet and lace befitting an earl, but to Saskia it was the subtle changes she saw that most distinguished the man he was now from the one she'd first met in the coffee-house. He put his arm around her in a gesture that had become as natural to him as breathing.

'You should be resting.' He kissed her temple.

'I'm not sick.' She laid her hand on her swelling stomach where she carried his child. 'I feel extremely well.'

'You look extremely beautiful.' He drew her back to lean against his chest, both arms around her as they looked out over the surrounding landscape. 'And you have made sure everything is ready for the arrival of Richard and his family.'

It would be the first time Richard had returned to Hawkminster since he and Harry had been taken from the priesthole by Swiftbourne, though the brothers had met on many occasions in London over the past year.

'Do you think he has nightmares of the castle?' Saskia asked. She knew that Harry's feelings about Hawkminster had gradually changed as he'd imposed his own authority upon it. She thought it might be a long time before he chose to sit and relax in the west parlour, but he entered and used the chamber without any visible reluctance during his normal routine, and she'd never again seen a hint of the savage response she startled from him the night his uncle had died. Though it hadn't been immediately apparent at the time, she suspected the worst of his nightmares had died with Stephen Ward. She was the one who still resented the damage Stephen had tried to do to his nephew.

They had been married quietly in Cornwall, two days after Lady Abergrave's funeral, and as soon as Benjamin was back on his feet they'd left Trevithick to start putting Harry's inheritance to rights. Peace had been formally declared between the Dutch Republic and England by then, and Harry and Saskia had gone to Amsterdam to make the arrangements for her move back to England. From there they'd gone to London where Harry had begun to re-establish the close friendship with Richard they'd shared as boys, a friendship that had now widened and adapted to include their wives.

Saskia had been relieved and very happy to discover her godfather was recovering well from his bout of acute ill health after Tancock's visit. She'd been fascinated to meet Lord Swiftbourne for the first time, but she'd enjoyed her reunion with Johanna at the coffee-house more. Then, just as Harry had predicted, they'd travelled frequently between Hawkminster in Dorset, the Yorkshire estate and London until they'd been sure that all of Stephen's malicious handiwork had been undone and Harry's inheritance was being well managed.

Stephen's debts had eaten into Harry's fortune,

but the situation had not been as dire as Stephen had intended, though they didn't know whether that was because he'd underestimated Harry's fortune or because he'd become too sick to continue actively pursuing his plans.

'I wasn't aware of Richard being troubled by nightmares of this place when we were boys,' said Harry. 'I don't think he would have concealed them from me—not in the days before we went to the Levant. Later he might have done. He was behind me in the priesthole. He saw Martha crying when Swiftbourne released us, but never saw what happened to her.'

Saskia liked Richard and his wife, and she was glad Harry was once more on easy terms with his brother. But in her private opinion, though Richard hadn't been as physically robust as Harry when they were boys, he was less sensitive to the feelings of others. She could easily imagine that even if Richard had seen what happened to their nurse, he might not have felt her suffering as deeply as Harry. She had taken silent note in preparation for dealing with the sons she hoped she would one day have. It was perfectly possible for a boy—or a man—to be adventurous and brave, yet feel things very deeply.

'Richard was eight when we left here,' said Harry. 'From what he's said, he has quite cloudy recollections of much of the castle. Those two years between us made a big difference to our memories and our understanding when we were young.'

Saskia turned in his arms to smile up at him. 'You will make him very welcome on his return,' she said. 'Soon his memories of Hawkminster will only be happy.'

'Like mine,' said Harry. He looked down at her, a quiet, intense expression in his eyes. 'There is something I must tell you.'

He sounded so serious, Saskia felt a flicker of apprehension, yet she could not imagine what was worrying him. 'Have you had bad news about the shipment of silk?' she asked.

'I haven't had any bad news at all.' He put his hands gently on either side of her head. 'But it has occurred to me that, for all the many things I have told you this past year, there are some words I haven't spoken.'

'Oh?' Saskia's pulse quickened. She held her breath in anticipation of what he might say.

He smiled down at her. 'I love you.'

'Oh, Harry!' She flung her arms around him, covering his face with kisses. 'I love you too! I love you so much.'

He kissed her back, before holding her close. She felt as much as heard his soft, rueful laugh. 'You noticed the absence of the words, then?'

She drew back a little so that she could look at him. 'I did notice,' she confessed. 'At first I was a little afraid—'

'Afraid?'

'In case you discovered that most ladies…' She paused and lowered her voice to a whisper, though they were alone on the top of the gatehouse. 'Most ladies would be happy and content in your bed. And if you realised that, I wouldn't be your miracle any more.'

'*Saskia!* You will always be my miracle,' he said fervently. A shadow of regret flickered in his eyes. 'I'm sorry.'

'No, I did not tell you to make you feel guilty.' She hastened to reassure him. 'When I thought a little longer, I realised you tell me you love me every day, all the time in so many ways. When you put my comfort before yours. When you ask me what I want, rather than assuming you know. When you reach for me every night. So many ways of telling me you love me.' Her voice faltered at the deep emotions filling her as she tried to express the confidence she felt in Harry's love.

'Except the words themselves,' he said. 'What I feel for you is so large it is beyond words, so I never spoke them. I told you all the words that describe the different parts of me, but not the ones that describe the whole of me. I love you.'

Joy soared through Saskia. Tears of happiness misted her eyes as she smiled up at him. 'When did you realise you hadn't told me?'

'When I realised you'd never told me you loved me. I put it down to womanly modestly—until it suddenly occurred to me I'd been equally reticent on the matter.' Rueful humour gleamed in his eyes.

Saskia stroked his mouth with her finger. 'We've managed to communicate well in other ways,' she said.

'We have, and we will go on doing so,' he said. He kissed her, then lifted his head at a shout from below and looked along the road. 'Richard and his family are nearly here,' he said. 'Let's go and greet them. And tonight I will show you I love you again.' He took her hand and led her down the stairs to wait for his brother by the open drawbridge.

* * * * *

HISTORICAL

LARGE PRINT

THE RAKE'S WICKED PROPOSAL

Carole Mortimer

Lucian St Claire, one of the wickedest rakes around, needs an heir – so it's time to choose a wife! Opinionated Grace Hetherington is definitely not the wife he wants. Yet there's something irresistible about her – and, when they're caught in a rather compromising situation, he has no choice but to make her his convenient bride!

THE TRANSFORMATION OF MISS ASHWORTH

Anne Ashley

Tomboy Bethany Ashworth's innocent dreams were destroyed by Philip Stavely's betrothal to her cousin. Years later, Bethany has grown into a beautiful woman, tragedy has left Philip knowing exactly what he wants – he's now determined to marry the woman he should have swept up the aisle six years ago!

MISTRESS BELOW DECK

Helen Dickson

Wilful Rowena Golding needs Tobias Searle's ship to chase her kidnapped sister, but the boarding price he's asking is one night in his bed! Rowena is determinedly immune to Tobias' lethal charm and so, dressed as a cabin boy, she's prepared for the dangers of the high seas…but is she prepared for the notorious Tobias Searle?

HISTORICAL

LARGE PRINT

THE PIRATICAL MISS RAVENHURST

Louise Allen

Forced to flee Jamaica disguised as a boy, Clemence Ravenhurst falls straight into the arms of Nathan Stanier. The heat between them sizzles, but honour demands Nathan resist Clemence. However, she seems determined that their adventure will be as passionate as possible!

HIS FORBIDDEN LIAISON

Joanna Maitland

To restore his reputation, rakish Lord Jack Aikenhead undertakes a covert intelligence operation in war-torn France. However, silk weaver Marguerite throws his plans into disarray! Jack needs the French beauty's help on his mission – though she will be hopelessly compromised...

AN INNOCENT DEBUTANTE IN HANOVER SQUARE

Anne Herries

Debutante Helene has one season to find a husband and save her family. Her compassionate nature leads her into the path of handsome, secretive rake Lord Max Coleridge. He's intrigued by innocent Helene – but with his life in danger, how can he put her at risk? Max determines to solve the mystery – and make Helene his bride!